"Blake, what happened last night—"

"Was a mistake," he interrupted.

"Thank God you understand," Lily breathed.

His lips quirked. "I understand, all right," he drawled, his eyes sparkling. "You want to forget everything that happened between us. You don't know what hit you, because you've never done anything like that before. Besides, we hardly know each other. So you want me to act as if everything's the same as it was before, right?"

Surprised and grateful, Lily nodded with eager agreement. He did understand!

But when she looked up into his face, she remembered the raw passion that had gripped her in his arms. Desire pulsed hotly through her at the memory of Blake's powerful body crushing her, cradling her, caressing her.

How could *anything* be the same...after *that?*

Dear Reader,

What better way to enjoy the last lingering days of summer than to revel in romance? And Special Edition's lineup for August will surely turn your thoughts to love!

This month's THAT'S MY BABY! title will tug your heartstrings. Brought to you by Ginna Gray, *Alissa's Miracle* is about a woman who marries the man of her dreams—even though he doesn't want children. But when she unexpectedly becomes pregnant, their love is put to the ultimate test.

Sometimes love comes when we least expect it—and that's what's in store for the heroines of the next three books. *Mother Nature's Hidden Agenda* by award-winning author Kate Freiman is about a self-assured woman who thinks she has everything...until a sexy horse breeder and his precocious daughter enter the picture! Another heroine rediscovers love the second time around in Gail Link's *Lone Star Lover*. And don't miss *Seven Reasons Why,* Neesa Hart's modern-day fairy tale about a brood of rascals who help their foster mom find happily-ever-after in the arms of a mysterious stranger!

Reader favorite Susan Mallery launches TRIPLE TROUBLE, her miniseries about identical triplets destined for love. In *The Girl of His Dreams,* the heroine will go to unbelievable lengths to avoid her feelings for her very best friend. The second and third titles of the series will be coming your way in September and October.

Finally, we're thrilled to bring you book two in our FROM BUD TO BLOSSOM theme series. Gina Wilkins returns with *It Could Happen To You,* a captivating tale about an overly cautious heroine who learns to take the greatest risk of all—love.

I hope you enjoy each and every story to come!

Sincerely,

Tara Gavin,
Senior Editor

Please address questions and book requests to:
Silhouette Reader Service
U.S.: 3010 Walden Ave., P.O. Box 1325, Buffalo, NY 14269
Canadian: P.O. Box 609, Fort Erie, Ont. L2A 5X3

KATE FREIMAN

MOTHER NATURE'S HIDDEN AGENDA

Silhouette®

SPECIAL **EDITION**®

Published by Silhouette Books

America's Publisher of Contemporary Romance

Thanks to my critique partner, Doretta Thompson; my agent, Alice Orr; my editors, Tara Gavin and Cathleen Treacy; Mary Jean Vasiloff, breeder of Whippoorwill Morgan horses; and my real-life heroes, Mark and Ben.

In memory of my beloved Morgan mare, Lauralee Merribelle (1969-1994). Her beauty was matched only by her sweetness and generosity of spirit.

 SILHOUETTE BOOKS

ISBN 0-373-24120-8

MOTHER NATURE'S HIDDEN AGENDA

Copyright © 1997 by Kate Freiman

Books by Kate Freiman

Silhouette Special Edition

Jake's Angel #876
Here To Stay #971
The Bachelor and the Baby Wish #1041
Mother Nature's Hidden Agenda #1120

KATE FREIMAN

began creating stories with happy endings even before she could read or write, after the old movie *Frankenstein* gave her nightmares. She believes she holds the record for rereading Louisa May Alcott's *Little Women,* and, of course, grew up wanting to be Jo, the writer.

A casual meeting with one of Kate's graduate professors—to discuss a book, of course!—turned into true love, marriage and emigration from Connecticut to Toronto, Canada. Her husband, Mark, became a lawyer, and they have one teenaged son, Ben, who can usually be found with an open book in one hand.

Kate received the Romance Writers of America "Golden Heart" Long Contemporary Romance award in 1990. She says, "I love the optimism of romance novels. I feel it reflects the strength and courage of everyday women, the real heroines." Write her at: Kate Freiman, c/o The Alice Orr Agency, Inc., 305 Madison Avenue, Suite 1166, NY, NY 10165.

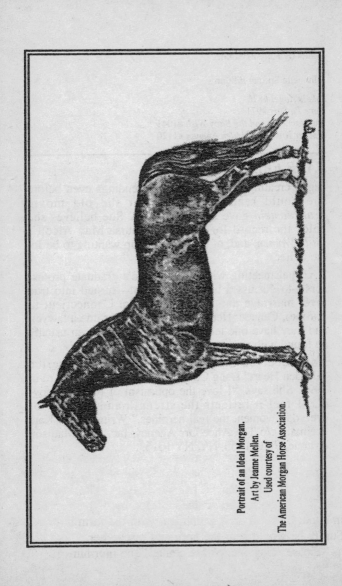

Portrait of an Ideal Morgan.
Art by Jeanne Mellen.
Used courtesy of
The American Morgan Horse Association.

Chapter One

A thump outside the MG's left window distracted Lily from the aging car's subsiding gasps. She turned her head, looked out the window, and stifled a scream. A monster with bared fangs and black, foaming lips snarled at her through the glass. Evil eyes glinted behind tangled black fur, greedily measuring her throat.

Lily shrank back into the car seat and pressed the heel of her hand on the horn. At the sound, the beast raked at her window with huge, hairy black paws and howled. The little car rocked under the assault. With a whimper of pure terror, Lily leaned farther away from the window and held down the horn. Her heart hammered painfully in her chest. Desperately, she glanced from the large white house to her right to the smaller white house on her left. Not a soul in sight. She had an appointment with the farm's owner. Surely he would hear the horn and rescue her.

"Please, someone, please come," she murmured.

She tried not to look at the creature's snapping, cavernous jaws, but even so, she imagined the heat of its foul breath through the mud-streaked glass. This was the stuff of nightmares, but she was definitely awake. The beast was all too real. So was her fear. In the distance, through bare black trees, she saw two large dark green barns, but not a single person in the yard between them and her car. She doubted anyone that far away could hear her horn, anyway. The beast let out another cry, half bark, half howl. Lily cringed. Certainly someone could hear *that*.

Until someone did, however, she was stuck in the car, late for her appointment, cowering in fear and praying for deliverance. She shivered, wishing she was anywhere else. No one in their right mind would get out and face this monster. She hit the horn for one more blast.

Suddenly, from the gravel lane leading to the parking lot, a man on a black horse burst into view. The horse's legs churned under it, spraying dirt, and steam plumed from its reddened nostrils. Its long black mane and tail flowed on the brisk, damp wind as if it were a demon Pegasus just landed. The rider, dressed all in black, looked almost as fierce as the beast still scrabbling at her window. Lily felt her jaw drop, and snapped it shut.

Horse and rider bore down on her car. The beast at the window barked sharply, then disappeared. Seconds later, Lily found herself staring through the muddy glass at a tall black boot adorned by a silver spur with a lethal-looking spiked wheel at the back.

As rescuers went, this one didn't look at all promising.

Lily's overriding hope was that the rider was not her client. She couldn't imagine a contemporary of Uncle Bill's tearing around like this throwback to Zorro. Her uncle had finally given up driving the last relic of his mid-life crises, the dilapidated MG that at the moment was all that came between her and the man on the horse. And Uncle Bill's reluctant request that she postpone her vacation to help him prepare a client for an audit had been a saddening sign that he was slowly conceding to his age. But she'd do anything for Uncle Bill.

Well, anything short of being torn to shreds or trampled by Count Dracula and his dragon.

Lily waited a moment for the horse and rider to move away from the car so she could risk getting out—as little as she wanted to take her chances again with the salivating monster. The horse and rider stayed beside her window, the horse's sides heaving, the boot bumping the car door when the horse shifted closer. Uncle Bill wasn't going to appreciate the mud on his vintage MG. She wanted to tell the man to let her out, but she wasn't about to roll down the window and get that boot in her face.

She also had no interest in this totally unnecessary assertion of power. The high rollers she dealt with daily back in New York City swaggered more than enough for her taste—or her patience. She certainly didn't have to travel to upstate New York to find more of the same.

Well, she knew the rules in the concrete jungle, and she didn't think they were that different out here in the boondocks. Never show weaknesses, but find the other guy's soft spots and use them. Get control of confrontations and turn them to your own advantage without being obvious. But first, she had to convey to the rider that she had something to say to him, not to his boot. To do that, she'd have to get his attention without risking her health and safety. Lightly, she beeped the horn.

The horse suddenly backed away and lifted its front end high above the hood of her car. Lily cried out as its legs thrashed the air, revealing its mud-splashed belly. As that powerful body descended, she cringed back in her seat and closed her eyes, certain that its feet would crash through the windshield and the convertible top and smash her into oblivion.

Seconds passed in silence. Nothing happened.

With her heart racing, Lily dared to open her eyes. Horse and rider had moved far enough away from the car that she could see them clearly. The rider's dark eyes met hers; his expression was contemptuous. As she watched him move his lips, her cheeks burned with anger and embarrassment. They stung even more when she saw the raging beast that had attacked her trot docilely to a spot near the still-dancing horse and sit, magically transformed into a huge, grinning shaggy black dog. With a smug lick of its chops, the creature swept the ground with its tail and gazed adoringly up into the face of the rider.

Sitting up straighter now, Lily studied the man on the horse and realized with profound relief that he couldn't be her client. Jonathan March, owner of March Acres Morgan Horse Farm, was in his sixties, like her uncle Bill. Whoever this man was, he was probably in his mid-thirties. Now that she was certain he wasn't Uncle Bill's friend, she didn't really care who he was, as long as he kept that dog and horse away from her.

She had to get out of the car to keep her appointment, but she was still shaking too much to work the door latch on the first try. The rider met her eyes again. The contempt was gone, but there was no mistaking his amusement. It was bad enough to be so afraid of dogs, but to have this arrogant rogue laugh at her because of it was too much.

Lily shoved open the car door and climbed out to face him, her gaze shifting nervously between him and the dog. Before she could do more than draw a breath to tell him what she thought of his behavior toward visitors, he shook his head.

"Don't you know better than to roar down a farm lane like a drunk in a stolen car?" He spoke quietly, but his deep voice carried authority. "There are children, horses and dogs around."

Lily's breath came out in a whoosh. He was right, of course, much as she hated to let go of her indignation. She owed him an apology, but his attitude made the words stick in her throat. Her cheeks burned again.

"That's not a dog," she blurted defensively. "That's a hound of hell."

The man's laughter rang out, warm and rich. "Dolly? She's as gentle as a kitten."

A stiff breeze cut through her coat. Lily hugged herself to control the shivering. Now that the worst was over, she didn't want to admit just how terrified she'd been. "Tell that to the car," she suggested, not quite ready to forgive him.

He grinned, devilishly handsome, and probably all too aware of it. A dimple showed in his right cheek. "I'll get the mud off the window before you go."

The combination of smile and good humor took her breath away. Whoever he was, he was very, very attractive. His shoulders were broad under a heavy black sweater, and whenever the horse moved beneath him, his powerful thigh muscles flexed and contracted within skin-tight black pants. The wind tossed his dark hair into unruly curls. And he patted the horse's neck with a hand that looked large and strong inside its black leather glove. Masculine and self-confident. Definitely attractive, despite his arrogance.

But in her world, attractive men were a dime a dozen, and worth just about as much. If she wanted to spend time with an attractive, insensitive jerk, she didn't have to look farther than her colleagues. Particularly her ex-fiancé, Jeffrey Conklin, who had loved her brains and decorative potential far more than he loved her. It might be true that a woman had to kiss a lot of toads before she found her prince, but Lily wasn't convinced that she needed a prince. "Cinderella" was just a fairy tale. The only rewards Lily wanted were the ones she earned herself.

"Ah! Lily, my dear!" another male voice called heartily. Grateful for the distraction, she turned to see a gray-haired man, lean and energetic, striding across the parking area from the direction of the large white house. She recognized his voice from their brief phone conversation and smiled in relief. This was definitely Jonathan March, Uncle Bill's best friend, and now her new client.

"Mr. March," she said as he reached her side.

He took her hand in both of his, and his distinguished face creased in a welcoming smile. "Call me Jonathan, my dear. I see you've met Blake already."

She smiled again, liking her uncle's friend immediately. "Actually, I've only met, um, Dolly," she answered gamely. If she was lucky, she'd be able to bluff her way around her embarrassing fear of dogs and escape before anyone was the wiser. No point in asking why Uncle Bill hadn't mentioned the beast. He knew darn well that if he even hinted she'd be facing a huge canine maniac, she would have found a substitute and taken her vacation after all.

"An excellent start. Dolly thinks she's the boss," Jonathan told her with a boyish grin. "Blake Sommers, my farm manager. Blake, this is Lily Davis, Bill Connell's niece. She's going to prepare our books for that blasted audit." Jonathan patted her hand before releasing it.

Lily turned to offer a conciliatory smile to Blake Sommers. He stared down at her from the shifting black horse, his previous amusement replaced by an expression of distaste. His dark eyes gleamed. "So you're the hotshot big-city accountant. I thought you were one of my daughter's friends."

At his obviously deliberate insult, her own smile faded. After gazing in palpable disapproval at her for another few seconds, Blake nodded and wheeled the horse away in a spray of gravel that would have done credit to an old-time movie cowboy. He whistled sharply, and the dog leaped into a run, following horse and rider toward the barns.

Lily turned and reached into the car for her briefcase and purse, puzzled by Blake's remark. Hotshot accountant, indeed! Anyone with half a brain would know that was a contradiction in terms.

And that comment about being a friend of his daughter's... She had learned to take in stride being mistaken for less than her actual thirty-one years. She'd even learned to turn that first disarming impression to her benefit when negotiating on behalf of her clients. But how old could this man's daughter be? Eight? Ten? Was this Blake person implying that her behavior over the dog had been childish?

Taking Jonathan's arm, Lily dismissed Blake Sommers from her mind. She was here to work, to do a favor for her uncle and his friend, not solicit a good opinion of her or her profession from an arrogant stranger. Besides, she had no use for married men who flirted. But she pitied his wife and daughter if he was always so moody, judgmental and positively rude.

"Dumb, dumb, *dumb*," Blake muttered. He halted Pride of March in the wide center aisle of the stallion barn and swung down off him. Pride nudged him with his muzzle.

"Okay, so I put both feet in it. I was ticked off about the horn." Pride blew through his nostrils and rubbed his face on his foreleg. Blake tugged on a rein to bring the horse's head back up. "You acted like a jerk, too. Showoff." Pride sighed deeply, as if implying that Blake just didn't understand.

Blake unbuckled the girth and removed the saddle. Working automatically, he cleaned the sweat and mud off the stallion's coat. "An accountant. Humph. Accountants are supposed to be plain and dull, with glasses," he grumbled as he worked. "They aren't supposed to look like Christmas angels."

"Hi, Dad. Talking to yourself again?" Carrie came up beside him and gave him a kiss on the cheek.

"No." He turned away to hide his burning face. "I'm talking to Pride. How was school?"

"It was okay. I got an A on my zoology exam and an A-minus on my English paper."

He grinned at her. "Good girl."

Carrie grinned back, and the dimple in her right cheek deepened. "So I can have a party, right?" She slipped the stallion a piece of crunch. "That was the deal, right?"

He sighed. In a lot of ways, he and Carrie had grown up together, but now his baby was growing up too fast for him. Carrie had given him so little grief and so much pleasure in her seventeen years that he knew he couldn't complain, and shouldn't even hesitate about this party she wanted to throw. It wasn't like she was a child and this was going to be her first boy-girl party. Hell, she'd been dating for years now, in groups and in pairs. Maybe it was because he was becoming more aware of the fact that she was about to try her wings. Seeing her with her friends, all poised on the edges of their own nests, planning for their futures, made him feel old in a way he'd never anticipated. It wouldn't be long now before Carrie didn't need him anymore. She probably hardly needed him now, but pretended to just to make him feel better.

"We'll talk about it over dinner. You've got work to do."

"Okay." She gave him a loud kiss on his other cheek, then patted his shoulder. "Who looks like a Christmas angel?"

He swore under his breath. She would have to hear that. "Jonathan's accountant," he admitted, more sheepishly than he expected.

Carrie shot him an odd look. "A *guy* who looks like a Christmas angel? Dad, you've gotta get out more often."

"Very funny. No, a woman who looks like... Never mind."

"The accountant is a woman?" He grunted. "Is that her car in the yard? Is she nice? Maybe she'd come to the career conference."

Before he had a chance to remind her again about the horses it was her job to groom and exercise, Carrie was off and running toward Jonathan's house. Blake shook his head and grinned. She'd worked so hard on her school's career day, looking so serious and grown-up as she explained to him that young women—not *girls*, thank you very much—needed strong female role models. Now she was racing like a puppy after a Frisbee, to ask Ms. New York Accountant to talk to kids at a high school in the boonies. Considering the look of pure disgust Lily Davis had given her surroundings when she got out of Bill's car, he couldn't see that happening in this lifetime. He just hoped Lily didn't make Carrie feel foolish.

Pride stamped his foot, demanding attention. Blake put

a hand on the stallion's powerful chest, checking to see if his coat was dry and cool. Against his better judgment, he conjured up an image of Lily Davis, then looked for reasons not to find her attractive. Unfortunately, his mind filled with the memory of her porcelain skin, full lips, deep blue eyes, and slender legs, shown off very nicely in high-heeled shoes, which was all he had seen of her in the straight red coat she wore. He'd guess she was small all over.

To erase the tantalizing image of just what that little female body might look—and feel—like, he tried to think of reasons not to find her attractive. Probably ate bunny food and rice cakes, afraid to gain a few pounds and look like a real woman. She wasn't much over five-two, trying to compensate in those ridiculous high heels. Her silvery-blond hair was pulled back and coiled up, very prim and businesslike. She probably never wore it loose, so a man could run his fingers through it.

Definitely not his type. Definitely out of place on a horse farm. Hell, she'd been afraid of Dolly. Well, okay, he had to concede she'd had good reason, under the circumstances. He also had to concede she'd stood up for herself. She had spirit, and a dry sense of humor. Okay, he liked that. The smile she'd given Jonathan—not him—could have melted an iceberg. He liked that, too. And her voice...soft and low. The kind of voice that could give a man all sorts of ideas.

"Maybe Carrie's right, old man," he muttered as he led Pride to his stall. "Maybe I've been around too many horses and not enough women lately. I should have my mind on my work."

But his mind wouldn't obey. It snapped back to images of Lily like a short rubber band. Her bare hands had been ringless. Well, hell, he wasn't seeing anyone seriously at the moment. And there was no law that said he had to be immune to a beautiful female accountant just because Jonathan didn't believe he could handle that audit himself. Well, it was true he hadn't taken a woman out—or accepted any of the many offers extended by the local single women—in a while. Maybe he'd drop into Jonathan's house for a coffee and casually ask Lily to dinner or something.

And just maybe, after he'd ridden her down in her car, laughed at her for being afraid of Dolly, insulted her about her profession and told her she looked like a teenager, she'd be willing to speak to him…sometime after hell froze over.

Jonathan poured tea into mugs decorated with horses and the words Pride and Product of America. He passed a mug to Lily, and settled himself in the chair across the golden oak kitchen table and smiled warmly at her.

"I hope you'll forgive Blake for being a little brusque. He's been doing the farm books for years, with Bill giving the tax returns a final polish. I'm afraid his nose is out of joint because I've brought in outside talent."

She closed her hands around the mug, enjoying its warmth, and smiled. "Ah. I thought perhaps he'd been frightened by an accountant at an early age."

Jonathan chuckled. Lily sipped her tea, feeling at ease with this genteel man.

"Blake has gathered our tax returns for the years in question, along with the relevant ledgers and files. I've cleared my desk for you," he told her. "I'm sure you'll be very comfortable."

"Fine. Do you use ready-made software, or was it customized?"

Jonathan drew his brows together. "Software?"

"For your computer."

He shook his head. "Surely Bill mentioned we don't use a computer. I prefer good old-fashioned ledgers. I don't trust those electronic gadgets."

Lily stifled a sigh. Uncle Bill's computer had every bell and whistle he could need, and a few she suspected he'd added just for fun. It would have been reasonable for him to encourage his friend and client to join the twentieth century before it was over. Checking five years' worth of financial records for an IRS audit would be painstaking enough without having to decipher longhand. It could take her ages. At least a couple of weeks of that long drive to and from the farm. And daily encounters with that expletive-deleted dog.

The past few months of this year had been more demanding than ever. She was exhausted by the stress of being up for partnership soon, which her mentor was confident she'd make. And she was on the short list for a fabulous foreign posting. Sometimes she felt tempted to pinch herself, to make sure she wasn't dreaming that everything she'd hoped for was coming true.

But Uncle Bill was the only person in the world for whom she'd have given up her precious R-and-R time. She'd promised him she'd handle this case, and he really was too weak from his heart attack, mild though it had been, to push himself toward a deadline. There was no question that she'd do whatever had to be done, however it had to be done. For Uncle Bill, she'd do this and more. She just hoped she could finish in time to relax a little before getting back to her own files. Becoming a partner was going to increase her work load exponentially.

Lily nodded over her mug at Jonathan. "I'll have to bring a computer tomorrow," she said. "Today, I'll see what needs to be done. Do you have an outlet near your desk?''

Jonathan's frown eased. "We'll see as soon as you've finished your tea. If necessary, Blake can run a line from the service box downstairs. He's very clever that way.''

"Fine. I—"

The kitchen door flew open. A teenager in jeans and a heavy blue sweater burst into the room, her dark hair flying around her face. She swooped down to give Jonathan a quick kiss on his cheek, leaving him chuckling. Then she smiled warmly at Lily, and a dimple flashed in her right cheek. There was no doubt that this energetic girl was Blake Sommers's daughter. At least that took some of the sting out of his thinking of Lily as one of the girl's friends.

"Hi. I'm Carrie Sommers. You must be the angel." Lily frowned in confusion. Carrie blushed. "I mean the accountant.'' She held out a hand for Lily to shake.

Lily shook Carrie's hand and decided to overlook the girl's odd comment as a simple slip of the tongue.

"So you're going to cover Dad's tracks with the IRS." Carrie grinned mischievously. "He pitched a total fit about being audited. Like it was a supreme insult." Her eyes sparkled and her dimple deepened. "Dad's kinda old-fashioned and macho. He's not too crazy about needing help with anything.''

"So I gather," Lily replied, liking the girl immediately.

Carrie shoved her hands into her back pockets, her dark eyes alight with interest. "My school's having a career conference in a couple of weeks. Do you think you'd be interested in speaking on a panel or something? You know, women in professions? I'm on the speaker committee, and I've been pushing for some strong women to participate.''

Thinking of her recent brush with Blake's diabolical dog, Lily didn't consider herself to fit the description of *strong*. Nevertheless, she smiled and said, "I'd be glad to, if I'm in town. It depends on how soon I can get prepared for the audit."

"Excellent! I'll get the guidance counselor to call you here tomorrow, if that's okay." Lily nodded. "Thanks." Carrie helped herself to a cookie from the plate Jonathan had placed on the table earlier. She nibbled at a corner, studying Lily with bright dark eyes. Then, dimple flashing, she grabbed an extra cookie. "Gotta go. I've got horses to exercise, and a ton of homework. See you."

As quickly as she'd arrived, Carrie dashed out the back door. Lily looked at Jonathan. He smiled and shook his head.

"'Hurricane Carrie,' we call her. Perpetually in motion, and smart as a whip. Keeps poor Blake on his toes."

"What about his wife?" The words just slipped out, before her brain could hold them back. Trying to avoid Jonathan's eyes, she reached for a cookie she really didn't want.

"No wife. Blake's been a single father since right after Carrie was born." In her peripheral vision, she could see Jonathan watching her curiously.

Lily suspected that any other living, breathing woman between the ages of twenty and ninety would be thrilled to hear that Blake Sommers was unattached. Personally, she couldn't have cared less, except if it made things awkward between them. She'd probably have to consult him about entries in the ledgers. And he'd probably be peering over her shoulder possessively whenever he could, to see what she was doing with his precious accounts.

She bit into the buttery shortbread and chewed thoughtfully. Really, there was no problem, she concluded. She had a job to do, and that was all. Blake Sommers's single status and drop-dead good looks were of no interest to her. She'd just keep pretending he was Jeffrey. Anyway, after their first encounter, he probably thought she was a neurotic shrew. Lord knew, she hadn't had reason to revise her opinion of him as an arrogant jerk.

"Well, lead me to your records," she told Jonathan brightly. "The sooner I start, the sooner I finish." And the sooner she could get back to the rest of her life, which was all she really wanted or needed.

At six that afternoon, Lily was more than ready to leave for the day. The work was going to be even worse than she'd first thought. Blake and Jonathan had kept meticulous records—of everything. All jumbled together. By the time she finished wading through five years of relevant and irrelevant information, she was going to need a vacation. Unfortunately, she reminded herself, this *was* her vacation.

Head down in concentration as she crossed the parking lot to her car, hugging herself against the sharp wind, Lily didn't notice Blake standing in her path until they nearly collided. She stepped back in surprise, and a piece of gravel gave way under her heel.

"Oh!"

Blake caught her shoulders before she actually lost her balance. Her head snapped upward, her eyes meeting his. His hands seemed to engulf her, their grip unbreakable against her momentum. Silently he held her gaze. He wasn't terribly tall, maybe just a shade under six feet, but that was tall enough for her. His touch made her feel small, and very much aware of herself as physically vulnerable. There was something exciting about his strength, something vaguely primitive and disturbing, an earthiness that made him totally different from the men she knew back in the city. Compelling. And a little frightening. She didn't want to be excited, disturbed or compelled. She certainly didn't want to be frightened.

Lily tensed. Breathlessly she waited for Blake to release her shoulders, unwilling to let him know that the physical contact had affected her.

"Easy, there," he murmured, in the tone he probably used on frightened animals. She wanted to resent it, but to her chagrin, she found his voice, his touch, surprisingly comforting. That was *not* good, she scolded herself. She didn't need soothing. She needed her personal space to remain inviolate.

"I'm fine. Thank you." She strove to sound gracious, and even managed a smile, unwilling to let him see her discomfort.

Blake dropped his hands. Irrationally, she missed the warmth and firm gentleness of his touch when he released her. Thoroughly irritated with herself, she took a half step back and shoved her hands into her coat pockets.

Blake stood his ground, his legs braced, a completely masculine figure in black. Images of highwaymen, pirates and demon lovers flitted through her mind. Then his full, generous lips curved into a smile that transformed his face with stunning results. A dimple flashed in his right cheek. The fine lines fanning out around his dark eyes deepened, and there was a sparkle in those eyes that was like the sun breaking through gray clouds. Unbidden, unwanted, delicious warmth spread through her. Before she could stop herself, she'd answered his smile with her own.

Blake watched Lily's slow-blooming smile light her face. He felt as if he'd been blindsided by some mysterious force. He'd expected her to feel as fragile as she looked. Instead, she'd felt resilient, willowy, like a dancer, when his hands gripped her shoulders. It had been a long time since simply touching a woman had produced the kind of warmth that tingled through him as he held her arms and breathed in the scent of her. Subtle. A little sweet. A little spicy. Just hinting at the female musk of her skin.

Awareness hummed in his nerves. He wondered again what was under the straight lines of her woolen coat. He looked at her mouth, and her lips parted. How would it feel to kiss her right then?

He met her eyes and knew she was aware of him, woman to man. It was there in the way her pupils darkened, the way her lids drifted down as if to hide her interest. He clenched his hands to keep from reaching for her again, wondering what it was about her that made him feel like a randy teenager. Maybe it was spring fever, pure and simple, that had his libido and his brain tied up in knots.

"I...I was just leaving," she said, with a little catch in her voice.

"Will you be back in the morning?" She nodded. He swallowed. "We got off on the wrong foot before."

"It was my fault. I owe you an apology. I've never been on a farm before. I didn't think about children or animals."

He smiled, touched by her willingness to apologize. "No problem." Her answering smile was shy. This was the time to ask her out. Something simple, so she wouldn't feel rushed. So he wouldn't feel like a fool, on the off chance that she turned him down.

"How about—"

"See you tomorrow," she said at the same time, stepping past him as if she couldn't get away fast enough.

He snapped his mouth shut and nodded. Lily walked to

her car and slid behind the wheel without looking at him again. He watched her drive slowly away, the little sports car's engine knocking badly, and whistled softly. Lily Davis was one cool, self-possessed lady. And one beautiful, intelligent woman, as well. It was a potent combination.

He knew he had to be more appealing than an IRS audit. Of course, there was the little complication of Lily's apparent indifference, but he had at least a couple of weeks to wear down her resistance. He didn't have any plans for what he'd do once he got past her defenses, but he did love a challenge. If there was one thing he was a master at, it was the gentle, persistent overcoming of even the most entrenched resistance. Granted, his expertise was mainly with horses, dogs and small children, but he was willing to give Lily Davis a damn good try.

Chapter Two

The next morning, Blake went back to his house for a second cup of coffee after feeding the horses and cleaning some of the stalls. At nine, he heard Lily's car crunch slowly across the gravel and felt a little hum of anticipation. By the time he got outside, however, there was no one near the old MG, so he headed toward the barn.

A scream that sent shivers down his spine stopped him in his tracks. He spun and sent a spray of gravel from his work boots as he sprinted toward the sound. Another scream was answered by a sharp bark. Dolly. He reached the front of Jonathan's house in time to see Lily back hard into the solid barrier of the closed front door as Dolly reared up on her hind legs to brace her forepaws on Lily's shoulders.

"Dolly, off!" he bellowed as he ran. "Down! Now!" The dog dropped onto her belly in front of Lily, her tail submissively tucked between her legs. Blake slowed to a walk. No need to rush, now that Dolly had retreated. "Good girl," he praised the dog automatically. Lily's overreaction would have the poor dog confused enough. She'd be humiliated by more scolding. Well, there was no harm—

Lily slid bonelessly down against the door. Lunging forward, he caught her just before she hit the flagstone step. Off balance from reaching out, he almost fell with her. Her scent filled his head as he clutched her to his chest. The light pressure of her head on his shoulder trapped his breath in his lungs. His heart pounded like a drum.

The image of her arms slipping around him, of her face tipping up for his kiss, flashed into his mind. The idea refused to fade as he straightened, lifting her with him. She stirred, her slender body brushing against him, striking sparks. He clamped his teeth onto his lower lip as his body responded to the light, intimate pressure of hers.

"Oh!" The barely audible gasp could have been made in passion. One of her arms slid around his waist, and her face tilted up toward his. Her silvery hair spilled across the front of his black sweater like moonbeams. A gear in his mind slipped. His body tightened. Through her thin sweater, he could feel warmth and pliant strength. Then he registered the fear in her dazed eyes and cursed his imagination.

"Shh..." he soothed, struggling against his awareness of her in his arms. "You're okay now. Don't try to move too fast."

"I hate when that happens," she muttered, then pressed weakly against his chest with one small hand.

For a long moment, her palm lay on his chest. Blake held his breath. Suddenly, she pulled her hand away and stiffened, breaking the enticing contact between them. He relaxed his hold, but didn't let her go yet.

"Why didn't you tell me you're afraid of dogs?" he asked gently.

"I'm not." Her chin went up a notch as their eyes met. "Not all dogs. Just big ones." She looked away and her face turned pink. "And...medium-size ones," she added, so softly he could hardly hear her. He gave her credit for trying to make light of the situation, but she was still trembling. His instincts told him to keep supporting her until she was steady, but when she pushed on his chest again, he reluctantly released her.

She cleared her throat. "Dolly is...very big."

"She's half Irish wolfhound and half Bouvier." Lily looked at him blankly. "She really loves people. She was trying to make you feel welcome," he explained.

"I thought she was trying to make me feel like dinner."

He smiled. "Nah. She's just a big, hairy goofball. If you pat her, she'll be in heaven." He glanced at the dog still lying sheepishly near their feet, but he was thinking that if Lily patted *him*, he'd be in heaven, too.

Lily backed away a step. He could see the fear in her eyes again. "I'll take your word for it."

He hated the thought of anyone being afraid of animals. "You know, when we're working with a horse that gets spooked by something, we always give it a second chance to check out what scared it."

Her soft lips curved up. "Last time I looked, Mr. Sommers, I wasn't a horse."

He grinned. "Where's your imagination?"

A full smile lit her face, giving him hope that she was beginning to warm up to him. "On the ground, with my dignity." She shook her head. "Another time, perhaps. I've got a lot of work to do, and very little time to do it."

That wasn't exactly the response he'd been hoping for. "Soon. You wouldn't want Dolly to be traumatized for life, would you?"

Lily's quiet laugh was low, husky. "Perish the thought. Can you do me a favor? I was going to get my computer from the car." She glanced past him toward Dolly. "I can carry it myself, but…"

"No problem."

She gave him a soft smile that made him think again about how her lips would feel under his. "Thank you, Mr. Sommers."

"Blake," he corrected.

She gazed up into his face for a long moment. Unable to read her expression, he held his breath, a little surprised by how important it was to hear her say his name. Under her sense of humor and her smiles, he sensed that Lily was tightly controlled. Anything she gave up would be that much more valuable for being difficult to win.

"Blake," she finally echoed in that devastating voice, her eyes wide and almost black.

He gazed back, a little stunned by the effect of his name on her lips. Lowering her gaze, Lily turned and opened Jonathan's front door. Blake walked out to her car, imagining her saying his name as he tasted the silky skin of her neck and gathered her slender body close to his. When he reached for the computer case on the front seat, his hands were trembling.

Damn! He hadn't reacted to a woman this way since he met Carrie's mother. None of the local women, with their frank interest and open flirting, had ever shaken him like this. And he couldn't even claim that Lily's few quips amounted to flirting. She was beautiful, but so were a lot of women who didn't make his pulse race. Whatever it was Lily Davis did to his equilibrium and his libido, he liked it, and he wanted more of it.

That afternoon, when Jonathan suggested they take a break, Lily was surprised to see that the time was twenty past four. She flexed her aching shoulders. "I'll keep going and save my questions until you're ready to join me again. There's plenty—"

"Nonsense, child. You need a break, too." He flashed a boyish grin. "Let's call it a day. I want to show off some of the horses you've been accounting for." He arched an eyebrow. "I'll shut Dolly in the office."

Lily felt herself blush. "So much for deep, dark secrets. I suppose Blake told you I acted like an idiot this morning."

Jonathan regarded her with sharp blue eyes. "Blake said nothing of the sort. I witnessed the incident from the window."

"Oh," she said, feeling humbled.

"You should have said something, my dear. Dolly is good-natured, but impulsive. Now, get your jacket so I can show you the mares who are the cornerstone of my breeding program."

Reluctant as she was to find herself in a barn full of dirty, smelly horses, she didn't want to hurt Jonathan's feelings. So, with only a small sigh of resignation, Lily joined him in the hallway. Outside, he offered her his arm and walked her briskly down the gravel lane toward the barns. At least today, she mused, she'd had the good sense to wear slacks and flat shoes. Back in New York City, she thought nothing of marching to work in a designer suit and running shoes, but she hadn't expected to trudge through a muddy farmyard. She *expected* to sit in a warm, dry office in Rochester. Uncle Bill had omitted some crucial information.

As they walked, Lily took in her surroundings. The damp bite of yesterday's wind had mellowed pleasantly in the afternoon sunlight. The trees, black and lifeless only a day ago, had magically sprouted tender green shoots. They looked like lace against the sky, she thought. Did the trees in the City look like this? Somehow, she'd never consciously noticed. Nor had she ever really noticed the symphony of bird songs that filled the air. Some chirped, some trilled, some tweeted. Without the noise of traffic and machines, of radios blaring out of cars and the babble of people, the birds' calls sounded cheerful and full of life.

Striding beside Jonathan, she took deep breaths. The air smelled sweet. There was an undertone of earthiness, a scent that made her think of fertility. Well, of course, she thought, laughing silently at herself. She was on a farm. Plants. Animals. Things grow on farms. Even a city woman—even a *hotshot accountant*—knew that.

Jonathan left her at the entrance to the first of the three large barns. Lily stood in the doorway to a wood-lined hallway, amused that a Mozart violin concerto was playing softly. Down the hall to the right, through an open door, she saw a file cabinet and guessed that was the office where Jonathan had promised to lock Dolly. Strange odors filled her head—rich, earthy, woody, unmistakably animal smells. To her surprise, she found them almost pleasant, not revolting, as she'd expected.

A sharp whistle was answered by a distant "Woof!" Lily stiffened and stepped back outside the doorway. She heard the sound of hands clapping, heard another deep bark, then Jonathan's voice, muffled. The memory of that huge black dog coming at her, its fangs bared, its breath hot on her face, started her shaking. When Jonathan called her name from inside the barn, she had to draw several breaths before she could release the door frame and step inside.

"All safe, my dear," Jonathan said. "Follow me. The horses are all inside for supper. Blake is in a grooming stall, working on one of our oldest mares. Patsy has produced some fine sport horses for us."

Lily followed Jonathan along the dusty concrete floor, into the barn. It was a huge square building with a high metal ceiling. Bars, like those on basement windows in the city, topped a half wall that ran all around three sides of the inside. Through some of the bars, she could see dark forms, silhouetted by the sunlight filtering in through windows. Except for the side of the barn where she and Jonathan stood, the floor in the center was dark dirt mixed with wood chips. Chirping birds swooped around the rafters, then settled in nests she could just see on the high beams. Now that she was inside, the smells of animals and earth were stronger, but still not unpleasant. As long as she didn't step in anything...

"This way," Jonathan prompted, smiling. It was touching how proud he was of his farm and his horses. Lily smiled back. A bell chimed. "Oh, drat! The phone." He turned and hurried past her, calling, "Just keep going along there, my dear. Blake will look after you. I'll be back in a moment."

Her pulse gave a funny jump that she didn't want to attribute to being alone with Blake. She frowned. She'd always thought physical attractions—especially instantaneous attractions—were definitely overrated. It was silly and adolescent, at best, and dangerous, at worst, to let her hormones take control of her head. She certainly wasn't desperate for male companionship. And she certainly wasn't interested in the inflated charms of a macho hick like Blake Sommers!

With that resolve in mind, Lily cautiously walked in the direction Jonathan had pointed. In the shadows, she could hear the faint rumble of Blake's low voice. She passed an empty cubicle that looked like a self-service car wash with faucets, a hose rolled on the wall and a drain in the black rubber floor mat. Above, two large amber light bulbs dangled. The next cubicle was the same as the first. Did horses take showers? What an odd notion. But then, all she knew about horses, after beginning work on the stable's ledgers, was that they ate enormous amounts of costly food and required the services of rather expensive experts.

A few more cautious steps brought her to a third cubicle, but this one had none of the washing equipment of the first two. It did contain a real live horse, the rich auburn color of a chestnut, standing facing out toward the center of the barn. And, with his back toward her, dressed again all in black, Blake stood with his arms around the horse's neck. The horse's eyes were almost closed, and its ears drooped limply, as if it were totally relaxed, completely trusting the man who embraced it.

The unexpectedly disarming sight made her smile.

Blake inhaled the familiar warm horsey scent and rubbed his hand against the crest of Patsy's neck, enjoying the quiet friendship of the old mare. If he lived to be two hundred and ten, he'd never tire of the company of these noble animals.

"Hello." Lily's soft voice greeted him. "I hope I'm not interrupting anything."

His face grew warm at the amusement in Lily's tone. He dropped his arms and stepped away from Patsy.

"Nope." Oh, hell. He sounded like Gary Cooper in an old cowboy movie.

He turned to look at her. She'd come closer and the deep blue of her eyes held his. For the first time, he noticed that there were tiny black and white flecks in her irises, lending them the mystery of lapis lazuli. He lowered his gaze. The peach-colored sweater under her open navy jacket looked soft. Her navy slacks had a knife-edge crease right down to her simple flat shoes. She looked expensive but not showy. Classy. And every inch a woman, even if she called herself an accountant.

Blake raised his eyes to her face again. Her mouth was bare. She'd pulled her hair back tightly, but he remembered how silky it was, and his fingers itched to release it and feel it flowing over his skin. Awareness started his pulse racing, but he knew he wouldn't get anywhere with her unless he forced himself to be patient. Think of her as a skittish mare, he counseled himself. Move slowly. Speak softly. Touch carefully. Clenching his jaw, he turned away.

"You'd be more comfortable in jeans and boots," he told her, more gruffly than he intended.

"The boots I have are too good to wear in a barn," she replied stiffly.

Angry at himself for putting her back up again, he unsnapped the rope tie attached to Patsy's halter, ready to take the mare back to her stall. Lily hurriedly stepped away, losing her balance as she went from the firm cement of the grooming stall to the soft arena dirt of the center. He reached for her arm, but she righted herself. Patsy, friendly and curious, stuck her nose toward Lily. Lily moved back even farther, her eyes wide.

Blake held back a smile. "Patsy won't hurt you. She just wants to say hello. Morgans are people horses."

"She's huge." Lily's voice was barely over a husky whisper. Her brave but fearful expression sent protectiveness surging through him.

"Actually, Patsy's pretty small. Thirteen hands, three and a half inches to here." He placed his hand on the withers of the mare waiting patiently at his side. "She's a half inch below the legal limit for ponies, even though she's considered a horse."

Lily's eyes followed his hand as he stroked Patsy's broad, warm back, then looked up at the mare's face. "She looks huge to me," she said with touching stubbornness.

"She's solid." He ran his hand down the bone and muscle of the mare's shoulder, and Patsy rubbed her muzzle against his hair. His quick glance at Lily was a mistake. He couldn't help wondering how it would feel to run his hand along her curves and have her nestle close to him in response. Immediately, his body tightened, threatening to give his primal reaction away. He angled away, not wanting to make Lily any more uneasy than she already was.

"She wouldn't bite you, would she?"

Would you? Blake caught himself before he said the words aloud and shook his head. "Not this gal. This is mutual grooming. She's paying me a compliment by treating me like another horse. Sort of like I rub her back, and she rubs mine." Lily rewarded him with a small, skeptical smile. He grinned, enjoying the subtleties of flirting with her. "Horses are vegetarians."

Lily's eyebrows arched, and her smile widened a little. "Are you trying to assure me I'm not on the menu?"

Desire clawed at him, and he decided to drop his pretense of polite distance. To hell with subtleties. "Depends on whose menu," he told her softly.

Her smile faded and her eyes turned dark. "Blake, please don't," she said huskily, but her gaze dropped to his mouth, and he knew she was feeling the same hunger that was coursing through his veins. He could see the pulse beating in the hollow of her throat. If he moved a few inches, bent his head just a little, he could be tasting that delicate spot....

"Is there someone else?" He had to ask, but the words came out choked. It was the only reason he could see for keeping his distance. But how could she be involved with someone else, when the attraction between them crackled like summer lightning? He'd lived too long to think this was all one-sided.

"Only me," she said.

He smiled. "Then there's no problem."

Her eyes flashed. "You mean, I'm fair game if no other man has staked his claim?"

Uh-oh. Her voice stayed low and husky, but he heard anger vibrate in it. He could backtrack, but that wasn't his style. Instead, he stepped closer, forcing her to tilt her face up toward his. Her lapis eyes darkened, softened, the anger suddenly gone. She looked surprised. A little confused. Her lips parted. If she wasn't thinking about kissing him, he was a Martian. But he had a feeling she'd deny it. Why, he wondered? Wasn't he as good as the three-piece-suited high-finance types in New York?

"Blake, my boy!" Jonathan's voice startled him. He looked past Lily to his friend of sixteen years. The old goat was grinning slyly. "Is there a reason Patsy is roaming around the barn on her own?"

Blake felt the sting of heat in his cheeks and cleared his throat. "Yeah. I was, uh, showing Lily how smart the mare is, to find her own stall."

Lily's eyes sparkled, obviously amused at his expense. She turned to face Jonathan. "I'm very impressed."

"I can see where you would be, my dear," the older man said smoothly.

Blake gritted his teeth.

"That was Dora Simpson in New Jersey on the phone," Jonathan told him, catching his interest. "She's been having trouble keeping the farm going since Edward's death, so she's thinking of selling out and retiring. She was kind enough to offer us first choice of her stock, and those antique vehicles I've been coveting. I'd like to go down there and see what she has in her herd."

Edward Simpson had bred some fine, athletic Morgans, Blake knew. He nodded his agreement to Jonathan. This might be his chance to pick up some foundation mares for his own breeding program. It never hurt to think about the future.

"It's going to be hard for her to adjust. I promised her any help she might need." Jonathan turned to Lily. "While Blake is retrieving Patsy, let me show you around and introduce you to some of these fine ladies. We have fifteen foals due in the next few weeks. Perhaps you'll have the opportunity to see a foal born. It's quite the miracle."

The queasy look on Lily's face told Blake she was hoping to skip that particular experience. Well, he'd make sure she got to see a foaling, if any of the mares cooperated. It was the kind of miracle that people needed to witness, to remind them what life was all about. Not money, not paper-pushing and number-crunching and lights blinking on a computer screen, but nature, survival, feelings, awe. The things that made life worth living.

While these thoughts ran through Blake's head, Jonathan made a big deal of offering his arm to Lily and leading her off toward the west side of the barn. With a grunt, Blake strode toward the opposite side where Patsy was standing in front of her own stall. Pausing with his hand on the mare's halter, he glanced across the barn to where Lily stood beside Jonathan. At that moment, she looked over her shoulder and met his eyes. Even at a distance of forty feet, he could feel the electricity.

The day after her tour of the mare's barn, a commotion in the kitchen pulled Lily's attention from the ledger she was studying. She heard Carrie greet Jonathan and looked at her watch. Three o'clock! Where had the afternoon gone? She'd been working steadily all day, and had barely made a dent in sorting the financial records from the breeding, training and horse-show records. At this rate, she'd be at March Acres until the turn of the century.

"Tea or hot chocolate, my dear?" Jonathan called from the doorway of his office. He wore an apron that read Kiss The Cook.

Lily smiled, unable to find even a shred of impatience at his interruption. "Hot chocolate, please," she answered, even though she normally drank coffee. "I'll be right in." She put a marker in the ledger and closed it, straightened her pencils and scratch pad, then saved the work in the computer.

Carrie, in bright orange overalls and a white long-sleeved shirt, sat sprawled across two kitchen chairs, the bottom half of an Oreo cookie in one hand. As Lily entered the kitchen, Carrie smiled warmly and sat up. It was impossible not to see the resemblance between Blake and his daughter, especially in their eyes and their smiles. And equally impossible not to like both of them.

"Hi!" Carrie called. "Nice sweater."

Lily glanced down at her cream-and-blue pullover.

"Thanks." She took the mugs Jonathan handed her and set them on the table.

A wistful look came into Carrie's dark eyes. "I wouldn't look good in a sweater like that. I'm too big and clunky."

Jonathan paused halfway across the kitchen, pivoted and returned the pot of hot chocolate to the stove. Lily guessed he was leaving her to deal with a delicate topic.

"But you're not clunky, Carrie. You've got the kind of looks that can be sporty, or very dramatic. Like Julia Roberts, for example," Lily assured her. Carrie's wide-eyed expression at the comparison to the popular film beauty made Lily smile. "On the other hand," she added, "if I wore an outfit like yours, I'd be mistaken for a preschooler."

Carrie smothered a snort of laughter.

"It's true," Lily assured her. "A few weeks ago, I had to show my driver's licence to get a glass of wine. My date wasn't amused."

"My dad would have laughed," Carrie declared. "He's got a great sense of humor."

Behind Carrie, Jonathan again started across the kitchen with the hot chocolate. At those words, his face split in a grin Lily couldn't miss, even with her attention on the girl. Blake certainly had a fan club.

"Sometimes," Carrie added, drawing her brows together and twisting her mouth. She stared down at her half-eaten cookie.

Again, Jonathan halted halfway across the kitchen. Lily caught his eye. He nodded slightly, then turned around and set the hot chocolate back on the burner. She understood that he was encouraging her to get Carrie to confide in her, but this was hardly her area of expertise. Being without a mother, Carrie probably needed another woman to talk to, but they were relative strangers. Lily couldn't think of anything to say. Carrie solved the problem for her by meeting her eyes and speaking first.

"He always taught me not to judge people before I got to know them, but if a guy he hasn't known since kindergarten asks me out, Dad's convinced he's Jack the Ripper."

Lily smiled gently. "I think most fathers have trouble when their daughters start to grow up."

"Did your dad get weird about guys you dated? You know, asking them questions about their family, and what college they're going to, and what they're going to do with their lives?"

"My dad died when I was twelve, but I think he would have," she confided. If her mother's intense jealousy hadn't kept her and her father on thin emotional ice, she added to herself.

"Oh. I'm sorry. That must have been hard. I never knew my mother, which probably made it easier for me. She died right after I was born." Carrie smiled sadly. "I think a lot about what she must have been like. I think she was probably very special, but I don't know much about her. It always made Dad unhappy to talk about her, so I stopped asking. He even destroyed their wedding pictures, so he wouldn't be reminded of her."

Lily realized she felt vaguely...jealous?...of Carrie's mother, even though—of course—she had no romantic interest in Blake herself. It was the idea of a love being so strong, so long-lasting, that appealed. A fairy-tale kind of love. Not the kind of love that could exist in the real world. With her parents always arguing and hurting each other, until her father's untimely death, and then Jeffrey's devastating betrayals, she'd become cynical about love.

"She must have been special," Lily commented gently. "Her daughter certainly is."

Carrie blushed, but shrugged. "Dad's gotta be over her by now. It's been over seventeen years. He better find someone soon," she said casually, but her eyes focused brightly on Lily. "Before he gets too old." A troubled expression darkened Carrie's eyes. "I'm going to college next year, and he's going to be lonely." The girl smiled brightly again. "He's not so old yet, and he's pretty good-looking. Don't you think so?"

Again, behind Carrie, Jonathan beamed as he stirred the more-than-ready chocolate mixture. Lily realized Carrie was hinting—with the subtlety of a neon billboard—that Blake was available, and that she approved of Lily as a candidate.

"No, not at all," she said quickly. Carrie's mouth dropped open. "I mean. No. He's not so old," Lily stammered. "Ah, Jonathan! Can I help you with the hot chocolate?"

"Relax, my dear. Everything is under control." He walked over, filled the mugs and then walked back to place the pot in the sink. "When we finish, would you like to take a walk and clear your head?" he asked as he sat down.

At the moment, Lily mused, her head was perfectly clear. If she encountered Blake, however, she was likely to find herself in a fog of attraction. "Thanks, but I still have a lot to get through today. Maybe tomorrow."

"Great!" Carrie replied with a grin. "Tomorrow, I'll show you some of the horses Dad's training. He's one of the best in the country. The horses would do anything for him. You'll see."

Touched by Carrie's eagerness, Lily gave in to the inevitable. "Okay. Tomorrow, I'll take a longer break." It couldn't hurt her schedule that much to spend an hour away from the ledgers. And she had every confidence that she was immune to the earthy appeal of Blake Sommers.

Chapter Three

At five forty-five, Lily closed the ledger and shut off the computer. Once again, she'd worked longer than she'd intended. She didn't relish the hour drive home at dusk, when her eyes were so tired she could hardly see straight. Every fiber of her body ached to catch up on the sleep she hadn't gotten for the past few months. And Uncle Bill's car didn't seem to have a cooperative nut or bolt in its rusty little body. If she didn't know how it would hurt his feelings, she'd rent something sensible and easy to drive. But her uncle loved that silly car, and honestly thought he was doing her a favor by insisting she use it. Oh, well, as sacrifices went, it was small and relatively painless.

After slipping into her coat, she found Jonathan in the kitchen, reading the latest issue of *Redbook* magazine. He set it down on the table and grinned. "I only read it for the recipes," he quipped, making her laugh.

"Sure. That's what all the guys say," she teased. Standing in the doorway, she buttoned her coat. "See you tomorrow."

Lily let herself out of the house and into the cold evening air, feeling somewhat bemused. Despite her best attempts, she couldn't chase Blake from her mind. It was irritating and puzzling that she found him attractive. She was so obviously, laughably, out of her element on the farm. He might think he was attracted to her, but he'd certainly be just as much a misfit in a museum or at an evening of theater as she was in a barn.

Seated in the chilly sports car, Lily turned the ignition key. The engine's *wah-wah-wah-wah* slowed ominously. She pressed the gas pedal and something under the hood made a muffled *thunk*. Hitting the steering wheel did nothing to help the engine or her frustration. She'd been irresponsible enough to let tact prevent her from getting a rental car. Why hadn't she ignored Uncle Bill's blithe assurances and gotten this bucket of bolts tuned before taking it out of storage?

A light tap on her window made her jump. Cautiously, she turned to look out, expecting Dolly's bloodthirsty face. Instead, she found herself at eye level with a brass belt buckle and the fly of formfitting black pants. *Oh, my!*

She rolled down the window and peered upward. "Hi."

Blake braced both hands on the roof of the car and leaned down. He smelled of fresh air and horses. "Hi, yourself. Pop the hood. I'll see what's wrong."

She did as he instructed. Without another word, Blake went to the front of the car and lifted the hood, obscuring her view of his black-sweatered torso. Irritated at being cast as the damsel in distress, Lily sat and fumed while Blake did whatever men did when they reached under the hood. The car rocked as he leaned against it, and without intending to, Lily found herself imagining how the car would also rock with the movements of lovers—assuming anyone was foolish or desperate enough to try.

"Let's try it," Blake said into the window. Lily's cheeks burned at how his words fit in so neatly with her fantasy. She turned the key, and the engine caught after only one sputter. "She's got bad plug wires, and could use a tune-up," he told her over the rattle of the engine.

Why did men always assume cars were female? As far as she was concerned, this car was male: stubborn, unreliable and selfish, with a bottomless pit for oil and gas.

"As long as it lasts until I'm finished here, I'll be happy," Lily replied.

Blake frowned. "Then you better plan to finish in a few days, because this old gal is on her last legs."

Even without a Texas drawl, he sounded so much like a movie cowboy that a laugh burst out of her. "Well, Doc, I hope I don't have to shoot her."

Blake snorted. "You won't think it's so funny when she dies on you. Tomorrow, I'll take a better look at those wires and see if I can do anything with the timing."

Lily opened her mouth to protest his assumptions, but the expression in his dark eyes silenced her. "Seriously, Lily, this car isn't reliable. Why don't you stay at the farm until you're finished? Jonathan has plenty of spare rooms, and he'd love the company. So would Carrie." His eyes held a world of sensual promise that sent ripples chasing over her skin. "I would, too."

Too much, too soon, her instincts warned. "I can't," she said curtly, to shield herself from the heat in his gaze.

He gave her a slow, lazy smile. "Why not?"

"I have a life outside work," she protested lamely.

"I know you do," he said softly, his voice husky and

low, making her think of kisses in the moonlight. "I'm trying to be a part of it."

Lily closed her eyes against the temptation in his, but it didn't help. She couldn't block out the memory of his arms around her when Dolly had frightened her. He'd made her feel safe and protected and deliciously aware of herself as a woman. And of him as a man. It was more than anyone else had ever done for her, she mused, remembering her parents' self-absorption and Jeffrey's hollow promises and spiteful demands. But Blake had nothing to offer her except a romantic diversion she didn't want or need. She wasn't about to sacrifice her self-respect for a roll in the hay, no matter how appealing this man was.

She opened her eyes to find Blake's face even closer, inches from the window opening. She could smell the spice of his cologne under the earthy scents of horse and leather, and could hear his steady breathing. "Blake, I don't do flings, and I don't have room for anyone serious in my life. I don't *want* anyone serious in my life. Not now. My work is very demanding, but I love it. I have everything I want, and I'm happy. Please don't make this hard."

He reached one hand into the car and caught at a loose strand of her hair. Her scalp tingled when he tugged gently. She fought the urge to lean her head back into his hand and seek his caress. That, too, was a danger sign because she never liked being touched by strangers.

"You're the one making things...hard." His eyes held hers, and she couldn't miss the double meaning behind his words. Her cheeks grew warm. "For the record, I don't do flings, either. And I don't think you have everything you want."

"Give me a break." She spoke in a deliberately scornful drawl. He grinned smugly. "Don't tell me *you're* what's missing in my life." His grin held steady. "I have to leave," she snapped, blinking back the sting of sudden, inexplicable tears.

Blake released her hair and touched his fingers to her cheek. She recoiled, glaring at him, but part of her yearned for more of the contact. He smiled—a lazy, sexy smile that told her he knew exactly how she was reacting to his touch. And knew she didn't want him to know.

"I'm not going to chase you around the haymow. You'll be as safe here as you want to be." His expression told her he also knew she wasn't sure how safely distant from him she wanted to be.

With his gaze smoldering into hers, he touched her cheek lightly, the feel of his slightly rough fingertip leaving a trail of warmth along her skin. His gravelly murmur conjured up images of rumpled sheets tangled around heated bodies. The impulse to throw away safety for that promise of passion made her shiver. What on earth was wrong with her? She didn't even *like* sex, and here she was entertaining X-rated fantasies about an arrogant stranger!

Blake suddenly straightened beside her. Lily took the opportunity to shift into first gear. Before she could release the clutch, a muddy pickup truck pulled into the parking area and halted near the path between Jonathan's and Blake's houses. Outside her still-open window, Blake swore sharply under his breath. A few seconds later, Carrie jumped out of the truck, waved at the driver, then turned to hurry toward her father and Lily. The girl's expression wavered from guilty to sheepish and worried.

Thinking back to her conversation with Carrie, Lily guessed that the driver of the pickup was one of those boys Blake didn't approve of. As the truck drove away,

Blake's low muttering confirmed her guess. Not for anything, Lily mused, would she want to be a teenager again.

"Hi! What's happening?" Carrie greeted them with exaggerated cheer. Her smile, aimed at Lily, looked positively desperate. Lily smiled in sympathy, but there was no way she intended to get involved in this family argument. She'd had enough of that hell in her own life.

Blake grunted. "You tell me," he growled. "Was that the Preston boy?"

"His name's Rick, Dad."

"Around here, his name is mud. I've told you before, I don't want you going anywhere with him. He's wild and irresponsible."

Carrie cast Lily a pleading look, then turned back to Blake. "You don't know him. You don't know what he's like. You hate him because of his parents and his brother, but he's not like them." As she spoke, Carrie's voice grew shrill. "It's not fair."

"We'll discuss this later. Lily doesn't need to witness a family squabble. She's got a long drive back to Rochester."

Carrie's cheeks turned pink. "Sorry."

Lily shook her head. "That's okay, Carrie. But I do need to get back. Uncle Bill holds dinner until I get in." She smiled at the girl. "See you tomorrow." Carrie gave her a little halfhearted wave.

Then, Blake did something unexpected and, to Lily's mind, wonderful. He hugged his daughter and ruffled her hair. Long after Lily drove away from the farm, the sight of Blake with his arm casually draped over his daughter's shoulder lingered in her mind. Much as she hated to admit it, she admired Blake's ability to show his affection for his daughter, despite his disapproval of her actions. Maybe she'd misjudged him, she thought uncomfortably.

* * *

The next morning, Lily was again bent over the March Acres books, even though it was Saturday and she could have used a day off. She didn't want to waste a second she could be investing in an early finish. The night before, Michael Mason, senior partner and her mentor since she joined the firm, had phoned to alert her that she was number one on the shortlist for the firm's Far East office. Her dreams were closer than ever.

It would be naive, she knew, to assume that no one else in the firm wanted that assignment as much as she did. There was Jeffrey, for one, who believed he deserved the promotion and the opportunity involved. His overt attempts to manipulate her into withdrawing, to increase his own odds, had convinced her to break their engagement. Michael was a very powerful ally, but competition was keen at every level. She simply had to go back to her own work, the sooner the better.

And, she warned herself, daydreaming about her chances at the Hong Kong posting was not getting the work at hand done. With a quick stretch, she turned to the next page of the ledger and started entering figures into the computer.

"Hi, Lily!" Carrie called from the doorway of Jonathan's office.

Startled, Lily looked up and blinked at the grinning girl. Carrie wore a deep green sweatshirt emblazoned in white with March Acres Morgans on the front, tight-fitting black riding pants and yellow leather work boots. Her long, dark hair had been pulled back into a ponytail, revealing classic features that would keep Carrie beautiful long into her life.

"How can you work inside on such a beautiful day?"

Lily smiled. "Don't you know how dull accountants are?"

Carrie's dimple deepened. "I'm here to save you from yourself. Come to the arena. Dad's going to work one of the more advanced horses, and he said we can watch. You'll love it."

"Carrie, I have so much to do...." The disappointment on the girl's face reminded Lily of all the times she had pleaded with her own mother for a little time together. "But," she added, "I guess I could use a break. And I did promise you yesterday that I would go see the horses." She wasn't at all interested in gawking at Blake, but she was getting stiff from working, and she honestly enjoyed Carrie's company.

"Excellent!" Carrie watched as she saved her work and exited the computer program. "Why did you become an accountant?"

Lily reached for her jacket. "I always did well in math, and I thought there'd be a lot of opportunities, especially in international investments." She snapped off the light switch as they walked out of the room. Holding the front door open for Carrie, Lily met the girl's eyes with a rueful smile. "And my favorite uncle, who just happens to be an accountant, gave me a part-time job when I was fourteen."

Carrie chuckled. "I guess that's why I want to be a vet and breed Morgans, too. Dad was going to go to vet school, but after my mother died he brought me here and went to work for Jonathan, instead. He's super with animals. It's like he's got some sixth sense to communicate with them."

Lily pondered that information. She was less interested in Blake's talent with animals than she was in his sacrificing his career plans to raise his daughter after losing his wife. That must have been hard on him, she reflected.

She knew women who combined demanding careers with motherhood, and others who had opted out of the rat race to raise children. Blake was the first man she'd met who had managed to balance his work with being a father, a *single* father. And he'd sacrificed a dream of his own to do it well. One more reason to suspect she'd underestimated Blake Sommers. She would have preferred to discover something that would help her dislike the man!

Carrie was still chattering. "I gave your business card to the guidance counselor for career day. She said she'll call this week, while you're still here. But I was wondering. Why does the card say you have a law degree? I thought you're an accountant."

"I am, but I also have a law degree. I'm a specialist in international tax law."

"Is that good?" Carrie's voice revealed her skepticism.

Lily chuckled. "It has been for me, although it's probably an acquired taste." Carrie giggled. "Honestly, it's an exciting field. My firm has multinational clients based in all sorts of exotic places. There's always the possibility that an assignment will involve traveling to Europe or the Orient, or even living overseas for a year or two, sometimes longer. I'm hoping for that kind of assignment as soon as I get back to my office."

"Wow!"

Carrie fell silent, as if mulling over what she'd heard. As Lily walked beside the girl toward the barns, she drew a deep, soul-cleansing breath. The air was damply sweet, warm from the sun but cool underneath. Patches of white and purple crocuses spread between the path and the brown, matted grass. Dampness from the ground oozed coolly through her flat leather shoes, and she gamely tried to ignore whatever was seeping into the cuffs of her wool slacks. A bird chirped a cheerful song over and over in the trees above their heads. In the parking area, several cars stood lined up beside Uncle Bill's antique MG and Blake's Jeep.

"Who's here?" she asked. She still didn't know much about the daily routine of the farm, even after nearly a week. "I must have been working too hard to hear anyone drive up."

"Just some of the boarders. Saturdays and Sundays get pretty busy in the mornings, but only a few people ride in the afternoons. Dad and I give lessons in the morning, and usually he'll do some private teaching later. During the week, there are a few people who ride mornings, but most of the other boarders ride in the evening. Dad trains horses during the day and gives lessons at night."

"So what is it that I'm going to love seeing now?" *Besides Blake,* she thought, not missing the point of Carrie's pitch. It was flattering, but misplaced.

"Dad's been training one of the boarders and his horse to go Grand Prix in dressage."

"Translate, please," Lily said with a light laugh.

Carrie stopped in her tracks and shot her an incredulous look. "Dressage is a type of horse training, a little like ballet and a little like gymnastics. It's also called classical or flat riding, because it dates back to the ancient Greeks, and because it doesn't involve jumps."

"Oh," Lily replied, still not sure what to expect. Somehow, she couldn't picture horses and riders doing cartwheels and back flips together.

Carrie smiled and started walking again. "Grand Prix is the highest level of international competition. It's what they do in the Olympics and the world championships."

It was beginning to make more sense now. Lily had

been in gymnastics from the age of four until fifteen, when biology had defeated her mother's attempts to starve her into prolonged girlhood. Maybe Blake would turn out to be a cold, demanding coach, giving her something to dislike about him.

"I guess I'll understand better when I see whatever it is Blake is going to do," she commented. "You can explain it to me."

"Dressage is a beautiful sport," Carrie declared, her eyes shining. "Most of the horses in serious competition are big breeds, like Thoroughbreds or the European warmbloods. Morgans are just starting to make a name for themselves at the upper levels, and Uncle Jonathan and Dad have bred and trained some of the best."

"And what about you?"

Carrie beamed even brighter. "Next year, my horse should be ready for Intermediare One, and maybe Two. It takes years to get really good. Dad won't rush a horse or rider, so the first lesson is patience. And he never tries to force a horse or rider to do more than they can. He's big on enjoying the work, or it isn't worth doing."

Ah, well, Lily thought, resigned to admiration. It seemed Blake was a compassionate coach, not a slave driver. Too bad for her quest to find serious faults with him, she mused as she walked, but she wouldn't give up hope. There had to be *something* wrong with him, besides that irritatingly attractive arrogance. Maybe, as with chocolate, it was a case of too much of a good thing, except she wasn't willing to gorge herself on Blake's attentions to find out!

They passed the first barn, the mares' barn, and approached the wide, open doorway of the middle barn. It looked more like two buildings attached. When Lily followed Carrie inside, she immediately saw that it was indeed two separate buildings joined by a common wall. To her right, rows of stalls with iron bars on top of cinder-block walls lined two wide aisles running perpendicular to the wide aisle from the doorway. Muffled noises similar to the ones she'd heard in the mares' barn, thumping, brushing, low murmuring and snuffling sounds the horses made, mingled with the occasional human voice, although she couldn't see either people or animals.

Past the wide-open sliding door in the middle of the wall, Lily could see a wedge of dirt surface, much like the one in the center of the mares' barn. Voices drifted unintelligibly toward her, and the air smelled of sweet hay, leather and earthy horse, with the distinct aroma of beeswax mixed in. Once again, she was surprised to realize she didn't dislike these smells.

"Hang on," Carrie said. "I'll see if Dad's in the arena."

A moment after Carrie disappeared around the corner, a young man led a gleaming auburn horse with a flowing ebony mane and tail past Lily. This horse looked much bigger than the mare Patsy, and had the musculature of a classical statue. She pressed herself against the cabinets to get out of their way, then, curious, followed them at what she hoped was a safe distance.

Standing in the doorway between the two banks of cabinets, Lily peered inside. Sunlight poured through sky-lights in the roof and along the three outer walls. The ceiling and walls were unfinished, except for the bottom four or five feet of the walls, where boards had been placed at a slight angle, covering the exposed beams. From speakers hanging from overhead beams, a voice identified a local soft-rock radio station, then introduced Heart's newest single. Lily smiled at the choices of music. Mozart for the expectant mothers, rock for the performers.

The horse and young man who had just passed her joined two others already in the arena. As Lily watched, the new man patted the horse's arching neck, then swung himself into the saddle. The horse began to walk quietly, its neck stretched forward as if it were about to fall asleep on its feet. The thought made Lily smile. The other two horses certainly didn't look sleepy. They were moving in different directions at what seemed like a pretty fast speed to her.

"Craig, keep that outside rein on." Blake's voice came suddenly from deep in a corner of the arena. "Give a little inside. Good. There, he's softening and getting round. Beautiful! Praise him and give him a break."

One of the horses slowed to a walk, and the rider gave it a hearty pat on the neck. She didn't know anything about horses, but at that moment, she would have sworn that Craig's horse knew it had done something well. There was a soft look in its large dark eyes, almost like pride. Until that moment, she wouldn't have considered whether animals had emotions. It was curiously touching to witness.

"Come in," Carrie said, reappearing at the arena door. "Craig and Doug are almost finished, and Lance is warming up."

Lily followed Carrie into the arena. As soon as she stepped into the dirt, her shoes filled with the stuff. A quick glance around told her that dirt wasn't the only substance working its way into her stockings. Best not to think about it.

Blake glanced at Lily then, and their eyes met. His smile started in his dark eyes, sending warm little currents of excitement tingling through her. His mouth curved upward, and his dimple flashed. She smiled back, hoping she didn't look like a teenager with a crush, which was embarrassingly close to the way she suddenly felt. She shouldn't be doing this. She should be finishing her work here so she could protect her career.

"Isn't Dad a hunk for an old guy?" Carrie murmured.

Lily nearly choked. "He's...he's not really old, Carrie."

The girl chuckled. "Not for a tree, huh?" She laughed at her own joke. "No, seriously, he's only thirty-eight. My girlfriends all think he's awesome. So do their mothers. What do you think?"

Thank goodness they were out of Blake's hearing range—if they kept their voices low. He'd turned his attention back to the horses and their riders. Without his smile, Lily felt as if a heat lamp had been turned off.

"You two would look great together," Carrie babbled on, apparently not aware of Lily's discomfort, or her failure to answer. "He's big and dark and you're small and light. He's calm and you're pretty intense. And you know how opposites are supposed to attract."

Desperately, Lily tried to think of something—anything— tactful and intelligent to say to stifle Carrie's enthusiastic matchmaking. The last thing she wanted was to inadvertently hurt this delightful girl. She'd had too much experience with disappointment to take lightly someone else's.

Lily stopped walking and put her hand on the girl's shoulder, slightly disconcerted to find she had to look up to meet her eyes.

"Carrie, a relationship has to be based on more than looking good together. Your father is very attractive, and he's very nice, but he and I have absolutely nothing in common, and I'm not going to be here much longer. I have a life I love in the city, and a career that I've worked very hard to build. I'm flattered, but..." She couldn't think of a way to explain herself, and she finally shrugged helplessly.

Some of the light went out of Carrie's eyes. "That's okay. I get the picture." She shrugged, too. "It's no big deal. C'mon, we better get out of the way."

Following impulse, Lily touched Carrie's cheek lightly with the backs of her fingers. To her surprise and dismay, the girl's eyes filmed over with tears. Then Carrie blinked, smiled and moved away.

Disconcerted, Lily followed Carrie to a padded bench in the corner of the arena. Carrie casually swept her hand over the dust covering the seat, then sat down. Lily decided she'd rather get whatever that stuff was on her pants than on her hands and sat down gingerly without further cleaning the bench. Blake stood, dressed in black as usual, legs braced apart, about a quarter of the way into the middle of the arena, his entire body focused on watching his student and horse.

"Inside leg on, Doug," Blake called. "Get her flexing first. Now, outside leg. Press, press, press. Right! There you go." The little horse moved briskly on a diagonal line across the arena, her legs crossing over smartly, almost as if she were marching sideward. It was surprisingly beautiful. Lily smiled at Carrie.

"That's enough." Blake said, and Doug brought his horse to a prancing walk. "Don't ask for too much at once when she's just learning. Praise her and call it a day. You and Craig can cool your horses down outside. Go have some fun on the trails."

Lily found herself smiling at his final instructions. She'd had several tough coaches during her years of gymnastics, but only a few who had remembered to praise, who had cared about feelings, as well as performance. She didn't have to see any more to know that Blake was tough but caring, the kind of coach students turned themselves inside out trying to please.

It really would be gratifying, she thought yet again, considering her desperate need to *not* like the man, if he could be a little less perfect.

Chapter Four

Blake sucked in a breath and counted to five before turning to walk toward Lily and Carrie. He was still trying to sort out the impact of seeing them together. Whatever female stuff they were talking about, Carrie's enthusiasm for Lily had been unmistakable. And when Lily touched his daughter's face, the gesture had been so purely maternal, the expression on Lily's face so sweetly concerned, that he was stunned.

He'd never thought Carrie needed a mother as long as she had him. Hell, it hadn't been easy, but he'd been determined from the start to do his best. At first, he'd been too busy cramming two years of college into one and trying to find time for his baby girl. Back then, and for a long time afterward, he'd been too upset about Carrie's mother to even think about getting serious with another woman. After he moved to March Acres, Jonathan and his wife had taken over where his own parents had left off when they retired to Arizona. With no children of her own, until she died two years ago Rachel March had showered Carrie with love. He had dated over the years, but had never seriously enough to think about marriage. Had he been shortchanging Carrie without knowing it?

Had he been shortchanging himself, too? There was something about Lily.... Layers of humor and passion and strength that made him want to start peeling away her perfectly pressed and tailored armor. It would be a challenge to get through to her, but he thrived on that kind of challenge. He'd never met a mare, skittish or headstrong, that he couldn't win over with patience and attention. And a lot of stroking.

Blake reached the bench and sank down beside Lily, briefly pressing her leg with his. Her flesh was warm and firm and she smelled wonderful. It definitely wasn't just the armor around her sharp little mind that he wanted to peel away. But then what? Well, he'd have to see, wouldn't he?

When Blake sat down next to Lily, Carrie was in the middle of a complicated explanation of what Lance and his horse were doing. Lily tried to concentrate on Carrie's words and ignore Blake. It was virtually impossible with him so close. First, his thigh pressed along the length of hers, warm and hard through her wool slacks. Then his hip bumped hers. Lily inched toward Carrie, but there wasn't much room, unless she sat in the girl's lap.

She held herself stiffly. There was something comfortable and familiar, yet terribly exciting, about the heat and hardness of Blake's body against hers. Even when she thought she was in love, Jeffrey had never made her feel quite like this. No other man had. Why *this* man? Why, when she was trying so hard to resist?

"Lance will put Charlie through his paces for the Grand

Prix test first,'' Blake told her, his voice low and confidential.

He paused. Politely, Lily turned her head to meet Blake's eyes. Mistake. Big mistake. It was like staring into the sun, hot, and blinding her to everything else. She turned toward the horse and rider again. That only helped a little. She couldn't see his gaze on her, but she could feel it.

"Riding is the only sport where your equipment thinks for itself," Blake murmured. In spite of her acute awareness of, her acute discomfort at, his closeness, she smiled at the notion.

Lance halted his horse in front of them and smiled at Lily before looking at Blake. "We're ready."

Blake nodded. "Let's see."

Lily watched horse and rider trot to the far end of the arena. Intensity radiated from both Carrie and Blake, and she found herself unexpectedly eager to see this dressage test. While horse and rider went through their movements and Blake murmured explanations beside her, Lily let herself absorb the grace and beauty of the horse's movements.

"Excellent," Blake said when Lance finished and rode toward them. "Give him a rest while I get the music cued up." He turned and began fiddling with the stereo on the shelf over their heads. When he reached above her, he gave Lily an interesting glimpse of a dirt-smudged white undershirt and the flat, hard belly it clung to. Her face burned when she looked away.

"This next stuff is what Dad's been working on," Carrie murmured. "It's called a 'kur.' The rider makes up his own test from compulsory movements and rides to music."

"I think I'm catching on. I did competitive gymnastics for years. This seems similar."

"Oh, wow!" Carrie turned shining eyes toward her. Lily smiled self-consciously. Her own excitement had been leeched from her long ago. "Dad! Did you hear that? Lily is a gymnast!"

Blake looked down into her eyes, his expression amused, but whether at her or at his daughter's enthusiasm, Lily couldn't tell. "I heard," he said neutrally.

Lance jumped off Charlie and led him toward Blake. When they got closer, Lily could see that Lance was about twenty-one or so, a handsome young man with earnest gray eyes. He smiled at Lily and leaned against the wall beside her as Blake swung himself up onto Charlie's back and began a slow trot around the arena. Immediately, Lily saw an indefinable difference in the way the horse held his head and moved under Blake. It was as if they were fusing together, becoming larger than life.

At Blake's signal, Lance flipped on the tape player and a strong rock beat poured out of the speakers. Transfixed, Lily sat forward, watching Blake ride Charlie to the music. He used the same walk, trot and canter patterns as Lance, yet there was a magic to the horse's movements that had been missing with the younger man. Breathlessly Lily observed horse and rider, feeling the rhythms of the steps flowing through her own body.

The horse seemed to defy gravity. His feet barely touched the ground. Blake sat so quietly that at first, Lily thought he was motionless, letting the horse do all the work. Then she realized that his movments were barely perceptible. His legs shifted slightly against the horse's sides. His seat rocked with the horse's motions, the two of them in such perfect harmony that Lily could believe they had become one entity, a living, breathing centaur.

Blake would make love like that.

Unbidden, the thought echoed in her mind and refused to fade. She felt her cheeks turn pink. What was *wrong* with her? She was trying to find reasons *not* to be attracted to Blake Sommers. The image of him making love so spiritually, so sensuously, so *sensitively,* did nothing to discourage her confused libido. It wouldn't be so hard to ignore if the impression were strictly physical, but she could feel something deep inside her responding to the insight. She really had to get out of here!

Blake halted the horse in the center of the arena. Lily couldn't take her eyes off the smoldering expression in his eyes. Breathlessly she watched him ride closer, saw him pat the horse's neck and swing out of the saddle. She was hardly aware of Lance taking the horse from Blake and walking away. She'd all but forgotten about Carrie sitting beside her. All she saw was the dark fire in Blake's eyes. All she felt was the excitement shimmering through her.

He stood in front of her and peeled off his black leather gloves. His hands were square, long-fingered, strong-looking. Meeting his gaze again, she thought about the way he'd held her when Dolly jumped on her. His eyes darkened, and she knew his thoughts mirrored her own.

"So, what did you think?" he asked, his voice husky.

"I think..." She swallowed. "I think that was the most beautiful thing I've ever seen."

His smile started in his eyes, and curved his mouth in a very appealing way. "Come up to the house for coffee," he said.

She didn't dare. Her nerves were raw with awareness, tingling from the erotic beauty of his riding. Her only defense from making an utter fool of herself was to escape quickly.

"Thanks, but I have to get back to work." She forced herself to break eye contact, then smiled at Carrie. "Thanks for reminding me to take a break," she said, gently touching the girl's arm. "I'll see you Monday." Carrie chewed her lower lip and nodded. Lily suspected the girl was wondering what else she could do to bring her father and Lily together. Once upon a time, she'd also been a romantic teenager. She hoped Carrie would never experience the disillusionment she had.

Shaking off unpleasant thoughts, she stood, which brought her squarely in front of Blake. He stepped closer and captured her shoulders in his strong hands. "Don't forget what they say about all work and no play," he murmured, in a lover's intimate tone.

Lily saw her opening and smiled. "I'm *so* flattered you think I'm dull, Mr. Sommers," she said sweetly.

Blake grinned, his dimple showing. "I think you're about as dull as a new razor, *Ms. Davis.*" His fingers tightened through the thick layers of her coat, giving her just a hint of contact, and then he released her. With a wink, he turned and sauntered away.

Lily closed her eyes against the sight of his powerful leg and buttock muscles flexing under the tight fabric of his riding pants. It didn't help. She opened her eyes and sighed.

"What on earth was that all about?" Carrie said beside her.

"Nothing," Lily replied lightly, but she knew that was a lie. She and Blake had had an entire dialogue without words, and she hadn't done very well at maintaining her defenses. The sooner she finished working for Jonathan and got away from the attractions of Blake Sommers, the better.

"Bad news, my dear," Jonathan announced from the doorway to his office. "The rain is starting to freeze."

"Oh!" Lily glanced at the schoolhouse clock on the wall. "Oh, no!" Five-thirty! What had happened to four o'clock, when she'd planned to leave and beat the storm? She'd have to phone Uncle Bill to warn him she'd be late for dinner. Again.

"I think it would be wise for you to consider staying the night, Lily. According to the radio, there are already a dozen or so accidents, and the rain is coming down quite hard."

She knew he was right, but she hesitated to accept. The more time she spent at the farm, the more comfortable she felt there. That wasn't good. If she grew too fond of the farm and its inhabitants, she'd be sorry to leave. And she didn't want anything to spoil her joy over her new work assignment. Still, the MG didn't have snow tires—the poor thing barely had a transmission. She didn't want to go home in a body cast after sliding off the icy road into a tree or a ditch.

Reluctantly, she said, "Thank you, Jonathan."

The elderly man flashed the boyish grin that was so at odds with his professorial manner. "Don't worry, my dear. Bill understands this weather, and he knows what it's like to get lost in his work. Say hello to the old rascal for me when you call. Carrie can lend you nightclothes, and I'm sure I have an extra new toothbrush." He started to leave, then turned back. "It's Blake's turn to cook tonight. I'll tell him to bring dinner over at half past six. Can you make biscuits?"

His question sounded so innocent that she did a quick double take. "Yes, if you've got a recipe."

"It's on the box of biscuit mix. I'll get everything ready, and call you at six. Do you have enough light?"

She started to say she did, when a fork of lightning lit the sky. A second later, thunder exploded, seemingly overhead. "Oh, dear. I have to turn off the computer, in case the electricity goes out."

"Good idea. Although the ice alone can be enough to knock the power out. I'll be in the kitchen stoking the wood stove whenever you're ready." Jonathan disappeared down the hall.

Quickly she saved her last work and exited the program. Without the hum of the computer, the rain sounded like hail against the windows. Lightning flashed again, followed by deafening, rolling thunder. The sky had turned a spooky purple. Thank goodness she wouldn't have to drive an hour or more in that weather, even if it meant having dinner with Blake. After all, she'd also be having dinner with Jonathan and Carrie. And after dinner, she could retreat to safety by running the computer on the battery. Or plead exhaustion and escape to bed early.

Once the biscuits were cut and in the oven, Lily offered to set the table, but Jonathan refused, insisting instead that she take a few minutes to freshen up and make the bed in one of the four spare bedrooms upstairs. She chose the front corner room, with white eyelet priscilla-curtained windows overlooking the tree-lined driveway and the sweep of front lawn. The violet-scattered wallpaper and lace bedspread added to the room's old-fashioned feminine atmosphere.

Just as she was leaning over the double mattress to tuck the far corner of the fitted sheet under, the lights flickered and went out. Lily waited, hoping the lights would come back on. She wasn't scared, but she didn't know her way around the room, or most of the house, for that matter. She didn't want to knock anything over or walk facefirst into something solid. At least she could finish making the bed by feel.

"Lily?" It was Blake's deep voice, coming from the hallway. She saw a glimmer of light and called back. A moment later, he appeared in the doorway, the dim light of a candle casting shadows on his handsome face. "Are you all right?"

"Fine, thanks." Lying, she mused, was becoming much too easy for her. She wasn't fine now that he was there. She was jumpy and nervous and feeling utterly foolish that he could have this effect on her. And she wouldn't have admitted it for anything.

He stepped into the room, seeming to grow larger and yet less easy to see clearly as he came closer. She caught a shallow little breath and smelled the spice of his cologne. The candle cast a circle of shimmery golden light in the center of the room, drawing her closer to Blake.

"I brought you this," he said, his voice low.

She couldn't see anything besides his face. "What is it?"

"Hold out your hands."

She extended her hands in front of her, unable to stop their trembling. The first touch of his arm burned her fingertips. She pulled her hands back.

"Try again," he murmured. "I'm right here."

That was the problem. But she wouldn't admit that to him. She held out her hands again. Soft fabric folded over them. "What's this?"

"A nightgown and robe of Carrie's." His low voice vibrated with intimacy. "For tonight."

Lily clutched the clothes to her chest. "Oh. I'll go thank her."

"She's not here. She's stuck overnight at a friend's house."

"Oh." At least Jonathan would be with them for the evening. In the spell of the candlelight, alone with Blake, she was afraid she'd make it too easy for him to see through her pretense of disinterest.

"There's a painting in the Frick Collection in New York City," Blake said softly, "called the *Education of the Virgin*. You can see the glow of a candle through the fingers of the girl's hand." Lily felt her jaw drop. "Seeing you in candlelight reminds me of that painting. Your skin looks translucent."

His fingertip left a trail of fire down her left cheek. She stared up at him through the golden shadows and clutched the bundle of clothes tighter. Oh, God, had she really considered him a hick, and assumed he was allergic to culture? Contrite, she bit her lower lip to prevent herself from blurting an apology. His lips curved into a crooked smile, as if he knew anyway.

"I think we better get downstairs," he murmured huskily, then turned away.

Lily tried to breathe. If he'd touched her again, she might not have agreed to walk away from the seductive moment. She *needed* to walk away, to stay free of entanglement, so why did she *want* him to try once more to tempt her?

Blake's hand closed around hers, warm, strong, hard, yet incredibly gentle. It felt right. Too right. Keeping her hand limp in his, she followed close behind Blake's steps so that she could see the stairs in the dim, flickering light of his candle. With only inches between them, the smell of burning wax couldn't cover the spicy scent of his skin.

She had to clench her free hand at her side to stop herself from reaching out to touch him.

The instant her feet touched the hardwood floor at the bottom of the stairs, Lily tried to pull her hand away from Blake's. His fingers tightened slightly, and he rubbed his thumb across the back of her hand. She could feel him looking at her in the shadows, waiting for a response, but she refused to look up, refused to let him know her skin tingled from the streak of heat his touch had left on her hand.

The heady aromas of biscuits and roast chicken wafted out of the kitchen. Her stomach grumbled embarrassingly. Blake gave one last caress to the back of her hand and released it. She could feel him smiling at her before he turned away. Rubbing her hand against her pants, she followed him toward the cheery sound of Jonathan whistling Mozart.

The kitchen glowed warmly from the light of several oil lamps on the table and counters. A bottle of white wine stood open in a Lucite chiller between the basket of biscuits and a platter of chicken. Soup bowls sat on dinner plates at three places on the table. Jonathan clearly saw this as a festive occasion. Lily felt as if she'd been caught in an invisible trap.

Jonathan grinned at her. "Come have some vegetable soup while the wine is gasping," he invited. He sat at the head of the table, leaving her to sit across the table from Blake. "Wonderful biscuits, my dear."

"Jonathan's late wife, Rachel, always wanted to teach Carrie to cook," Blake said, helping himself to another portion of chicken, "but my daughter was happier in the barn or on a horse."

Lily sipped her wine and smiled. "Not every woman likes to cook."

Blake shot her an exasperated glance. "Don't tell me you're one of those feminists who think boiling water is slavery."

The sour look on his face made her laugh bubble over. "Actually, I love to cook. And I can't remember the last time I assaulted a man who held a door for me," she added, piling on the mock sweetness.

"Very funny," Blake muttered.

Jonathan snickered. "Forgive him, my dear. Blake's an old-fashioned soul who isn't sure what to do with the new, liberated woman."

Blake reached for another biscuit, then met her eyes. "Oh, I wouldn't say that, exactly. But I wonder if the new, liberated women know what to do with me?" Lily dropped her gaze to his hands, unwillingly fascinated by the way his capable fingers cradled the biscuit as he broke it open. "Think you can teach Carrie to make them like this, instead of like hockey pucks?"

"If she wants to."

"Good." He grinned. "I'll teach you to ride in exchange."

"What if Carrie doesn't want to learn to make biscuits?"

His eyebrows lifted. "Don't worry. She will."

The arrogant way Blake spoke for his daughter, without consulting her, struck a sour note with Lily. It brought back memories of the innumerable times her mother had answered for her, made decisions for her, as if she were a puppet with no will of her own. The challenge in his self-assurance seemed to carry over to his easy assumptions about Lily herself. Finally, she was finding something to dislike about the man!

"And what if I don't want to learn how to ride?"

"Don't worry. You will." Blake flashed her a grin that

told her he'd followed her thoughts and was enjoying baiting her. She opened her mouth to deny any interest in learning to ride, but Jonathan cleared his throat before she could utter a sound.

"You know, my dear," he said, a serious expression in his eyes, "tonight's ice storm started me thinking. Rochester's weather is so changeable in spring. It's not unusual to have snow and ice into May. I'm concerned about you commuting in that little car of Bill's. Blake says it's not terribly reliable. I'd like you to consider staying here until your work is finished."

"Oh!" She was looking at Jonathan, but she could see Blake nodding. "I couldn't...."

"It's the smart thing to do," Blake said, a subtle reminder in his tone that he'd already told her this once. He must have felt her readying a retort to that arrogant assertion, because he quickly added, "Besides, if you don't have to drive two hours a day, you can finish faster."

"That definitely has appeal," she conceded, biting her tongue so she wouldn't fall into his trap about being smart, or not. She didn't want to make the meal unpleasant for Jonathan, and she didn't want Blake to know he could irritate her so easily. Although he'd have had to be comatose not to notice.

Jonathan refilled her wineglass. "Good decision, my dear."

Blake's dark gaze rested on her with unsettling intensity. Lily looked away, to find Jonathan watching her, amusement in his eyes. "It would be a pleasure to have company in the house," Jonathan told her. "Carrie will love having another woman at the farm. I wouldn't be at all surprised if she decides to learn to cook, under your influence." He rose from his chair. "Now, if you young people will excuse me, I'm rather tired. I'll turn in early."

Jonathan cleared his dishes from the table and piled them in the sink, then walked out of the kitchen. Lily glanced at Blake. His smile caught her like a burst of sunlight. Suddenly, the large country kitchen seemed claustrophobic, much too dark and cozy. She hastily gathered her own dishes and put them in the sink with the others. Without waiting to find out what Blake intended, she turned on the water, but only a trickle came out.

"Power's out," Blake said. "The pump won't work. I'll start up the generator later, if the power doesn't come back soon."

"Oh." Lily stared at the sink, dismayed. She'd needed the distraction of washing dishes to delay having to face Blake alone.

The silence between them pulsated with its own energy. It certainly wasn't what she'd have called a companionable silence, but the tension was more exciting than unpleasant. She didn't feel she had to make conversation and, obviously, neither did Blake. On the other hand, she would have liked to know what he was going to do next. And talking—about anything—might just be safer than whatever he had in mind.

"Why don't you go join Jonathan in the living room. I have to check the barns and feed the night hay."

"Do you need help?" The offer was out before she thought.

Blake looked as surprised as she felt. "Do you think you're up to it?"

His doubt irritated her. "I'm hardly a weakling or an invalid. I wouldn't have offered if I didn't think I could help."

He smiled, and she wondered if she'd been subtly manipulated. "I'll bring you some of Carrie's clothes. You can't slog through the mud and carry hay dressed like that.''

''Fine.''

His gaze lowered, traveling slowly over her rosy sweater and straight white wool pants. Heat tingled on her cheeks.

''On the other hand, maybe you should come with me and go through Carrie's things yourself. I haven't a clue what will fit you. I'll get a poncho of Jonathan's for you to wear.'' He grinned, his dimple a quick shadow in the soft light. ''Back before you have a chance to change your mind.''

Minutes later, Blake wrapped a heavy waterproof poncho around Lily's shoulders, then looked down at her black patent leather shoes. With the rain and ice out there, she really needed hip waders, not flimsy, expensive-looking party shoes. There was only one solution that made any sense. The trouble was, he didn't think it would make sense to her. Not the way she'd been trying to avoid him all evening. Nope, he didn't think she was going to like his idea at all. Too bad.

Without giving her any warning, any time to object, he scooped her up into his arms. She gave a little yelp and grabbed him around the neck. It might have been a promising position, if not for the thick layers of coat and poncho between them. But, man, she smelled wonderful! Soft. Mysterious. All woman. If his heart pounded any harder, Lily would probably mistake it for an earthquake.

''Aren't you going to tell me you can walk by yourself?'' he prodded. His ego might not be seriously damaged by her attempts to keep her distance from him, but it did feel a little dented.

''No, thanks.'' She laughed softly, and he had the uncomfortable feeling that she'd just read his mind. ''I offered to help you feed the horses, not to sacrifice a pair of two-hundred-dollar shoes.'' Her breath stirred warmly against his neck when she spoke.

Not daring to say anything with that wave of heat clutching at him, Blake stepped into the biting rain. Lily was light in his arms. Her head pressed against his shoulder, and she held on tightly. He moved quickly across the yard and hurried up his porch stairs.

Out of the wind and rain, he stood and held her, breathing hard. For a long while, she kept her face tucked into his shoulder. Then, slowly, she lifted her head and let it tip back until the hood of the poncho slid off. Her eyes were like a midnight sky in the darkness of the porch. If he didn't put her down that second, he was going to kiss her and ruin any chance he might have for anything more than a brief taste.

Even knowing that, it wasn't an easy decision.

Chapter Five

Lily stood shakily, one hand on Blake's hard arm for support. She couldn't remember ever being carried like that, even as a child. He made her feel safe and cherished, which was ridiculous, since he hardly knew her well enough to cherish. He also made her feel desirable *and* desiring. Another moment in his arms and she would have given in to the temptation that radiated from his dark eyes. He made it all too easy to forget why she should be running the other way.

She took a step back. Blake held open the door to his house, and Lily stepped into a dark foyer. Where, she wondered, was that enormous salivating beast, Dolly? If she asked Blake, he'd probably tease her again about being afraid of dogs. Unwilling to remind him of her weakness, Lily fought down a wave of panic.

"Hang on," he muttered. "I've got flashlights in the kitchen." He disappeared into the shadows, then reappeared a moment later carrying two large flashlights. In the yellow circles of light they made, she could just see a faded Oriental carpet runner leading toward stairs that went up into the dark of the second floor.

She took the light he held out to her. His fingers brushed the backs of hers, trailing sparks. Her beam of light wavered on the paisley carpet. Silently she followed Blake up the stairs, praying that she wouldn't disgrace herself again if Dolly suddenly appeared out of the darkness. To her relief, there was no sign of the dog.

While Blake held the flashlight, Lily searched through Carrie's dresser and found dark sweatpants and a sweatshirt. She held them against her, then stood with her breath trapped in her lungs when he gazed at her, his dark eyes seeming to seek more than whether the clothes would fit her. Finally, he turned away and fished a pair of thick socks from a wicker basket.

"I'll wait for you downstairs with boots."

Lily clutched the clothes to her chest until Blake had shut the door behind him. Moving quickly, trying without success to ignore the fact that she was taking her clothes off with him mere footsteps away, she changed into Carrie's sweats and socks. The pants and shirt hung on her, so she rolled up the sleeves and cuffs. Grabbing the flashlight, she hurried down the stairs. A pair of small, scuffed tan work boots sat in the foyer in front of the door. She slipped her feet into them and tied the laces.

"How do those fit?" Blake asked from the shadows.

Her heart leaped and raced, choking her when she replied, "Pretty well."

"I keep everything Carrie outgrows," he told her as he came closer. "It comes in handy to have extras. Ready?"

"As I'll ever be." Which wasn't exactly what she'd have called *ready*. She still had no idea what she'd volunteered for, in addition to the foolhardiness of being alone with Blake. She could still feel the pressure of his hard arms around her, could still feel the heavy pounding of his heart against her. Worse, she could still feel her own hunger for the taste of his mouth on hers. Hadn't Jeffrey taught her anything about hidden danger? Apparently not.

Lily welcomed the sudden, sobering cold of the freezing rain. After a mad dash through the storm from Blake's front porch to the mares' barn, Lily shook off the poncho with a laugh. The barn was dark. The rich earthiness of the air filled her head. She could hear the soft sounds of animals moving in their stalls and sighing. One horse made a low, eager sound, which was promptly echoed by several more. The barn felt somehow safe and cozy, despite the cold and the storm outside.

Lily stood back and watched Blake heave several tightly bound bales of pale green-gold hay onto a flat cart, scenting the air with their grassy sweetness. He'd taken off his jacket and poncho, and his sweater lifted to bare his waist with every bale. His shoulders were broad, his hips just slender enough to be perfectly proportioned without being reedy or thin. Under the dark denim of his new-looking jeans, his thigh muscles flexed and bunched. She'd seen many spectacular physiques during her years in gymnastics, but there was something extraspecial about Blake, something beyond mere physical beauty.

He turned to look at her at the exact moment she let her gaze stray to his firm backside. Her cheeks burned. Grinning smugly, he explained how to feed the horses while she struggled with her composure and a pair of coarse yellow leather gloves he'd handed her. He was obviously enjoying her discomfort. Damn the man!

The work boots felt comfortable but heavy as she

trudged through the thick dirt of the center of the barn. She switched on the flashlight Blake had handed her. A neatly printed card on the door of the first stall indicated that the horse inside, named March Acres Darlene Love, got one flake of hay at night. After fumbling with the latch, Lily managed to slide the heavy door open a few inches. Immediately, a dark brown horse face shoved itself into the opening, almost touching her. Warm, sweet breath huffed out at her. Lily froze.

"Blake!" she practically squeaked. "What's she doing?"

"She's just looking for her snack. She won't trample you," Blake said from the doorway of the next stall down.

As if to confirm Blake's comment, Darlene made a soft *whoof* sound, followed by a low nicker. Hastily Lily tossed the thick flake of hay past the mare's body and into the stall, then slid the door shut as the horse nodded her head and moved over to begin munching. By the time she'd fed almost half the horses, she was feeling oddly touched by the way the horses seemed to appreciate her visits. Without even thinking about it, she'd begun speaking to them as she opened their doors, pausing briefly beside each one to watch them eat, like a hostess eager to please her guests. She wasn't, however, quite ready to *touch* them. One giant step at a time.

"Now what?" she asked as Blake dragged the cart back to the corner where he'd loaded it with hay.

"Boarders' barn and the stallion barn. You holding up okay?"

"I'm fine. Actually, I'm enjoying this," she admitted, surprising herself. "There's a special feeling in here now. It's different from the daytime," she said as they stood in the doorway, braced to go out into the storm once again.

"Cozy and private, as if the barn now belongs to the horses."

Blake grunted, then touched the small of her back, a gesture she normally hated from a man. It usually made her feel as if they were going to shove her along if she didn't go willingly. But Blake didn't touch like that. Blake touched in a way that said, *Thanks* and *Stay with me* and made her feel special.

It had to be too good to be true. Only a fool would try to think otherwise. Shrugging away from his hand, she stepped out of his reach. The freezing rain pelted them in the open space between the mares' barn and the boarders' barn, hitting her shoulders and head like pellets of hail through the rubberized fabric of the poncho. The air outside smelled of wet earth and ozone.

The boarders' barn, with its cement floors, made rolling the hay cart easy. While Blake checked each horse over, shining his flashlight and running his hands over their necks, backs and legs, Lily distributed the hay. They met at the last stall.

Lily stood in the open door, watching Blake stroking the burnished copper coat of the horse, listening to the low murmur of his voice. How would his hands feel on her own neck, back, legs, with his voice crooning love words in the dark? A shiver ran through her, and she had to catch her breath at the power of the image.

Blake straightened. She couldn't see him clearly in the darkness of the stall, but she could feel his gaze on her. *This way lies danger,* her mind whispered. *Fall for this man and all your plans, a lifetime of work and dreams, will wither and die.* She knew the truth of that warning, but some deeply buried, barely understood instinct urged her to turn traitor. Common sense couldn't dull her keen awareness of the electricity between them. It could be very easy to fall for this man.

"Finished?" he asked. The mundane question helped her regain her self-control. She nodded. "Me too. There are only four in the stallion barn, so I can handle it easily alone, if you want to get back to the house."

The sensible thing to do would be to accept his offer and put as much distance between them as possible. But as she hesitated, torn between good sense and impulse, the rain intensified against the roof of the barn.

"I think I'd rather wait that out in a dry barn," she told Blake, tipping her head toward the doorway, where the rain spattered on the concrete entry. As suddenly as the rain had begun to increase, it slowed, as if holding its breath to see what would happen next. She knew how *that* felt! "Hurry up," she urged him. "I'll be right behind you."

"Yes, ma'am!"

Head down, Lily scurried the short distance between the barns and raced into the large square stallion barn. Nickers and thumps greeted them from the dark. The beams of their flashlights played off muscular dark horse forms within large stalls.

After feeding hay to the first two horses, Lily opened the third stall door. A velvety muzzle came out of the shadows to sniff at her face. Whiskers brushed her skin, tickling her. Like a deer transfixed by car headlights, Lily froze, when she wanted to jump back out of reach. The owner of the velvety muzzle continued to sniff and rub her cheek. Then a huge, soft tongue swiped wetly up her face.

"Oh!" Then she did leap backward, scrubbing at her cheek with the back of her wrist. "Oh, *yuck!* I thought you said horses are vegetarians."

"That's Cuddles," Blake told her, laughter lurking in his voice. "He's thirty years old, and a Romeo. Morgan stallions tend to be easier to handle than a lot of other breeds, but this fella is a real baby. I think he used to be one of those fluffy lapdogs in another life."

"Oh. I thought he was just checking to see if he wanted dessert." She tossed the horse his two flakes and stood aside for Blake to step into the stall. "Speaking of dogs…"

A low chuckle wafted out of the shadows of the stall. "Dolly the Avenger is hiding under Carrie's bed. She's petrified of storms."

In the span of a heartbeat, the liking she'd begun to feel for Blake vanished.

"Hiding under… Blake Sommers, do you mean to tell me you deliberately let me lock myself into a room with that monster? What if she'd attacked me?" Her voice sounded shrill, but she didn't care. She was too busy shaking and being angry.

"It would take a wrecking ball to get her out from under there during a storm, Lily. I'm sorry I didn't tell you, but I'm so used to it that I didn't think to mention it until you'd been in there a few minutes. I figured if I said anything, you'd come flying out in your underwear, and that wouldn't exactly win me any points, either. It wasn't deliberate."

Too hurt by his insensitivity to listen or relent, Lily tossed two hay flakes into the last stall.

"I'm going back to Jonathan's house," she said, unable to keep her irritation out of her voice.

"The pump is working now. You can shower," he told her, his tone rebukingly neutral.

She gave him only a curt nod. "I'd appreciate it if you'd bring my clothes over. You can leave them in the kitchen.'' With that, she turned and stalked out into the rain and slogged her way across the muddy yard to the lantern glow in Jonathan's front window.

Told you he was too good to be true, her mind taunted with every stride.

Blake crouched and poked the log just catching fire in the well-worn fireplace of Jonathan's living room. Showered and changed into clean, dry clothes, he was waiting for Lily to come out of the guest bathroom. Her reaction to Dolly's presence in Carrie's room with her nagged at him. He wanted to get to the bottom of her fear of dogs and help her erase it. Fear of any domesticated creature struck him as such a waste, such a loss. Conveniently, he was ignoring the little voice reminding him that Lily would be out of his life soon, would be living in New York City, where she'd be contending with rats and cockroaches, not with sloppy, sentimental dogs and horses. And not with him, either.

A small sound made him look up. Lily stood at the top of the stairs, looking like an old-fashioned ghost in the shadows, her small figure hidden by Carrie's high-necked nightgown and robe.

''Come get warmed up by the fire,'' he invited.

She waited a long time to answer. ''Thank you,'' she said softly, then started down the stairs. ''I thought I'd have to go to bed with wet hair.'' In her raised hand she held a hairbrush.

He pictured her in bed—*his* bed—with her pale hair fanned out over the pillow, her lapis eyes fixed on him. Pictured himself leaning down to taste her mouth, and shuddered. He couldn't bring himself to believe that it would never happen. Not tonight, certainly, but soon.

He'd seen the softening, the yearning in those darkening eyes, even as he'd seen her fighting it.

Lily sank down beside him on the hearth rug. The skirts of the robe and nightgown swirled around her, covering her feet. She smelled faintly of strawberries. The firelight flickered on her pale skin, warming it, tempting him to touch, to discover the velvet of her cheek with the roughness of his shaking hands.

He had to clear his throat before he could speak. "Turn around. I'll brush it dry." She sputtered a protest, but he shook his head. "It'll dry faster. C'mon. Stop being stubborn."

"I'm *not* being stubborn!"

He grinned at the way her chin rose. "Then turn around."

Lily exhaled sharply and turned so that she sat with her back toward him. Biting his lower lip in a futile attempt to control the way his hands were shaking, Blake lifted the brush to the damp silk of her hair.

"Okay?" he challenged gently.

"Okay!" she snapped back, making him grin a little. For a woman trying her darnedest to be distant and disagreeable, Lily Davis was a lot of fun to be with. A helluva lot more fun than the women who tried too hard to please him. Go figure it.

He worked in silence for a while, letting the silky strands slide through his fingers, watching the firelight turn her hair to spun silver and gold. After a long time when the only sounds were the spattering of rain on the windows and the crackling of the flames, he heard Lily sigh. His heart tripped over itself.

"Feels good?" His voice came out raspy.

"Mmm."

He swallowed. "Lily, tell me why you're so afraid of dogs."

She stiffened. He maintained the rhythm of the brush strokes and waited. "I just am, that's all," she finally muttered.

He'd expected that. "There has to be a reason. No one *just is* afraid of something, especially dogs. Dogs and humans have too long a relationship for you to be born scared. Did you get attacked by a dog when you were little?"

"Not exactly."

He stroked the brush through her hair and wondered what she'd do if he kissed her neck behind her ear, where her skin looked translucent. He needed a diversion. "Then what *exactly?*"

"It was such a long time ago. I don't remember much."

He tugged her hair gently. "Lying doesn't become you."

"Nagging doesn't do anything for you, either."

A snort of laughter escaped him. Lord, he enjoyed sparring with her, almost as much as he knew he was going to enjoy making long, slow love to her. "If you'd stop being so stubborn, you wouldn't have to lie and I wouldn't have to nag."

"I'm not—"

"Being stubborn. Hell, no. Would you like a brandy?"

"No, thanks. I can deal with it without anaesthesia."

Guilt poked at him. "If it's that bad, let it go, then. I shouldn't—"

"I was exactly seven years, eleven months and two weeks old," she began softly, surprising him into silence. "I'd been asking my father for nearly a year for a puppy for my eighth birthday." Her voice sounded faraway.

"My mother said she didn't want a dog, but I swore

I'd take care of it myself. Daddy promised me he'd convince Mother, and I spent my penny collection on a book on dog training.'' She turned her head slightly, not quite enough to meet his eyes, but enough to still his hands. "I had my heart set on a golden retriever.''

Lily turned away again, and Blake stroked her hair with the brush, drawing on the patience that had won over countless difficult creatures, praying it would work with one small, sad, defensive woman. For a long while, she stayed tense. Then, with a relief that surprised him with its depth, he felt her relax. Had she decided, for whatever reason, to trust him? If the rest of her story was going to spoil this moment, he'd just as soon not hear it.

But Lily continued speaking quietly. "Two weeks before my birthday, Mother took me to some tacky warehouse studio where some sleazy guy was photographing child models. Mother desperately wanted to get me into TV commercials, but I always froze up and ruined all my auditions. She was hoping I'd be better at photographic work.''

Her back stiffened briefly. Then she sighed. "We had to walk by some place with a high chain-link fence all around it. A junkyard or something. Behind the fence were two black dogs.''

For a long while, Blake continued to brush Lily's hair in a silence broken only by the patter of the rain and the hiss of the fire.

"I got so excited. I ran up to the fence and called to them. I wanted Mother to see how much I loved dogs. I thought that they would love me back. Instead, they charged the fence. I could feel their breath. I could see the hatred in their eyes. Their teeth looked enormous, and I imagined them tearing into me. I screamed and screamed, but Mother just stood there. I guess she was too scared to get me away. The owner finally came out and held me until I stopped crying. He was a fat, hairy man who was almost as scary as his dogs, but he tried to be nice to me. He hollered at Mother for letting me go too close to the fence, and made her cry, too.''

Blake sucked in a breath. He dropped the brush and cupped her slender shoulders in both hands. She was trembling like a frightened child.

"Mother never said another word about dogs. But on my birthday, when my father opened a basket and out ran a black Labrador pup, I freaked out. I screamed and screamed and wouldn't stop until he promised to take the dog back.'' Her shoulders sagged under Blake's hands. "Poor Daddy. He was so hurt. He never knew why I refused the pup. I guess I couldn't tell the difference between the Doberman guard dogs and a Lab. All I knew was, they were both black.''

Blake swore quietly and tightened his hands on her shoulders. He didn't know what to say after Lily's story. It made him sick to think of her terror as she faced two enraged guard dogs. What kind of parent didn't fight like a tiger, even scared spitless, to protect a child? Even Carrie's mother—Lord knew, Sandy had had her flaws, but she'd done her best to provide for the daughter she'd hardly known.

Lily twisted in his hands, turning so that she was almost looking back at him. He fought the impulse to draw her against him and soothe her pain with his hands, his mouth, his body. Neither of them was ready for all that making love implied, but he couldn't help wanting her.

"It's not such a big deal. Don't feel you have to pity me, Blake,'' she said softly, her voice lower than usual, smoky and sexy. "None of the Ten Commandments says a person has to like dogs. As long as you can keep Dolly out of my face for the short time I'm working here, I'll be fine."

He smiled at her brave words, and decided not to push the issue at the moment. He still had a little time to work on her fear of dogs. Right now, drinking in the fresh scent of her hair and skin, warmed by the firelight, excited by the gentle pressure of her shoulder leaning lightly against his chest, he had other things on his mind. Things like soft, slow kisses, sighs that promised that later, when they knew each other better, they could give in to the temptations those kisses were going to stir up.

He leaned closer, angled his head toward hers. A tremor ran through her small frame and shivered into him. Nuzzling the fine silvery hairs covering her small ear, he inhaled. When she didn't move away, he turned a little more and brushed his lips over the satin of her cheek. A few more inches and he'd be tasting her mouth. Anticipation had him shaking like an eager teenager.

Abruptly Lily wrenched out of his hands. She scrambled to her feet, gathering the skirts of the robe and nightgown around her. The glow of the fire made her look like some ancient goddess. Diana, perhaps. The virginal goddess of the hunt, caught between being all woman and trying to be one of the guys. The thought made him smile, despite his frustration.

"Please, Blake. This is the wrong time and place." Her voice came out low and urgent, a little unsteady. "I'm the wrong woman and you're the wrong man. There's no point in starting something we can't finish."

She stopped so breathlessly that he wondered if she'd run out of clichés.

"Who says we can't finish what we start?"

She drew herself up to her entire five-foot-two-inch height and glared down at him. "*I* say. I'm not interested in a short-term affair, and I'm not interested in a long-term commitment. That doesn't leave us with many alternatives except mutual respect."

He grinned. "Mutual respect? As the kids used to say, gag me with a spoon." He got up and let his grin fade as he looked deep into her midnight eyes. "I could feel you trembling, Lily, wanting to let yourself give in. You know you were wondering how it would feel to kiss me, to feel my hands on you, to feel what your hands could do to me."

She opened her mouth to protest, but he kept talking, enjoying the war between desire and caution that was so obvious in her expression. "Don't worry. I won't make you wonder for long."

Before she could say anything—or get her hands on anything she could wing at his head—he turned and went to the front door. "Sleep well," he told her with a broad wink, then slipped out the door and into the storm. Judging by the fire in her eyes, he was safer out there. But not for long. Nope. Not for long. Before Lily finished Jonathan's books, she was going to have a change of heart about a lot of things, beginning with dogs—and him.

A crack of thunder yanked Lily out of a deep sleep. Disoriented, she propped herself up on one elbow and peered into the dark. The lightning that flashed seconds later silhouetted a figure in the open doorway. In the darkness that followed, the image seemed burned into her unseeing eyes.

Uncomprehending, she opened her mouth to demand an explanation, but no sound came out. Thunder shook the house again, but not as hard as her heart pounded.

"Lily?"

Another flash of lightning threw Blake's form into bizarre relief. Was it some trick of the light, or had he really been standing there, stripped to the waist? Sensing him moving closer to the bed now, Lily scrambled to sit up and clutch the quilt tightly to her chest. Was it the disorientation of being awakened abruptly, or the distorting illumination of the lightning, or was she alone with a secret madman?

"Lily? I'm sorry. I..." He swore softly. "I need..."

Chapter Six

A roll of thunder covered the rest of Blake's words. She stared into the dark, straining to see what he was doing, and afraid to find out. A distant shimmer of lightning barely broke through the darkness. Suddenly, the lamps in the bedroom flooded the room with painfully bright light. The power must have been restored. She had to blink to keep watching Blake coming closer, carrying something bulky close to his chest.

He stood over her now, and she could see that he was holding a bunched-up, muddy white towel. His naked upper body glistened wetly. His dark hair streamed water onto his wide, muscular shoulders. His jeans were dark-streaked with water. His expression was grim. Her breath caught in her throat, and she didn't think she had a coherent thought in her head. Her eyes never left his. Fight-or-flight warred with shocked fascination.

"Sorry, Lily." He spoke again, quietly but urgently. "I need your help. It's sort of an emergency."

He leaned forward and lowered the filthy towel away from his broad chest. She could smell the rain and cold on his bare skin. Reflexively she leaned away, but her gaze shifted to the bundle he cradled in his arms. Now that her eyes were used to the light, she could see that some of the streaks on the towel were dark red, bloodred. Was he hurt?

"What happened?" she asked. "Are you all right?"

"I'm fine," he said. "It's Patches."

"Patches?"

"One of the barn cats. She was in a fight with a raccoon. I heard them over the intercom, but I got out there too late."

Lily took a few seconds to absorb what he'd told her. "Do you mean you broke in here, impersonating Norman Bates, scaring me half to death at whatever ungodly hour this is, to tell me about a cat fight?"

His mouth opened, then snapped closed. Guilt over her insensitivity softened her tone when she added, "I'm sorry about Patches, but what in heaven's name do you expect from me?" She heard a squeak. It was a pathetic, mouselike sound, followed immediately by another, much louder one. She met Blake's eyes again. Understanding dawned.

"Oh, no! No, Blake. That's out of the question."

He held out the bundle. "They're too young. They won't make it if you don't take care of them."

"What about Jonathan? He must be an old hand at this kind of thing."

"Jonathan is a lot more fragile than he's willing to let on. I don't want to wake him." His words made her bite her lip at her thoughtlessness. "Look, if Carrie weren't stuck at her friend's house, I wouldn't have to ask you. It's nearly five-thirty, so it's just for a couple of hours. I'll take them off your hands when I finish with the horses. By then, Jonathan will be awake, anyway.''

She felt panic rising like bubbles inside her. He was asking her to accept responsibility for two tiny, fragile lives. What if she failed? ''Blake, I'm a tax expert, not a mother cat. They're even less likely to live if I take care of them. I can't even keep plants alive.''

Lily edged away from Blake's reach, but the desperate cries coming from the towel tugged at her heart. She glanced down at the towel cradled in his big, strong hands, then looked up into his face. ''I wouldn't know what to do,'' she told him. ''I...I haven't got a maternal bone in my body. I never played with dolls. I didn't know how. Honest. My mother made Lucretia Borgia look like a positive role model.'' She drew a breath to stop her babbling. ''Isn't there another cat...?''

His silence, the patient expectation in his dark eyes, told her more eloquently than words that she was losing the argument. And if she was honest with herself, she knew there was an irrational part of her that didn't want to disappoint him. She crossed her legs under the covers, making a nest for the kittens. Blake leaned down and placed the weightless bundle in her lap. Their eyes met with all the electricity of the passing storm arcing between them. One wet lock of his dark hair fell over his forehead. Lily suppressed the urge to reach up and push it into place. She felt all too vulnerable to the intimacy of the moment.

Instead, she let the incredibly piercing shrieks from inside the towel draw her attention away from Blake, grateful for the interruption. After some frantic scrambling, two dark kitten faces peeked out of the sheltering cloth. Wide-eyed, they stared up at Lily, then opened their pink mouths and wailed. She really couldn't blame them for their lack of confidence.

"Oh, Blake! They're so tiny! What if I—?"

"Don't underestimate yourself. You can do whatever you put your mind to," he said firmly, and she wanted to believe him. "There's canned kitten formula and bottles in the kitchen. Just pour and feed. They'll know what to do. I've got to bury Patches and start chores. I'll be back in a couple of hours."

Before she could anticipate his intention, Blake leaned down over the bed and brushed his mouth across hers. She gasped at the cool heat in that brief touch and looked up at him. His dark eyes held promises of longer, hotter kisses. Shivering under the intensity of his gaze, she turned her head away. The floor creaked, and when she looked again, he was gone.

The kittens' piteous wails demanded her attention. She watched them swaying on unsteady little legs, then scooped them up together into her hands. She felt the warmth of their tummies and the rapid beating of their tiny hearts.

"Hush, babies. I'll do my best, and you'll just have to hope it's good enough." They cried even louder. "Poor babies. Mommy can't hear you."

Sudden tears filled Lily's eyes as she recalled the times her mother had simply ignored her pleas for attention. All those times she'd ached for a kiss, a hug, a gentle hand stroking her hair. With a long, shuddering sigh, she brought the kittens to her cheek. Their fur was as silky as mink. Tiny velvet paws pressed against her chin as if the kittens were asking for reassurance. The gesture melted her reservations.

"I'll try, babies," she promised as she slid her legs out

from under the quilt. "I may not have any maternal instincts, but Blake thinks I can do this, and damn him, he's usually right. You deserve better, but I'm all you've got, so bear with me."

Lack of sleep made his head feel heavy as Blake made his way into the kitchen of Jonathan's house. He figured Lily would be feeling as chipper as he did, after playing nursemaid to the kittens. The least he could do was put on a pot of coffee. If Jonathan was awake yet, he'd ask him to take over the orphans as soon as Lily got up.

The house was still quiet. Maybe he should check on Lily and the kittens before he tackled the coffee. She might want to hand them over now and sleep in a little later than usual. He could feed the little guys before he started turning horses out. He couldn't keep dropping everything to feed them every hour or so, but once was no big drain on his time.

Cautiously he made his way up the stairs. The third step creaked loudly under his weight. He'd have to fix that loose nail one of these days.

At Lily's partially open door, he paused. Images of her asleep and then awake before dawn, burned into his brain by lightning, had haunted him for the rest of the night. The brief taste of her mouth, the scent of her sleep-warmed skin, had lingered, carrying him through the unpleasant task of taking care of poor Patches in the freezing cold. No other woman had affected him like this, and for the life of him, he still didn't know why Lily, why now. What he did know was that she had awakened something inside him that had been playing Rip van Winkle for so long he'd forgotten about it. And, damn it, he wanted more of it.

He took a deep breath and peered around the edge of

the door. What he saw in the diffused light trapped the air in his lungs. Lily was still asleep, lying on her right side, facing the door. The nightgown had opened at the top, exposing the pearly skin of her throat. The kittens slept on a clean towel, curled together, cuddled against her breasts. Her left arm curved protectively around them.

He stood in the doorway, devouring the sight of her. He wanted to touch her, to finish unbuttoning the prim nightgown and seek the ivory satin skin hidden inside. He wanted to lift the kittens away and slide under the quilt beside her delicate curves, then kiss away her surprise. He could feel himself barely brushing his work-rough hands over her, carefully awakening her passion.

Suppressing a shudder of desire, he turned and went back downstairs to the kitchen. Not yet, he told himself. Not yet, but soon. Before her return to New York became reality.

Something cold and wet touched her neck. Something soft tickled her skin. Something sniff-sniff-sniffed, then set up an all-too familiar duet of high-pitched wails. Lily cupped her hands around the warm, furry bodies squirming to get closer.

The clock radio still flashed twelve o'clock. She hadn't reset it after the power came back on. Her watch read 7:15. She'd better get up, feed the kittens, make about a gallon of coffee and start working.

"Okay, you two, stay put!" she ordered softly.

Lily wrapped the quilt around their towel so they couldn't wander off the bed, then slipped into Carrie's borrowed robe and staggered to the bathroom. When she came out, feeling slightly refreshed, the kittens were crying desperately and rooting around in their towel. Sudden tears stung her eyes. She scooped the towel up and held the kittens close to her cheek, murmuring reassurance. She'd rather be tortured than admit it, but she was already in love with the little creatures.

She sniffed away her tears and smelled ambrosia. Coffee! The aroma of fresh coffee lured her toward the kitchen, the thought of finding Blake there turning into flustered anticipation. She had dreamed of that brief kiss over and over. Now here she was in a nightgown and robe, her hair like a bird's nest, without the protective armor of her professional clothes.

Lily paused at the closed kitchen door. She didn't want to think about the domesticity of the scene, Blake lingering over a second cup of coffee while she sat, Madonna-like in flannel and lace, feeding surrogate infants.

The implications of domesticity, of intimacy with Blake, made her uneasy. Since breaking up with Jeffrey, she'd renewed her promise to herself never to become a household convenience for a man, yet one quick kiss, a sudden flood of guilt, and she was mothering orphaned kittens. If she wasn't careful, she'd be sewing shirt buttons for Blake next.

Not to mention that she suspected she wasn't going to be immune to his seductive intentions if he kept up this tantalizing pursuit. She'd had to struggle not to give in to the temptation in his soothing touches when they sat by the fire last night. She'd longed to taste him, to feel his hard strength against her, to test the limits of her own sensuality with him. She'd had to summon all her anger at the people who'd exploited her over the years to find the strength to resist him.

Ironically, her success had left her with a hollow ache that refused to fade. Another woman might have given in to curiosity or primitive sensuality, and settled for a fling, but, as cynical as she was about love, she still couldn't separate it from sex. Perhaps, she thought with some surprise, her cynicism was really a cover for a hidden idealism. Ah, well, perhaps she was just suffering from interrupted sleep.

Resolutely she pushed open the swinging door and walked into the bright, immaculate kitchen. Jonathan, seated at the table reading the newspaper, a cup of steaming coffee at his elbow, looked up and smiled. Swallowing her disappointment, she smiled back.

"Good morning, my dear. What have we here?"

"Hungry kittens," she told him, with an answering smile that faded as she remembered the circumstances. Briefly she explained how she'd gotten charge of the kittens. Standing at the counter to pour the formula into the doll-size bottles, she shifted the bundled kittens into the crook of her left arm and worked one-handed.

"How about some coffee?"

"I'd love some, but I'd better wait until these two finish."

Jonathan poured a mug of coffee for her while she filled the bottles. When she sat at the table, he reached out a gnarled but steady hand. "Let me take one. You look like you've been up all night with them."

She grimaced and handed over the larger of the two kittens, the one with splashes of gold in its black coat. "Only a couple of times since five-thirty, but it feels like all night. Watch out for her. She's a real rascal. She starts kneading on the bottle cap and unscrews the thing." Jonathan smiled.

Lily sat and offered the bottle to the all-black kitten she held. The little thing stopped her shrieks and started sucking, making soft little humming sounds and opening and closing her tiny claws on Lily's supporting hand. Something deep and nameless inside her moved and expanded at the sight of the contented baby.

If an orphaned kitten could turn her to mush like this, she was in serious trouble. The faster she finished this job and returned to the city, the better.

The sound of footsteps on the back porch interrupted her lecture to herself. The door opened slowly, and Blake peered inside. He met her eyes, and his dimple flashed when he smiled. Lily froze, the memory of his kiss igniting a jolt of awareness.

"I see we made it," he said jovially. "Any coffee left? It's pretty brisk out there." Lily suddenly remembered he'd been outside before dawn, shirtless in the freezing rain, trying to save the barn cat.

"Plenty left," Jonathan answered. "Cute little things, aren't they? Too bad about Patches. She was a sweet cat. We'll miss her." He took the empty bottle from the kitten he'd been feeding. "I was about to suggest Lily might want you to drive her into Rochester to pick up her things. I don't think she should be working on the audit today." He turned to Lily and smiled. "Bill agrees you should stay here. He'll come to visit when the weather clears. Poor child, you look done in."

Blake grinned at her over his mug of coffee. "Yeah, she does look a little peaked. I'll be happy to drive her."

"Drive me nuts is more like it," Lily muttered to the kitten in her palm. The touch of its tiny wet nose on hers seemed to express agreement.

"Come get me when you want me," he told her, his suggestive wink assuring her that he'd meant the double entendre. "I'll be in the boarders' barn." Blake took another gulp of coffee. Lily watched his throat move as he swallowed, an unwanted image of her lips touching him there springing to her mind's eye. She suppressed a tiny shiver and forced herself to look away. "See ya," he said after putting his mug in the sink, then went out the back door.

Lily busied herself with the kittens, tucking them into a blanket-lined box Jonathan provided, while she considered Blake's offer. She would have to refuse. She didn't want to spend over two hours in close quarters in his Jeep, where the small talk would inevitably turn to more personal topics.

She didn't want to know him any better than she did already. Knowing more about him, she had a sneaky feeling, would lead to liking him more. No, she would refuse his offer. The MG could make the trip just fine.

"I think I'll go to Uncle Bill's now," she told Jonathan. "I guess I should call him first, so he won't be surprised."

"I'll call him again, child. You go get yourself ready. I'll tell him you'll be there by around ten."

She thanked Jonathan, then took her coat and boots from the front hall closet. Her deliberate deception bothered her, but she knew that he would fuss and worry if she told him she intended to drive herself. He wouldn't understand her reasons for avoiding Blake, and she didn't want to have to explain. She suspected that trying to express her reluctance in words would make her sound—and feel—foolish.

After ten minutes of scraping and gouging ice off the windows of the MG, cursing the weather and praying that Dolly wouldn't discover her, Lily finally drove down the icy lane to the street. Even at about three miles an hour, she felt the little sports car slipping and struggling. Her face already hurt from staring at the road. This was definitely going to be a four-aspirin drive.

The main road wasn't much better than the farm lane, she discovered a few minutes later. Speeding along at ten miles an hour, she was fine until the car in front of her suddenly fishtailed. Lily downshifted and feathered her brakes, but the MG had had enough. It spun completely around in slow motion once, then halfway around again, ending up half in a ditch and facing the wrong way.

For a long while, Lily sat shaking as the possibilities of the situation sank in. She'd been so lucky not to spin out into the thick trunk of the tree not three feet from her rear bumper. And no other cars had slammed into her.

While the interior of the car cooled rapidly, she called herself every kind of fool. Not only would she have to slink back to the farm, her pride trailing behind, but she'd have to accept a ride with Blake *and* ask him to pull the car out of the ditch.

With tears of frustration stinging her eyes, she slammed the car door, much too hard. It popped open as if mocking her. She shut it again with deliberate care, clenching her teeth painfully. Then she buttoned her top button and turned up her coat collar for the half-mile trudge back to March Acres.

Blake watched the MG skate down the lane and shook his head. The woman had stubborn down to an art. Would it be so hard for her to accept a favor from him? Did she think he'd keep score, expect something in return? Or maybe she was afraid he'd jump her delectable little bones over the gearshift lever of the Jeep, the minute they were out of sight of the farm.

Not that the idea wasn't tempting. But he was way past sexual acrobatics in a car. When Lily was ready, he'd take her on soft sheets, gently, slowly, the way she should be made love to.

The swift rush of arousal sent a wave of heat through him. The weather might be saying *winter*, but he had a bad case of spring fever. Gritting his teeth, he turned on his heel and strode to the Jeep. He'd better follow the little fool and make sure she got to Bill's safely. And back again. She didn't have to know he was there, but if she got into trouble, he'd be able to bail her out.

The sight of the MG turned wrong way around on the shoulder, not a half mile from the farm, made his heart pound. Was she all right? There was a solid tree right near the car, and he couldn't see the driver's side. If she'd hit that tree and spun around, in that flimsy old car, she could be badly hurt. After a storm like this, there were few people stupid enough to drive before the sanding crews came by. If he hadn't come after her, and she was hurt, she could be there for hours, and no one would know.... The thought made him feel sick.

As he drew closer, edging the Jeep toward the shoulder, the door of the MG flew open. Lily flung herself out and slammed the door. Blake bit back a laugh as the door swung open again. He could see she was mad as a wet hen in the way she closed the door again, with exaggerated care, but she didn't look hurt. Relief flooded through him.

He parked facing her front bumper. She looked up, surprise and fury mingling in her expression. While he swung himself out of the Jeep, she stood facing him as if he were a firing squad and she were trying to be brave. It was kind of cute.

"Is she still running?"

"Yes, *he's* still running," she snapped. "Off the road, as you can see."

He fought down a grin. "At least you're headed in the right direction." He leaned against the rear of the car, looking for the best leverage. "Get back inside and start her up. I'll push you off the shoulder and follow you to the farm.''

Her expression was pure dare; she didn't think he could move that flimsy tin can with her inside. A minute later, when the tires gripped what little blacktop showed through the ice, she looked furious. Shaking his head, an action he found himself doing a lot around Lily, he climbed into the Jeep and made a U-turn. If she'd spent most of her life hauling hay, shoveling manure, and moving half-ton horses around, she'd take pushing a car in stride. He was just grateful that he'd been there.

Back in the parking lot, Jonathan was holding Dolly by the collar as Lily flung herself out of the MG. Blake parked beside her and left the motor idling. He opened the window.

''Hop in. Which you should have done in the first place.''

''Smugness doesn't become you, Mr. Sommers.''

He caught Jonathan's eye and grinned. ''Stubbornness doesn't become you, Ms. Davis. All you had to do was ask.''

Her eyes flashed sparks. ''*May* I have a ride to Rochester to pick up my things?'' she asked, as if she were biting off each word and none of them tasted very good.

He couldn't resist baiting her. ''Anyone ever tell you you can catch more flies with honey than you can with vinegar?''

Behind Lily, Jonathan's eyebrows shot up. The old boy probably thought he'd gone too far. For a moment, seeing the cool blue flames in her eyes, he suspected he had.

Her smile surprised him. ''I'm not interested in catching flies, Mr. Sommers,'' she said sweetly. ''But if I were, whatever is on your boots would do the job quite well.''

Jonathan's laugh rang out across the yard. Dolly barked in agreement. Yes, indeed, Lily Davis gave as good as she got. And he intended to give her a lot more than word games.

Lily sat back in the corner of the overstuffed sofa, sipped at her wine and turned the pages of one of Jonathan's albums. It was almost eleven in the evening. Jonathan was in bed. Carrie and Blake were in their house after sharing dinner. The only light came from a lamp glowing behind her shoulder. The only sounds were the crackling and popping of the fire in the big, old-fashioned hearth. Unaccustomed peace and contentment made her feel lazy down to her bones.

The day had gone better than she expected, considering its beginnings. Miraculously, Blake had kept the conversation light on the way to and from Uncle Bill's house in Rochester. He'd talked about the horses, about Carrie, about Jonathan and his own family. He'd asked about her work and the assignment she was hoping to get. But not once had he probed beneath her comfort level. It had been as if he understood her desire to keep her emotional distance. He'd been discreet, tactful. So much so, in fact, that it made her even more nervous to be so close to him.

Still, she couldn't help getting to know more about him as a person, and, as she'd feared, he really was the rock-solid salt-of-the-earth type. Not that he said much about himself, but she could read between the lines to see what was important to him. Family. His daughter. His horses. His friends. Life.

The range of his interests surprised her, making her ashamed of prejudging him as a hick. He really did know the paintings and sculptures displayed in the Frick Collection in the city. He could discuss art, music, films, with

the same ease as he talked about horses. It had been sobering to realize that all she had ever discussed with the
men she dated over the years was work—mostly theirs.

Lily sipped at her wine and turned to the next page of
the album. The photograph in front of her made her heart
flutter. There was no mistaking the identity of the man in
the photo: Blake Sommers, clad only in ragged cutoff
jeans, heavy socks under his work boots, and leather
gloves. His body was streaked with dirt and shiny with
sweat. Powerful muscles in his legs, arms and torso
bulged as he strained beside a horse that appeared to be
dragging a thick tree trunk through mud and undergrowth.

The image was so sharp that Lily imagined she could
hear Blake groaning with his efforts. She ran her finger
over the plastic cover on the photo, as if she could feel
the heat rising from his glistening skin. She closed her
eyes, but she could still see him. The sheer animal mag-
netism of the man in the picture made her shiver and feel
overheated at the same time.

"Anybody here?" Blake's voice came from the
kitchen, hushed in the darkened house.

Lily's breath caught. Her pulse skipped, tripped and
raced. Heat stung her cheeks. How could she face him
coolly, distantly, when her blood was surging hotly with
an awareness she'd never felt for any other man?

On the second attempt, her voice croaked back that she
was in the living room. A moment later, she heard the
floorboards creak slightly under his steps. Then she
smelled the spice of his cologne and the musk of his skin.
He was standing behind the couch, hands resting on both
sides of her shoulders, leaning over her. Her velour robe,
even zipped to her throat, seemed to offer no protection.

"I'd almost forgotten about that picture," he said in a
low, gravelly voice. "Jonathan won a couple of awards

with it, but at the time, I was cursing him for playing with his camera while Caruso and I were clearing those logs.''

Not daring to look up, she swallowed against the sudden dryness in her throat. ''Why were you clearing logs with a horse? I thought people used tractors for that.''

Her own voice came out much too soft and intimate, and she knew she couldn't blame it all on the need for quiet, because Jonathan was asleep upstairs on the other side of the house.

''Some do,'' he conceded, his tone vaguely critical of those who would stoop so low. She smiled, but then the heat of him surrounding her stole her smile and made her shiver.

''We'd had a thunderstorm that turned the ground to pea soup and took down a few trees across a local road. We had to use the horse because the tractors bogged down before they could get close enough. It was a hell of a day. Ninety-eight in the shade, and the air so wet you had to wring out your clothes just standing still.''

She couldn't think of anything to say that wouldn't come out lame or patronizing. On the other hand, the silence was too dangerous. She was already trembling, her fingers barely able to grip her wineglass.

''We aren't holding you prisoner here, Lily. You can always borrow the Jeep,'' he said, his voice closer than before. She felt his breath stir the hair by her ear. ''Or Jonathan's Volvo. That tin can Bill lent you isn't good for much.'' The words he murmured didn't matter. It was the way he spoke, so softly, so intimately.

''I...I know. I...'' Ignoring the consequences, she tipped her head back to gaze up at him in the flickering shadows. ''I owe you an apology for the way I behaved this morning. It's so irritating when you're right.''

His dimple creased, and his lips curved up a little. ''I

think I understand," he told her softly. "You didn't want to be cooped up with me for the drive there and back."

His perceptiveness made her blush in shame. "It wasn't just that," she admitted sheepishly. "I hate to ask for favors."

The touch of his warm, callused fingertips on her exposed throat stole her breath. She couldn't have moved if a bomb had gone off.

"Is it so hard to accept a favor from me?"

She tried to swallow past her breathlessness. "It… It's not personal. I don't like to accept favors because I don't want to owe anyone anything."

His lips replaced his fingers on her neck. His soft hair brushed her face. His breath on her skin lit a fire deep inside, in a place that had been frozen forever.

"I don't keep score, Lily," he murmured, his mouth moving on her neck in a maddening caress. "You don't owe me anything. Except—" his tongue branded her skin with the lightest touch "—honesty."

Her breath escaped in a ragged sigh. "Honesty?"

Blake released her, leaving her confused until he settled beside her on the couch. "Honesty." He took the album from her lap, leaving her without the illusion of protection.

Lily gazed into his dark eyes until the intensity there forced her to lower her lids. His hand cupped warmly around her neck, holding her gently. She knew she could pull away, should pull away, but she couldn't make herself move.

Chapter Seven

His mouth brushed hers once, tantalizing, tempting. Lily gasped at the desire that flared from her breast to her belly. Afraid of the consequences, she still lifted her mouth for his kiss. Frightened as she was, she needed more than that teasing sample of the delights he was offering. But would he want to take more than she was offering? As if to reassure her, he released his light hold on the back of her neck, freeing her to move away. She didn't want to. Not now. Not yet.

Blake's lips were soft on hers. They caressed and stroked and warmed her lips. His tongue touched her lower lip, taking a tiny sip. She opened to him without waiting for his request, hungry for the taste of him. And, oh, he tasted wonderful! Dark and sweet-tasting, intoxicating as fine cognac, his tongue sought hers. Lily dipped into his mouth, seeking more, answering his low moan with a tiny cry from deep in her throat.

Time and place dissolved. All that existed was the firm softness of Blake's lips, the heady flavor of his warm mouth. Lily didn't know if she was breathing. She didn't care. Their only point of contact was mouth on mouth, yet she was melting, turning soft and aching to mold herself to him.

When Blake's hand cupped her face, his palm hard and warm, Lily let herself flow closer to him. Shoulder to chest, she nestled into his kisses, drifting. In a trance, she lifted her hand to his face. Trembling, she touched and traced the planes, the angles, the smooth-shaven skin. His silky hair brushed over the back of her hand. She slid her fingers into the thick softness of it and let a small sigh escape her. How long had she wanted to do that, without knowing her own mind?

Blake trailed kisses over her jaw and down to her neck. Heat suffused her. She gasped with it.

Then he gripped her shoulders and angled her against his chest. At the first contact between their bodies, a shock ripped through her. She felt an answering shock in the way he stiffened. Then he breathed her name against her neck, urging a tiny cry from her. A heartbeat later, his mouth covered hers again, his tongue seeking, offering, requesting. His gentleness was undoing her. She couldn't think of a single reason why she shouldn't kiss him like this until they both went up in flames.

His hand slid down her back, urging her closer. His kiss deepened, no longer requesting, but demanding. They were fast approaching the point of no return. Panic replaced sensual languor. Suddenly, Lily remembered a million reasons why she shouldn't be kissing Blake, shouldn't be allowing him to seduce her. She pulled away, weakly, as if her body disagreed with her mind, but he let her go immediately. Breathless and shaking, she hung her head.

"Lily?"

With a gentle finger under her chin, he tipped her face toward him. She closed her eyes against the probing light of his.

"I'm sorry, Blake. I...I can't. This isn't what I want. I'm sorry I didn't stop us before—"

His finger touched her lips, stopping her rush of words. "Honesty, Lily. That's all you owe me." He took his finger away and smiled. "And yourself."

With a single lingering stroke of his hand on her hair, he stood and walked out of the living room. A moment later, Lily heard the back door click shut. Alone with the dying fire, she hugged her knees to her chest and tried to get her trembling under control. Tried to get her responses into perspective.

It didn't mean anything. She was lonely. Vulnerable because of her isolation. Because of Jeffrey's betrayal. Blake was attractive. His kisses made her melt, but it was purely physical. Nothing more. She had to resist him. She would never let herself get involved with a man simply because of physical attraction. She needed more, more than Blake or any other man could give her.

She needed her independence, and that was the first thing loving someone would destroy.

The following day, Lily stood in her socks in the tack room of the boarders' barn. Cool air wrapped around her legs, and Lily shivered. What lapse of sense had allowed her to get talked into learning to ride? She couldn't even blame Blake. Carrie had spent the past two days cajoling, nagging, teasing and daring her, until Lily had given in just to get some peace. Truth to tell, she didn't mind the girl's company. It was like having a younger sister, something she'd yearned for as a child.

She felt exposed in the skintight suede-seated britches Carrie had loaned her. She hadn't felt so exposed since giving up gymnastics. Just when she'd made up her mind to leave, Carrie emerged triumphantly from the tack room, waving a pair of tall black leather boots.

"Get these on and I'll finish tacking up Patsy," Carrie told her. "You may need boot pulls. There's a pair in the right boot."

Typically, Carrie was out of sight before Lily could ask her what boot pulls were and how to use them. She stood in the hall and gazed at the boots, assuming a logical solution would present itself if she stuck her hand into the right boot. After a few tries, she figured out that the hooks with the wooden handles slipped into the loops inside the boots. Pleased with her discovery, she sat down on the nearby bench and slid her foot into the top of the boot.

A moment later, Lily had her foot wedged halfway down the tall stem of the stiff boot and her calf muscle was threatening to cramp. She tugged harder on the boot pulls but couldn't get her foot farther in. Biting her lip, she looked at Lance, hoping he'd have some suggestion.

From somewhere out of sight, Blake's voice cut into the room. "Stand up, Lily." A second later, he was beside her, one arm around her shoulders, hauling her up. She pulled away from his supporting grasp. The pain gathering in her calf shot all the way up to the back of her thigh, but she refused to let herself lean any more on Blake. Biting her lower lip, she bent to adjust her foot in its prison. Once again, Blake hauled her upright.

He surrounded her. His arm around her shoulder held her close to his side, where the heat of his body radiated through his sweater and the layers of clothes Carrie had loaned her. His thigh rested against hers, and his free hand rested on her hip. Her leg hurt like blazes, but her heart raced, because of Blake's touch, his scent, and her certainty that he would help her even if she was foolish and stubborn enough not to want him to.

"Grab the boot pulls and pull up hard while you jam your foot down," he ordered gruffly.

She did as he said, and suddenly her foot slid into the boot. The pain in her leg faded just as suddenly. "Thanks," she said softly. "I'll remember that for the other boot."

Blake released her shoulder, and she made the mistake of thinking he was going to move away. Instead, he sat behind her on the bench and slipped the boot pulls out of the loops. Trying in vain to ignore him so close to her skimpily clad backside, Lily balanced on one foot while she angled the other into the left boot. The first time she started to pitch to one side, Blake gripped her hips firmly in his big hands and held her steady. The second boot went on quickly, with no leg cramps.

"Some things work better slow and easy," he murmured as he stood behind her. "Others work better hard and fast."

His words sent a hot shiver through her. Why? she asked herself irritably. If some yuppie jerk in a bar handed her a line like that, she'd have torn a strip off him—or, more likely, she'd have walked away. She certainly wouldn't be entertaining the erotic images that flashed into her mind just now.

"Terrific," she muttered, wishing he'd release her hips. "A cowboy philosopher."

Blake's chuckle told her he'd taken no offense, even though she'd meant to annoy him. Why, in addition to all his other virtues, did he have such a ready sense of humor? Why couldn't she think of a single fault to make him less attractive? Why couldn't she stop imagining what might happen if she simply sank backward into his lap?

He released her, and immediately, irrationally, she missed the firm touch, the warmth, of his hands. He stood, his arm brushing her. She stepped away, awkward in the stiff, high boots.

"Let's go. Patsy's waiting for us."

"What do you mean, 'us'? Carrie's going to teach me." As she spoke, his dimple flashed and a devilish gleam lit his dark eyes. "Isn't she?"

"Nope. Carrie's going to videotape you. I handle all the beginners. House rules. No exceptions." Again, his dimple flashed, but he only put his hand on her shoulder and guided her into the arena.

Lily balked halfway across the dirt to where the chestnut mare stood patiently next to Carrie. "Wait a second, Blake." He stopped and turned toward her, his eyebrows lifting. "This was Carrie's idea. I only agreed because I thought it was important to her. I really don't—"

"Chicken?" he said softly.

"Oh!" Without another word, she stalked toward the horse and the grinning girl.

"Bend your left leg and put your knee in my hands. Then, grab the saddle by the front and back. On three, I'm going to boost you up."

Put her knee in his hands? Oh, Lord! This was nothing like the impersonal boosts to the parallel bars she'd gotten from her coaches. "Why can't I get up the way everyone else does?"

"Because you don't have stirrups." She looked and, to her dismay, he was right. "We don't use them on the first few lessons. Don't sweat it. You're a former gymnast, right? Should be a piece of cake for you."

With a sigh, Lily gripped the hard, smooth leather of the saddle and bent her left leg. Blake moved so close that his shoulder brushed her ribs. His hands closed firmly around her knee, and he counted. On three, she sprang up with her right leg when Blake lifted her left knee. Feeling as if she were going to be launched toward the ceiling, Lily clutched at the front of the saddle and all but fell into the unyielding seat.

Blake still had one hand on her left thigh. She glanced down at it, then wished she hadn't. With her inner thigh muscles registering the pull of straddling the horse, she felt Blake's touch magnified. It took only that awareness to trigger an image of Blake using his strong, warm hands to part her thighs, gently, irresistibly. In unconscious defense, her body tensed.

"Relax," he told her, and she almost laughed out loud at the impossibility of that. "Let me adjust your position. Let your legs hang from your hips." He ran his hand from her hip to her knee, straightening her leg, setting her nerves on fire with his touch. "Sit with your pelvis tucked under you." He poked at her bottom until she managed to squirm so that her hips were tucked under. "Let your weight sink into the saddle."

Then she felt his hand slide up her back. "Sit up straight." She complied. He touched her left shoulder, which, like the right one, was halfway to her ear. "Let your shoulders down and back." She tried to do what he asked. "Good." He rewarded her with a light stroke on her upper back that made her wonder if she was expected to purr or wag her tail.

"Head up," he ordered, with a soft brush of warm fingertips on the exposed back of her neck. She jerked herself up. "Tuck your chin in a little." His fingertip touched the point of her chin. "Tummy in, chest out," he added, lightly touching her pelvic bone.

Her gasp took care of sucking in her tummy. As for her chest... He wouldn't. Would he? Lily looked down into Blake's face and saw the dangerous glint in his eyes. The rat! He wasn't going to touch her, but he was making sure she was thinking about it.

"Ready? You look fine." He patted her thigh. "Relax and sit into her movement. We'll go as far and as fast as you want." He paused, then added, "You just have to tell me what you want."

Blake's double meaning didn't escape her, but when he stepped away, she was seized by a panic that drove away thoughts of anything but survival. He stopped about fifteen feet from her, holding a long brown strap in his hand. Carrie had already moved away, and was peering through the lens of the video camera mounted on a tripod in the corner.

"Wait!" Lily cried out. "I don't have anything to hold on to! And I never made out a will. Blake!"

He snorted. "Put your hands on top of your head."

"*What?*" She was going to die.

"I thought you were a gymnast. This will be a snap for you."

"I haven't been a gymnast for almost twenty years, and the only thing that's going to snap is my neck, when I fall on it."

"Trust me, Lily. I've trained hundreds of beginners and haven't lost a horse yet."

"Very funny. I need something to hang on to. Maybe a parachute?"

"It's okay, Lily," Carrie sang out. "You'll get your reins and stirrups when you learn to balance without props. You should be a natural. You look great from here.''

With a sigh, feeling utterly foolish, Lily put her hands on top of her head. Blake made a soft sound, and Patsy took a step forward. Lily lurched, and her knees shot upward. She almost brought her hands down to grab at the saddle, but the mare continued moving slowly, and nothing worse happened. Swallowing hard, Lily talked herself back into the correct position and let herself rock with Patsy's gentle swaying motion.

Lily glanced over to Blake, and their eyes locked. The intensity of his expression surprised her. He really seemed to think this was important. Had this riding lesson really been Carrie's idea, or had it been Blake's after all? She'd dismissed his offer to trade riding lessons for Carrie's cooking lessons as a joke. But if he was serious, why? Why did he want her to ride, knowing she was going to leave soon, and would probably never see another horse that wasn't a statue in a park?

The heat of his gaze drove all her questions from her mind, until all she saw was his eyes, and the slight smile on his generous mouth. He knew how to use that mouth to kiss a woman senseless. She couldn't afford to be senseless, but he'd tasted so good. Just remembering the feel of his lips on hers, the flavor of his mouth when his tongue had stroke and probed... She didn't understand what he meant by wanting honesty from her—she was always honest—but he'd understood and honored her demand to stop. That in itself was strongly seductive.

Lily closed her eyes and let the gentle rhythm of the horse move through her. She let her hips sway, following the movement, feeling herself becoming one with the horse. It was such an ancient bond, she found herself thinking: humans and horses. Almost as timeless as the mating bond between man and women. As easily as she joined the horse in its movements, she could be making love with Blake, rocking her hips to bring him closer, bonding them in body and spirit.

Her eyes popped open. Losing her balance, she grabbed for the front of the saddle. What on earth was going on in her head? How had she gone from riding in a circle at a sedate walk to bonding body and soul with Blake as her lover?

Lily dared a glance at him and knew he was reading her thoughts as clearly as he could have read skywriting. Her face burned.

Several days after Lily's first riding lesson, Blake leaned against the doorway and watched her guiding Patsy around the boarders' arena at a rhythmic sitting trot. He grinned. She was a natural athlete.

The woman was also a fraud. A complete and utter fraud.

In the past week, he'd seen more examples of her lies than fleas on a dog. Not just little white fibs, but great big whoppers, and all of them to herself. He'd never seen a person who knew herself less than Lily did. Or one who was more scared to find out the truth about herself.

For a woman who claimed not to have a maternal bone in her body, she'd taken over those orphaned kittens like a mama tiger. Blushed like a rose when he caught her crooning over them. God, that was cute. She called the tortoiseshell one Rascal, and the all-black one Panther, and they already knew their names. They trilled and mewled when they heard her voice, and those lapis eyes of hers went soft and misty. All the while, she was muttering that she didn't like cats and wasn't going to take care of them another day. Couldn't fool him.

Whenever he sought her advice about Carrie, she insisted she didn't know anything about parenting. Yet when he finally got an answer out of her, it always made sense. And Carrie was crazy about her. It almost made him a tad jealous, the way the two of them could talk and laugh about stuff that left him out. And it made him realize how much Carrie had been missing.

Come to think of it, everyone was crazy about Lily. Jonathan treated her like a favorite niece. Lance and a couple of the other male boarders fell all over themselves around her. The barn workers brought her flowers in exchange for the fresh coffee she brewed for them on her breaks from Jonathan's books. The horses nickered when they heard her voice.

Poor Dolly turned herself inside out trying to cuddle up to Lily, somehow perceiving Lily's fear of dogs but desperate to share her affection. He sure knew how that felt. He'd spent the better part of the week keeping his distance, and it was frustrating as hell. He was a physical man. He needed to express his feelings physically. Words were for poets. It didn't mean his feelings were strictly physical. It was just his way to use touch to speak for him.

And he had a lot to say to Lily. She was a fraud and a liar, all right, and the biggest lie she was telling herself was that she didn't want to be within two feet of him. They spent hours together every evening, going over the ledgers, or just talking, watching movies on television, playing cards or board games. He'd never enjoyed a woman's company as much. She even made doing the dinner dishes fun, which was no mean feat.

And the few times he breached her defenses and kissed her, held her, she'd melted against him, opened to him as if she wanted him as much as he wanted her. His heart went into hyperdrive just thinking about the softness, the tenderness, of her kisses. She kissed like a willing, hungry lover, then pushed him away like a nervous virgin.

Too much about Lily didn't make sense. She was a warm, generous, intelligent woman who tried to convince the world in general—and him in particular—that she was cold, self-contained, ambitious to a fault, unwilling to become attached to anyone. If that was so, then why, for starters, had she dropped everything in New York City when her uncle asked for her help? From the little she'd said, he guessed she had piles of work waiting for her, and she'd been exhausted when she arrived. But she hadn't groused once about pinch-hitting for her uncle on Jonathan's audit. Sure, she'd made a couple of snide cracks about farm dirt, but she'd just dived into the work like a trouper.

Talk was cheap. Actions counted, and everything Lily did told him she had love and caring to spare. Something—make that someone—must have done something pretty low to make her pretend she was allergic to relationships of any but the financial kind. It was the only possible explanation. Somehow, he'd get to the reasons behind her fears and prove how wrong she was.

Blake pushed away from the wall he'd been leaning on and headed toward the stallion barn. It was getting late, and not just for doing the day's chores. Time was running out for him to convince Lily to trust her instincts—and him.

Lily let Blake's kitchen door swing shut behind her with a grateful sigh. The noise of three dozen reveling teenagers had her ears ringing. Ripping open more bags of pretzels and potato chips, she smiled at Jonathan's wisdom in taking Uncle Bill to his friend Dora's horse farm in New Jersey for the weekend. If maturity was discovering the volume knob also turned counterclockwise, these kids had a way to go yet.

Still, she reflected as she poured the snacks into bowls, they seemed like nice kids. They'd been partying for a couple of hours, with only minor spills, and no fights. No one had crashed the party, no one was drinking. From what she knew about kids in cities like New York, she was witnessing a minor miracle.

"Hi, uh, Lily," a young male voice said over the sudden increase in noise from the other rooms.

Lily turned to find Rick Preston regarding her nervously as he shifted his weight from one foot to the other. She smiled, hoping to put him at ease. Rick's answering smile wasn't very convincing. She wondered why he'd sought her out.

Blake hadn't gone out of his way to be very hospitable to the boy, and Lily wasn't sure why. Rick had arrived early in the afternoon and worked like a galley slave to help Carrie get the house ready for the invasion. He'd been polite, but not obsequious, and it was clear he was crazy about Carrie. And just as clear that Carrie liked him a great deal.

Maybe, Lily reflected, that was why Blake treated Rick like a leper.

"Can I help?" Rick nodded toward the big bowls she'd filled.

"Sure. Just put them wherever there's a bare surface." She picked up a bowl, ready to tackle the dancing hordes again.

"Okay. Uh, Lily? Can I talk to you first?"

Surprised, she set the bowl down. "Sure."

"It's about Carrie and me…and Mr. Sommers. I really like Carrie, but he hates my guts." Rick looked down at his feet, his cheeks turning crimson. She had a feeling it had cost him a lot to say as much to a relative stranger, and a woman at that.

Lily waited for him to continue. When he did, the words came out in a rush. "Carrie says her dad thinks you're pretty smart and all. Do you think you could put in a good word for me?"

She believed in Rick's sincerity, but his request was like the tendrils of a tenacious ivy, reaching out, wrapping around her, drawing her into the folds of a family that wasn't hers. If she let it, the vine of involvement would bind her until she had to hurt Blake and Carrie to free herself.

"I think it would be better if you spoke to Blake yourself, Rick," she told him gently. "I'm hardly a close enough friend to broach the subject."

The look he gave her was one of pure desperation. With a sigh, Lily put her hand on Rick's shoulder. "All right. If you want to talk to him with me there, you set it up and I'll make myself available. Okay?"

Rick nodded. Lily forced a smile for him and handed him two big bowls of pretzels. Damn Blake! Carrie's relationship with her father and with Rick were none of Lily's business. And because they weren't, she couldn't give Blake a piece of her mind about what a jerk he was being about Rick.

Lily picked up the bowl of potato chips just as Blake pushed the door open. He paused, glancing from Lily to Rick, suspicion clouding his dark eyes. Rick cast a nervous grin at Blake and headed for the door.

Someone had switched the music to a CD of oldies. Lily perched on the corner of the couch and watched the kids bouncing around, trying to catch the beat while the Cascades sang "Rhythm of the Rain." Although the song went way back before her time, she had several friends for whom pop music stopped at 1980. Lily had learned to dance the locomotion, the mashed potato, the twist, the swim and other silly gyrations at their oldies parties. Her generation had lost much of the finesse of her parents' one, especially in ballroom dancing, but one look around the living room proved that Carrie's generation apparently didn't have a clue.

Suddenly, the music stopped. "Hey, guys, it's not hip-hop," Blake hollered, laughter in his voice. "It's a cha-cha. Let a couple of old folks show you how to dance to oldies."

Before she had a chance to register his intention and hide, Blake had her hands in his and was tugging her into the center of the living room. He pulled her against him amid whistles and whoops from the kids, and yelled, "Hit it!"

The song started again. When Blake began moving, Lily found herself following him as easily as if they'd danced a million times. She seemed to know exactly what he was going to do a second before he did it. Feeling unexpectedly daring, Lily embellished her steps, which seemed to inspire Blake to lead her into increasingly elaborate maneuvers.

By the time the song ended, she was laughing. It felt like the most natural thing in the world to stand in Blake's embrace and catch her breath. As the heat of their bodies mingled between them, a slow song started. When Blake stepped into a slow dance, Lily followed his lead as easily, as necessarily, as breathing.

His heat and scent surrounded her, his hard body cradled her. He lowered his head until his cheek rested against her head, his breath whispering in her hair. Bonelessly, Lily allowed Blake to wrap her arms around his neck. She closed her eyes, shutting out the grinning teen-agers, the topsy-turvy furniture, the bowls of snacks and cans of soft drinks. In the darkness, there was only Blake and the music and this dreamlike trance.

She felt alive, aware, shaky with just how aware she was of Blake. He affected her like champagne, making her lose her good sense, making her feel silly and giddy and sentimental. Making her want too much of a good thing, which was never wise. She'd have to keep remind-ing herself that she always regretted drinking champagne the next day, when her head ached. Except it wasn't her head she was afraid would ache if she let herself surrender to Blake. It was her heart.

"What are you thinking about?" he murmured.

"Champagne," she told him, then laughed at his puz-zled expression. "Never mind. It's too complicated."

"What did the Preston kid want?"

She recalled Carrie complaining that Blake never used Rick's name. "Rick? He wanted to talk. He's a nice young man." Then, after only a brief mental debate, she broke her vow to herself. "He likes Carrie, but he knows you don't feel the same way about him. I was wondering why."

Blake's shoulders stiffened, as if his whole body had gone on the alert. "He wanted you to butter me up, huh? Little chicken."

She pulled back and stared into Blake's face. "Aren't you being a little harsh? He's trying to do things properly, without sneaking behind your back. Can't you give him credit for that?"

"Sure. But I don't trust him, and I don't want him sniffing around Carrie."

"She's almost eighteen, Blake, and she's got a good, sensible head on her shoulders. You can't keep her a child forever. You have to learn to trust her, trust that you've done a good job raising her. The more you hold tight, the more she'll want to pull away. Isn't that what you keep telling your riders when they pull on the reins?''

So much for noninvolvement, Lily thought ruefully as she watched Blake's dark eyes for some sign of what he was thinking. Then she felt his body relax and she realized she'd been holding her breath. He pulled her close again, and she nestled against his chest as his cheek touched her forehead.

''You're right, I guess,'' he muttered. ''I suppose it won't hurt to listen to what the kid...Rick...has to say. A blind man can see he's nuts about Carrie. I don't want her taking the bit in her teeth and bolting. Lord knows, I've seen what can happen when two kids let the stars in their eyes blind them.''

Tears gathered behind Lily's closed eyes. She tightened her hold around Blake's neck briefly and nodded. He was a good man, trying to be a good father. This was a moment he should be sharing with a wife, with a woman who was a mother to Carrie, not with her. She had no place in their lives, and she didn't want to care so much about them that she could cry.

She'd done the right thing after all, this one time. But now she had to put more distance between them. Fortunately, she was almost finished reviewing Jonathan's books. The rest of the work shouldn't take her more than a week. And then she'd go back to her real life and try to forget about a girl with a smile like a spring morning, and a man who made her feel— almost—that caring was a risk worth taking.

Chapter Eight

The Sunday evening after Carrie's party, Lily shut off the computer. She'd put in an extra hour after the simple meal she'd fixed herself. On previous Sundays, Jonathan had made a large dinner, inviting Uncle Bill to join them. But tonight her host was in New Jersey with Uncle Bill, helping Dora Simpson prepare to sell her horses and farm. And right after finishing Sunday chores on the farm, Carrie had gone to a friend's house to work on a term paper.

That left Lily alone with Blake, not a situation she wanted to be in. So she'd begged off from his offer of steaks at his place, lamely explaining that she wanted to work late to make up for taking two hours off that afternoon to ride. She could tell by the expression in his dark eyes that he didn't believe her.

The phone rang as she was filling the kettle. Blake's intimate ''Hi'' sent unwelcome little ripples of awareness through her. Her answering greeting came out embarrassingly curt.

"I've got a cold bottle of wine with our names on it," he told her. "I can be over in two minutes."

"No! I... I mean, thank you, but..."

"Then you come over here, so you can go whenever you want."

"No, really, I—"

"Afraid of me, Lily?" he said softly. "Or of yourself?"

His tone told her he already knew the answer. Stupidly, her vanity didn't want him to think she was cowardly—or predictable.

"Neither. I'll be over in a half hour." Fool that she was!

"Good."

The dial tone purred in her ear. She looked at the receiver as if it held the explanation for what she'd just done. Or some hint for staying out of trouble. Unfortunately, the hunk of black plastic had no answers for her. Thirty-five minutes later, having changed from sweater and skirt to jeans and sweatshirt and back again several times, she threw on her coat and made her way across the dark parking lot to Blake's front porch.

He opened the door, a glass of white wine in one hand. When she stepped inside, he took her coat and, still without a word, offered her the wine. To her dismay, she was trembling when she closed her fingers around the stem of the glass.

"C'mon in. Carrie's still at her friend's, and I've got a fire going."

He waved her into the now tidy living room and slid the double doors to the hallway most of the way closed. "Helps keep the heat in," he told her, with a straight face she wasn't sure she should trust. Then he sank down onto the overstuffed sofa and patted the cushion beside him. "Come sit," he invited, "I don't bite." His dimple flashed. "Not hard, anyway."

He was just teasing, just testing, Lily told herself. He was hoping to get a rise out of her. Well, she'd call his bluff. She could sit a couple of feet away from the man without succumbing to his charms. That was, after all, why she'd ultimately chosen to wear jeans and a March Acres sweatshirt, rather than a skirt that would send the wrong signals. And make it much too easy for him to breach her defenses.

She settled herself on the sofa, the middle cushion between them, and drew her legs under her to face him. He smiled and raised his own glass to his lips. Despite her resolve, she couldn't stop watching his mouth, and his strong neck as he swallowed. This could turn out to be a mistake, she warned herself. She'd have to do something neutral fast. A friendly question about—

"Tell me about yourself," he said quietly, interrupting her thoughts. "What were you like as a kid? And how the hell did you decide to get into international tax law?" The smile in his voice softened his incredulous tone. "Help me understand why I make you so skittish," he added softly, but there was a hint of his own vulnerability that touched her. She'd never intended her rejection of his advances to hurt him.

Lily weighed refusal against complying. Finally, she decided that if Blake knew anything about her parents, he'd probably head for the nearest exit and stop trying to seduce her.

"As a kid, I was an afterthought, except when I was providing my mother with someone to live through, especially gymnastics. My mother was a hypochondriac.

She controlled us through her weaknesses. My father indulged her. He was what they now call an enabler, although back then, people thought it was sweet how he fussed over her and pampered her. Of course, those same people didn't hear them arguing and throwing things behind closed doors. I did, but I could never convince them to stop.''

"Sounds like they didn't have much left over for you."

She shrugged uncomfortably, unwilling to meet Blake's eyes and see his reaction. ''When did they die?'' he asked quietly.

"My father when I was twelve, and Mother eight years ago."

It had been a mistake to give in to the urge to confide in Blake. The old hurts she'd kept hidden so long now clamored to pour out, demanding that she acknowledge them. She sipped at her wine, letting the cool, crisp liquid slide over her tongue and down her throat. She wouldn't cry, she vowed. She wouldn't let him make her feel sorry for herself, so he could offer sympathy. She didn't want to be vulnerable to the temptation of leaning on Blake's strength, his generous warmth.

"My mother had ambitions for herself that she claimed she'd given up for my father and me. She wanted me to compensate her for them, but I couldn't, no matter how hard I tried. She took it out on my father, and he turned to bourbon to help him put up with her. They were very unhappy people who weren't terribly mature." She took another sip of wine.

"In the long run, I grew up and they didn't. I used to resent them, but now, I feel sorry for them. They couldn't help what they were. I'd like to think that if they'd seen themselves objectively, they would have tried to be better. I used to believe their unhappiness was my fault, because

I couldn't fulfill their needs. But I've come to believe they did love me, to the best of their abilities. Or their limits."

"I'd like to think you're right," he murmured. "You're a very lovable woman."

Suddenly choked up by Blake's softly spoken affirmation, Lily sipped at her wine again, forcing it past the ache in her throat. Damn! She didn't want to cry! If she talked any more about herself, she'd be drowning in self-pity. "Now your turn. Tell me..." She stopped and cleared her throat. "Tell me about you," she demanded, without looking at him.

"Okay. I'm from northeast Connecticut. My parents are still there, but my brothers and sisters and their families are all over the States. I majored in animal husbandry and minored in psychology at the University of Connecticut, and came to work for Jonathan sixteen years ago, when Carrie was a little over one year old."

She smiled at the typically masculine way he'd talked about his life without commenting on any of it. Just the facts, ma'am. Well, turnabout was fair play. She'd pump him for more.

"Carrie told me you were studying to be a vet when your wife died. It must have been hard on you to suddenly be a single parent so young."

Blake regarded her so seriously that she wondered what she'd said wrong. Had Carrie told her that in confidence, and was she now betraying that confidence? Was Blake upset that she and Carrie had discussed important details of his past? Was he still in love with his late wife? Carrie believed he'd gotten over her, but not before destroying all but a few photographs of her. Little remained for the girl to treasure.

He sighed. "I might as well come clean, Lily. My family and Jonathan always knew, but no one else does. I didn't want Carrie to know. I figured it would make her feel bad about herself. Carrie's mother and I were never married. She did die, but Carrie was about five, so by then I didn't know how to explain why I'd lied. It just seemed simpler and kinder not to backtrack.''

He took a quick sip of his wine. Stunned speechless by his confession, Lily waited for him to continue.

''I fell for a drama student, Sandy Owen, when I was nineteen, but we broke up because she didn't want to give up her dreams of an acting career to live in the boondocks with a poor but honest horse doctor. Nine months later, she showed up with a month-old baby and my name on the kid's birth certificate as the father. Then she took off for Hollywood. A year later, she was Zondra Van Owen, rising soap-opera star. And four years after that, she died in an accident during a taping on location. Fortunately, by the time Carrie was old enough to understand any of it, Sandy's death was old news.''

Before Lily could assimilate all that he'd told her, before she could react, there was a crash and the sound of shattering glass in the hallway outside the partially closed living room doors. Blake dropped his wineglass and bolted across the room. He wrenched the sliding doors fully open.

''Carrie? Honey?'' There was a world of regret in his voice.

Lily held her breath in the silence that followed.

''I *hate* you!'' Carrie suddenly cried out from the hallway. ''You *lied!*'' Her voice broke on a sob. *''My whole life is a lie!''*

Footsteps pounded up the stairs, and then a door above slammed shut. Lily sat still, aching for Carrie, aching for Blake. She wanted to go to each of them, to both of them, and take away the pain they'd caused each other, but there was nothing she could do.

Blake appeared in the doorway to the living room. He met her eyes with a bleak, helpless expression. Without thinking, Lily rose and crossed the room. She touched his arm, and he pulled her close and held her hard against his chest. She didn't know she was crying until she felt the wetness of his shirt under her cheek.

"Oh, God!" he groaned. "I didn't know she was home. With the doors half-closed, and you on my mind, I just didn't hear her come in."

Lily held him tighter, offering her silent support. She didn't think there were any words that could help him now.

"I never wanted her to know her mother didn't want her. I wanted to protect her from being hurt." His laugh was short and bitter. "Screwed that up, didn't I? Damn! What am I going to do, Lily? I have to convince her I did my best for her."

Lily pulled back from Blake a little. Looking up into his face, she saw the pain in his eyes. It hurt that she had no power to ease that pain for him. She didn't question her deep, urgent need to do so.

"Blake, come sit down. Give her a few minutes before you go upstairs. She needs to cry and to think. She won't be able to listen for a little while."

Blake's smile was hollow. He stroked her hair back from her cheek and wiped away the residue of her tears. With a nod, he let her lead him to the couch. This time, Lily had no second thoughts about sinking down close beside him. His arm came around her immediately. Wishing she knew what else to do, she wrapped her arms around him and listened to the beating of his heart.

"I thought I was doing the best thing for her," he said

softly. "No kid should grow up thinking she's so unlovable that even her mother doesn't want her. Especially not Carrie."

Not anyone, Lily thought, but she kept silent, giving him her tacit agreement with a gentle tightening of her arms.

He took a deep breath. "When Sandy shoved this pink bundle at me, I felt like my life had fallen down a hole. I couldn't believe it was happening. I never thought about it before, but I guess she felt the same way when she found out she was pregnant. I was raised to take responsibility for my actions, but what was I going to do with a baby? Then Carrie opened her eyes and looked up into my face, and I didn't care if I was her biological father. She was mine, and I loved her."

The simple way Blake told his story touched Lily. She'd never met a man who gave so easily, so completely. He didn't deserve to be hurt.

"What did you do, in school, with an infant?"

"My parents helped. They were great. Carrie was their first grandchild, and I don't think my mother cared if she came from the cabbage patch or not. But I wanted time with Carrie, and if I went to vet school, I'd be too busy for too many years. And I figured I had to start earning some real money, 'cause my parents had five of us to raise."

"How did you end up here?"

"UConn breeds Morgan horses, and everyone in Morgans knows Jonathan. I ran into him at a show in Syracuse and mentioned that I was looking for a permanent position. He said he could use a farm manager who knew Morgans, and his wife, Rachel, said she'd love having Carrie around. It was perfect. We came up here right after my graduation."

His chest moved under her as he took another deep breath. "I really thought I'd done the right thing, not telling her about *Zondra*." He said the name as if it left a bad taste. "When she asked for pictures of Sandy and me, I fed her that story about loving her mother so much I couldn't stand to keep our wedding album. And when she asked if she would ever have another mother, I fed her the same b.s."

"But, Blake, maybe it was better to tell her a good story when she was a little girl still believing in fairy tales."

"Like hell! I was really thinking about what was good for me. I liked being Carrie's only parent. I rationalized that she didn't need a mother, because I wanted to prove I could raise her by myself. The truth is, I didn't want to share her. And maybe I wanted to punish Sandy, too. Damn!"

Lily stroked his smooth cheek, wiping away the traces of moisture that trailed over the hard planes. "Blake, you really did do a wonderful job raising Carrie. She's one of the nicest people I've ever met."

"But maybe I shortchanged her. Maybe I should have tried harder to convince Sandy to stay with us. Or found another woman who wanted to raise Carrie with me."

Lily couldn't bear Blake's self-recriminations. He wasn't being fair to himself. "And risk Carrie hearing repeatedly that she'd ruined Sandy's life? I know firsthand what kind of a hell that is. My mother never let me forget what she gave up for me. I wouldn't wish that on a dog. Or would you have married just any woman so that Carrie could have a stepmother? What kind of life would that be for you and that woman? Be realistic, Blake. You made a choice from your heart, and you did a wonderful job of raising your daughter."

He sighed and pulled her closer. "I guess you're right.

But, hell, Lily, I didn't know she could use baby lotion to shave her legs. Girls need that kind of advice. Mothers know those things.''

Lily smiled at the memory of Carrie's embarrassment when her father had overheard that conversation. "Blake, I got that idea from a magazine. Anyone could have told her that. You gave her love. That's something you know a lot about. You can't find love in a magazine, and believe me, not all parents know about love." She gave him a little shake. "*You do.* Carrie knows you love her. And she loves you. That's why she's so hurt. But that's also why she'll find a way to reconcile it. You'll see."

Blake eased her away a little and gazed into her eyes. Lily offered him what she hoped was an encouraging smile. He stroked her face with his work-toughened fingertips and smiled weakly back at her.

"You're a very wise woman, Lily Davis. Thanks for being here." He captured one of her hands and brought her fingers to his lips. "Think it's time I went up to Carrie?"

"You can try." He placed a gentle kiss on her forehead and pushed away from the sofa. "But, Blake? Be patient with her if she's not ready yet. She's got a lot of sorting out to do."

Blake smiled ruefully, his dimple barely visible. "Don't we all?" He sighed. "Wish me luck."

She nodded. "I'll clean up whatever dropped and go back to Jonathan's. The kittens are probably hungry again."

"Forget the mess. I probably deserve to walk on broken glass. But wait a little while? I may need you if Carrie…" He shrugged. "You know."

"Yes, I know," she agreed softly, her heart aching for him. "Good luck."

Blake climbed the stairs as if lead weights dragged at his feet and a giant vise had fastened around his heart. He wished Lily's words could give him a glimmer of hope, but then, she hadn't seen the look of betrayal on Carrie's face.

He'd tried so hard to protect Carrie from the truth, but his silence had become a lie that hurt her worse than the truth would have. And now they would both have to live with that irony.

The lack of sound beyond Carrie's closed door echoed. No crying, no defiantly loud music, no smashing things. He could have dealt with those reactions. This echoing silence was worse, because he had no markers to help him find his way.

His knock, intended to be gentle, resounded in the still house. No answer.

"Carrie? Carrie, honey, may I come in? We need to talk."

He waited. Nothing. He knocked and called again. Again, no response. Not a sound. Could she have slipped out the window and down the trellis to run away? The thought set his heart pounding in his throat.

"Carrie? Please, honey, talk to me."

He put his hand on the doorknob, afraid she really had run away, rather than be in the same house with him. As he turned the knob, it was jerked out of his hand. The door swung open, and Carrie faced him, glaring.

Oh, God, his poor baby girl! The misery etched on her face broke his heart. Her eyes were red, her nose was running, tears had made black mascara trails down her cheeks and onto her shirt. Stupidly, he wondered when she'd started wearing mascara. Tongue-tied by the enormity of the situation, he regarded her.

"Leave me alone!" She choked the words out hoarsely.

"You lied to me!" Tears flooded her eyes again. "You stole my mother!"

"Oh, Carrie, I'm sorry. I'm so sorry. I thought—"

"I don't care what you thought! You were wrong! Leave me alone!" She started to shove the door shut. He blocked it with his foot. Anger flared in her eyes.

"Carrie, we need to talk. There's so much I should explain. You need to listen. I need to listen. Please don't shut me out."

He reached out to touch her cheek. She stepped back, out of reach. He dropped his hand, a vise tightening around his heart.

"Is Lily still here?" she asked curtly. Blake nodded. "I'll talk to Lily. I don't want to talk to you."

The door swung shut. There was no lock, but Carrie had turned a more powerful key against him. What would he do if he couldn't make her understand that he only wanted to protect her from hurt and disillusionment? Was it so wrong for a father not to want his daughter to know her mother had abandoned her?

He knew he couldn't keep her his little girl forever. She was growing up too quickly for that. But he didn't know what he'd do if he'd killed the sweet closeness he'd always shared with his sunshiny daughter. And he wouldn't forgive himself if he'd robbed her of the joy, the spirit, the light that glowed inside her.

Her rejection hurt, but he prayed she would listen to Lily. Somehow, Lily would know how to bring them together. The thought that had been simmering in his mind for weeks formed into words: Carrie needed a woman like Lily in her life.

And so, damn it, did he.

Lily perched on the edge of the sofa, willing Blake and Carrie to listen to each other. From the shrill sound of

Carrie's voice, that would take more time than Blake had allowed just now. But she knew that the love they had for each other would eventually heal the hurts they were inflicting on each other. That love would make all the difference.

Carrie was in too much pain now to understand how much Blake loved her. She thought she'd deserved the truth from the start. But Lily knew that a lifetime of unvarnished truth—especially the truth that a child wasn't wanted, that sacrifices had been made grudgingly—without love, was far more devastating than even this profound disillusionment. Carrie wouldn't ever have to fight to create her own identity, even though at this moment she thought she'd been living a lie. Lily prayed the girl would see the truth of that soon.

A soft, pathetic whimper from behind the sofa sent Lily's heart into her throat. *Dolly!* Had the monster been there all the time? Heart hammering, Lily stood and peered over the back of the sofa. The eyes she met were almost human in their sad anxiety. Did the dog understand that something awful had happened between the people she loved? Dolly whimpered again, and Lily almost believed she did.

"They'll work it out," she murmured, feeling a little foolish. Was she trying to reassure the dog? Or herself? Dolly apparently believed her. The dog let out a long, groaning sigh and lowered her huge head to her paws. Lily sank back onto the edge of the sofa cushion, waiting for Blake.

The slamming of a door upstairs made Lily jump. Dolly gave a quiet little yip, echoing Lily's dismay. A moment later, Blake appeared in the doorway, his expression unreadable in the dim light. But his posture spoke of defeat.

Lily crossed the room and let him pull her close to his chest. She held him tightly, feeling him struggle against his emotions, wishing he could allow himself to let them out.

"She won't talk to me," he told her hoarsely. "She won't even listen. What am I going to do?"

"Give her time, Blake. Keep loving her, and give her time."

"She wants you up there. Maybe she'll talk to you."

"Me?"

"Carrie needs you, Lily. She's crazy about you. She respects you." He exhaled sharply. "Part of me knows she'll listen to you, and part of me is jealous that she wants you, not me. Pretty shabby, huh?"

Lily briefly tightened her arms around him. "Not shabby, Blake. Perfectly normal. You're her father. I'm an outsider. I'd feel more than a little jealous, under the circumstances." The way, perhaps, her mother had felt when Lily slavishly obeyed her gymnastics coaches? That was an insight she'd have to mull over later, when this crisis was past.

"Will you go talk to her?"

Lily held her breath as the slipknot of involvement tightened. Her self-preservation instincts told her to refuse, now, before it was too late. But her heart told her it was already too late. She cared about Carrie. She cared about Blake. The rift between them saddened her, and she might be able to help them reconcile. She'd never been able to do that with her own mother, and the lack of closure still haunted her. Probably always would. The least

she could do was make sure neither Blake nor Carrie had
to live with that kind of burden.

"Yes," she said, exhaling. "But don't expect mira-
cles."

"I won't. But I'll be hoping for one."

Something bumped Lily's hip. She looked down, saw
Dolly's big head and pleading eyes, and froze. Blake
looked down, too.

"She won't hurt you, Lily. She's worried, too."

"I know. We, um, talked a few minutes ago," Lily
admitted, feeling heat wash over her cheeks. "I guess she
understands something is wrong."

Blake bent and pressed a kiss on her forehead. "You
are one very special woman. Take Dolly upstairs with
you. She may help Carrie talk to you. Dogs are great
listeners."

Lily braced herself. "She won't jump on me?"

"No. She understands you, now. She'll respect your
need for distance." He gave her a hint of a smile. "Even
if she doesn't agree with it."

He released her, and she skirted the remains of a shattered glass and the cookies and milk surrounding it. Dolly
followed at her heels as she climbed the stairs. Halfway
to the upper landing, she turned to look back at Blake.
Unsure of herself, she offered him what she hoped was a
reassuring smile.

"Go on, Lily. Carrie needs you." She nodded and
turned away, but she thought she heard him add, "So do
I." Her heart, already tangled in strings she had tried so
hard to escape, gave a strange little flutter at his words.

Chapter Nine

Dolly reached Carrie's closed door before Lily. She whined and scratched at it as Lily followed, hoping Blake had been right about Dolly not jumping on her. This wasn't the time for her phobia to swamp her. Somehow, for Carrie's sake, and for Blake's, she'd ignore her fear of the dog. She could fall apart later.

"Dolly?" Carrie called softly through the door.

"Me too," Lily answered, reaching the door. To her relief, Dolly settled herself several feet away, her eyes going from Lily to the door and back to Lily. "Blake said you wanted to talk to me. May we come in?"

The door opened slowly. Dolly pushed past Lily to rush inside. Carrie stepped aside for Lily to come in, then closed the door behind them. She hung her head, not meeting Lily's eyes. For a moment, Lily stood awkwardly, unsure of what to do next. What did Carrie need from her? Would she do the right thing, say the right things, or make the situation worse somehow? She'd never had a sympathetic older woman to guide her and comfort her, so she didn't have a clue how to go about being one herself.

Carrie lifted her head, her tear-streaked face a mask of misery and confusion. Instinctively Lily opened her arms, and Carrie flung herself into them, sobbing. Holding the girl close, Lily stroked Carrie's tangled hair and felt the sting of tears in her own eyes. Dolly paced beside them, whining anxiously.

Finally, Carrie's sobs quieted. "Let's sit down," Lily suggested, her back aching from supporting the much taller girl.

Carrie nodded against Lily's shoulder and moved like a sleepwalker to her rumpled bed. She sat down and made room for Lily to sit beside her. Without hesitation, Dolly leaped up and flung her big body down next to Carrie, her head on the girl's knee. Lily stiffened, but she tamped down her automatic impulse to scream and escape. Blake was probably right that Dolly's presence would help Carrie unburden herself.

"Would you like to talk?" Lily asked gently.

Carrie shook her head. Lily waited. Carrie stroked Dolly's head and sniffled. When she wiped her cheek with the back of her hand, Lily offered her a tissue.

"How could he lie to me my whole life?" Carrie suddenly blurted. "I thought I was one person, and now I find out I'm someone else. I believed that stupid fairy tale about him loving my mother so much that he could never replace her. I thought my mother was someone special. But the truth was, my mother was some bimbo who didn't want me."

More sobs choked off Carrie's further attempts to talk.

Lily took the girl's hand in her own and let her cry until she'd gotten some more of her misery out of her system.

"My father always talked about how important it is to tell the truth. No matter what. Unless..." Carrie's eyes met hers, and a sheepish expression replaced some of her earlier defiance. "Unless it would hurt someone unnecessarily," she finished dully. "But this hurts more. My mother didn't want me! And now she's dead, and I'll never be able to know her."

Privately. Lily thought the loss was more Sandra's than Carrie's, but she wouldn't say that aloud. Lily shifted so that she could sit beside Carrie, and put her arm around the girl's shoulders. Carrie leaned her head against Lily's. Dolly looked up at them and sighed. The dog's concern was so obvious that Lily almost smiled.

"I shouldn't presume to speak for your father, Carrie, but I believe he was trying to protect you from feeling that your mother didn't love you. I would have done the same thing, if..." *If you were my daughter*, she almost said. "If I were in his shoes."

"That's easy for you to say," Carrie muttered against Lily's shoulder. "Grown-ups always stick up for each other."

Maybe a little shock therapy would help Carrie put things into perspective, Lily decided. "It *is* easy for me to say. I know what it's like to hear day in and day out that you were an accident. That you ruined your mother's chances for an acting career. That you owed your mother an unpayable debt for simply being alive."

Carrie lifted her head and stared at Lily. "Your mother?"

Lily nodded.

"Oh, God, that's awful."

"She was very immature. I think she loved me, but she

was frightened by the responsibility of a child. Like your mother, she wanted to be an actress, and had to give up what she saw as her big chance when she discovered she was pregnant. My father and her parents pressured her into getting married, but she never came to terms with it. I grew up thinking I was unlovable, a failure. I worked like a demon to please her, but nothing I did satisfied her, because nothing could undo the fact of my birth. It took me over twenty years to understand her and figure out that it really wasn't my fault. She just wasn't meant to be a mother.''

Carrie rested her head on Lily's shoulder again, and a sigh shuddered through her. When Lily hugged her, Carrie hugged back, as if offering some of the comfort back to Lily.

"You know," Lily said gently, hoping she wasn't going to make things worse, "it's just possible your mother did the best thing for all of you by leaving before she started to hurt you like that. And your father raised you to feel loved and secure and self-confident, when he could have blamed you for ending his chances to be a vet. I'd say that makes you pretty lucky."

Carrie sniffed. "So I'm not supposed to be mad that he lied? Just 'cause he said it's for my own good. Is that it?"

"No. You're entitled to your anger. It must have been an awful shock. But while you're working through your anger, remember that your dad loves you very much. You're the most important thing in his life. Knowing he hurt you is killing him."

Carrie sat silently for a long time, occasionally sniffling, her face buried in Lily's shoulder. Finally, she breathed a long sigh and lifted her head.

"You really like him, don't you?"

Lily closed her eyes, weighing her answer. She didn't

want Carrie to feel even more betrayed than she already did.

"Yes, I do."

"He likes you, too. More than he's ever liked any other woman." She sniffed. "If he asked, would you marry him?"

Lily's eyes flew open. She'd handled some tough business situations, but nothing as emotionally entangling, as risky as this.

"It's not that simple, Carrie. I have a career that's vitally important to me, and I have to leave as soon as I finish preparing Jonathan for the IRS. Marriage isn't in my plans."

"Isn't that what my mother said?"

Ouch! "In a way, perhaps. I don't know what her life was like. I can only speak for myself. My career is definitely established, and I've invested too much to give it up."

"But is your career more important than anything else?" The words *Even us?* hung unspoken between them.

Lily picked up Carrie's free hand, the one that wasn't playing with Dolly's ears, and sought the right words to explain why her desertion wasn't the same as Carrie's mother's.

"I spent a lot of years trying to please people who couldn't be pleased. I did a lot of things I didn't want to do, and gave up a lot of things I wanted, whenever my mother said the magic words—'If you love me...' Since she died, I've been putting my own life together. I'm at a point in my career where I'm practically writing my own ticket, and I love my independence."

Carrie offered a weak smile. "I thought women were supposed to be able to have it all in the nineties."

Lily gave Carrie a brief hug. "Only in theory. In real

life, the choices can be tough." She leaned away to look into the girl's red-rimmed eyes. "How are you feeling now?"

"Can I stay at Jonathan's house with you tonight?" The quaver was back in Carrie's voice.

Lily sighed. "I guess. But Dolly has to stay here, please. I've got a scream inside me that could break loose at any moment."

Carrie giggled, and Lily marveled, a little enviously, at the resilience of youth. "Okay. I'll get my stuff." Carrie bounced off the bed and opened her closet. Then she turned back to Lily, her expression anxious. "Will you tell my dad? I'm still not ready to talk to him."

"Sure. Come down when you're ready."

When Lily went down the stairs, Blake was standing in the kitchen doorway, his body taut, his face drawn.

"Well?" Anxiety tightened his voice.

"She's still hurt and angry, but she's working through it. I agreed to let her stay with me tonight. I hope that's all right."

Blake reached out and took Lily's shoulders in his strong hands. His dimple flashed, and his mouth quirked into the closest thing to a smile she'd seen him offer since Carrie's appearance.

"Smart kid," he said, pulling Lily close to his chest. "*I* was going to ask you to stay with *me*."

"You'll have to settle for Dolly," she told him, glad for the teasing note in his voice. Maybe the worst was over for him and Carrie.

"She snores."

Lily laughed softly into Blake's shirtfront, trying not to notice how good he smelled. When he loosened his hold around her, she tilted her face toward him to offer a reassuring smile. She wasn't prepared for the heat in his dark eyes. His face came toward her, and his kiss swallowed her gasp.

She tasted Blake's desperation and let him find comfort in her answering kiss. Maybe she needed some comfort, too. He held her tightly, and his tongue pushed between her lips.

There was nothing seductive about Blake's kisses now. He was on the edge, seeking a lifeline. Without hesitation, Lily welcomed his hunger, offering her softness and her strength.

He broke the kiss slowly, leaving her breathless. He whispered her name, his breath warm on her skin. "I never realized how good it can be to have someone share something like this. You're right. We'll work this out together."

Blake covered her face with soft kisses, silencing her when she tried to tell him he couldn't count on her beyond the immediate future. Waves of heat melted her resistance, until she sought his mouth with her own and gave him back some of the sweetness he'd given her.

He tore his lips from hers and buried his face in her neck. "Lord, I want you," he murmured, sending tremors of longing through her. "It's not the right time or place, but I want you."

She wanted him, too, with the same desperate urgency she could taste in his kiss. But she didn't dare give in to that craving. Blake didn't deserve to be used like that. He deserved to be loved, deeply and forever. She couldn't give him that. She owed him the truth, but his mouth was plundering hers, silencing her protest. She could feel his need in the hardness of his body, in the iron hold of his arms around her, in the depth of his kisses.

"Lily?" Carrie's quavery voice from the upstairs hall broke the spell.

Lily shuddered against Blake, grateful for his strong hands spread over her back, supporting her. She eased away, torn between the desires Blake had awakened and the nagging of her conscience.

"Yes, Carrie?"

"I'm ready."

"Okay. Let's go."

Blake retreated into the darkness of the kitchen, but she knew he was watching for his daughter. Lily's heart ached at the sadness in his eyes. When Carrie reached the bottom step, she looked equally miserable. Lily felt torn between them.

As for herself, she knew they were both counting on her to help them. That scared her more than any number of large dogs.

Blake stared at the list of horses Dora Simpson was offering for sale, but he couldn't concentrate on bloodlines. He couldn't get the day-old memory of Carrie's tearstained face out of his mind. Like any child growing up, Carrie had shed her share of tears, but this was the first time *he'd* been the one to break her heart. This was the first time he hadn't been able to make things better with a hug and a kiss. This was the first time Carrie had rejected *him,* not just something he'd done or said.

He'd let her down big-time. And he couldn't think of a damn thing to do to redeem himself.

In disgust, he flipped the unread papers onto his desk and leaned back in his chair to think. The faint knock on his door brought him upright. Was it Carrie, coming to talk to him after a long day's silence? Or was it Lily, coming to offer sympathy? He could sure use both now.

"Come in."

"Dad?" The word came out softly, shakily.

Seeing his daughter in the doorway reminded him sharply of the first time he'd seen her, wrapped in a pink blanket, her dark hair mere wisps, her eyes huge and unfocused. His love for her was the same now as it had been on that fateful day: visceral, total, unconditional.

He had to clear his throat before he could answer her with a simple "Yes."

Carrie stepped inside and leaned against the door frame. Her dark eyes reflected the same troubled feelings that gripped his heart. His first impulse was to rise and wrap her in a hug, but something held him back. After talking with Lily, he was seeing Carrie in a new light. Now, he really had to acknowledge that she wasn't his baby anymore. He wasn't sure who she was, but he had a feeling he'd better shut up and give her a chance to tell him.

He sure as hell wished kids came with instructions.

"I, um... I'm sorry I blew up. I think I have a right to be upset, but I understand now that you did what you thought was best for me." She smiled, a sweet-sad smile that melted his heart. "You always do, Dad. It's just that what's best for me may change as I get older. So don't underestimate me, okay?"

Blake exhaled, unaware until that instant that he'd been holding his breath. "You've grown up, Carrie. Right under my nose, you've turned into a beautiful, intelligent young woman."

Carrie's cheeks turned pink. She grinned, dimple flashing. "It's a tough job, but somebody's got to do it," she told him, her voice a little shaky. She kept smiling, even when tears glistened in her eyes.

He stood up and opened his arms. "C'mere. This old man needs some reassurance."

Carrie dashed across the room, nearly knocking him over with the force of her hug. She gave a hiccuplike sob and buried her face in his shirtfront. With a sigh of relief, Blake wrapped his arms around her, thanking God and Lily that the rift between them was so easily healed.

"You're the best, Dad," she mumbled. "Even when you make a mistake, you're still the best."

He chuckled and tugged a lock of her hair. "Thanks— I think."

"I mean it." She broke loose and grinned up at him. "Debbie called. Can I go over there so we can study math together? She's got her mom's car for a couple of hours."

He was still enjoying the warm little glow her praise had stirred up. It took him a couple of seconds to catch up with her change of direction. But why, he wondered ruefully, should Carrie slow down for an emotional slow-poke like him? He'd sort of been hoping for a little more time with his daughter, but there was still a bright side. With Carrie at the library and Jonathan at Bill's, in Rochester, now he'd have the evening alone with Lily.

Which made him recall his own teenage years, and how he'd come to be a single father. An image of Rick Preston's pickup truck came to mind. "It's just you and Debbie, right? You're not planning to go anywhere besides the library?"

Carrie shook her head. "No. This project is due Wednesday, and it's worth fifty percent of the semester grade. We don't want to blow our A averages. Is it okay if I stay over? Debbie's mom needs the car later, and that won't leave us much time to work if she has to drive me home first."

"As long as it's okay with Debbie's mother."

"It is." Carrie flashed a grin. "We promised to look after Debbie's little brother while her mother's out."

Her cheek was salty when he kissed her. He watched her bounce out of his office, and grinned. The worst was over, and they'd managed to pull out of it without leaving any permanent scars on each other. Thanks to Lily.

It was one more reason not to let her walk out of his life.

That night, when Lily heard the bedroom door creak open, she didn't even bother to sit up. She simply turned her head to gaze at Blake's silhouette in the dim light from the hallway. They'd said good-night after watching an old cowboy movie on video. It had taken her forever to fall asleep, when her nervous system was short-circuiting all over from Blake's sweet, lingering kisses. He'd done that on purpose, she knew, but that knowledge didn't make those kisses any less tantalizing.

"Not again," she muttered, unwilling to betray the tiny shiver of excitement at his presence. Rascal squeaked. Panther yawned and meowed at the same time. "You should see a doctor about this sleepwalking."

"I've got a horse doctor on call," he answered, "but I need you in the barn right now. Bonnie's having trouble foaling. I can't help her alone, and Carrie's at one of her friends."

That got her sitting up. The kittens protested being dumped out of their warm nest. Automatically, she cradled them in her hands and calmed them, but her own nerves were short-circuiting.

There was no point in asking for Jonathan's expertise. He was staying at Uncle Bill's, claiming to have a score to settle about their latest chess match. Besides, Jonathan was in no shape to spend a night in a cold barn, which seemed to be where Blake wanted her to spend this night.

"You want me to play midwife to a horse?" The very thought made her stomach clench.

"No. I just need you to stand by, in case I need something. And I could use a little moral support. This is Bonnie's first foal, and she's earlier than we thought she'd be. I don't want anything to happen to her or the foal.''

The undercurrent of worry—deep, knowledgeable fear—in his voice propelled her out of bed. He didn't have to tell her how much he cared about his horses. There was no other choice. Blake needed her help.

After tucking the kittens into their box, she turned to Blake. He looked her over from head to toe, slowly appraising the violet satin camisole and tap pants she'd worn to bed, but she could tell his heart wasn't in his leer. Quickly, ignoring her awareness of his presence, she slid into a heavy sweat suit and pulled on a thick pair of socks.

''Let's go,'' she told him, walking past him into the hallway. ''My boots are in the mudroom. Do you want me to put up a pot of coffee before I come out?''

''Yeah. Thanks. Just get it ready here and plug it in at the mare's barn. We've got cups in the office. And dress warm. It could be a long night.'' He was gone before she could reply.

Bundled in an old jacket of Carrie's, Lily carried the coffee percolator across the yard. In the chill quiet of the night, the floodlights in the yard cast long, eerie shadows. Her borrowed boots crunched loudly on the gravel. The only other sound she could hear was the irritable chittering of some animal whose sleep she'd disturbed. She knew how it felt.

The lights in the mares' barn drew her with their welcoming golden glow, but her stomach knotted at the thought of what might be happening within the barn. She didn't want to let Blake down, but she wasn't exactly Nurse Nancy. Major surgery on a client's financial portfolio was one thing, but this...this was real life.

The last time she tried to take a splinter out of a friend's finger, she'd had to sit down with her head between her knees three times before succeeding. She wouldn't be much help to Blake or his mare if she keeled over. Maybe, however, all Blake really needed her for was company at a safe distance and an occasional cup of coffee.

As she stepped inside the barn, the high-pitched cry of an animal in fear and pain sent a chill up her spine. Swallowing hard, Lily set the coffeepot on the desk in the office, plugged it in and braced herself to find Blake. The cot set up in the farthest corner probably was as good a clue as any.

She could hear his low, soothing murmurs across the barn, whenever the mare Bonnie quieted. The other mares shuffled in the straw in their stalls, as if aware that one of their sisters was in trouble. A deep groan emanated from the large stall where Lily found Blake crouching beside the black mare lying on her side.

"Hi," Lily said softly, not looking into the stall. The smells and sounds were already turning her stomach. She didn't want to see what was happening. And she didn't want Blake to see what a wimp she was.

"Hi. The cordless phone is on the cot, if you hear it ring. I'm hoping the vet will call soon. This poor girl's having a pretty bad time."

She felt helpless, but compelled to offer, "Anything I can do?"

"Pray?"

Lily could hear the crooked smile in his voice, even though she didn't dare look into the stall to meet his eyes. The edge of worry in his tone touched her. He really felt for the mare. Oddly enough, she shared his concern. Maybe because the horses had people names, they had become more than objects in her mind. She knew she would find it terribly difficult to deal with if something happened to the mare or her unborn foal.

"I'm praying already," she assured him. "What else?"

"There are clean towels in a cabinet in the office. I'll need a couple of them to rub the foal down. I've got everything else I need in the first aid box next to the cot."

Grateful for the errand, Lily hurried to get the towels. When she returned, the mare suddenly scrambled to her feet, nearly trampling Blake. Heart in her throat, Lily gripped the towels and waited. It had never occurred to her that a foaling could be hazardous to humans. Her mother's oft-repeated tales of her own difficult birth had seemed harrowing enough without the added danger of broken bones.

The mare circled and paced in the big stall, the whites showing around her large, dark eyes. Blake stayed back a little, continuously murmuring to her. Lily found herself thinking that, if she was ever giving birth, she'd want Blake to be there to offer such comfort. The unexpected and uncharacteristic thought brought stinging heat to her cheeks.

Suddenly, the mare's legs buckled. With a groan, she sank to the straw-covered floor of the stall. Lily's heart skipped a beat.

"I think this is it," Blake muttered. "Stay close. I may need you in here."

The last thing she wanted to do was stay close. The sudden roaring in Lily's ears sent her grabbing for the stall doorway. She leaned against it and closed her eyes, praying for the mare and foal, praying Blake wouldn't need her. He swore softly, and Lily heard noises she didn't want to identify. The mare groaned.

There was a *whoosh*ing sound, and then Blake said quietly but triumphantly, "That's it! A beautiful filly!" His voice turned to a croon. "Good girl, Bonnie. Lily, come see her. She's a little beauty."

Hesitantly, Lily opened one eye. Then she opened both eyes in awe. Lying in the deep straw near the exhausted Bonnie was a small, dark, wet replica of the mare.

Lily knew she'd never witnessed anything more profoundly beautiful and moving. She felt as if she stood on the edge of some mystical cliff, peering into the uncertain and irresistible mists of life itself. She trembled with simultaneous fear and excitement, and looked to the man who had awakened her to these emotions.

Blake continued to murmur to the new mother, praising her and the foal, while he wiped the baby's muzzle. Bonnie lifted her head, as if it weighed a ton, and sniffed at her offspring. Then, slowly and carefully, she stood and nudged the foal until it, too, struggled to stand on spindly, wobbly legs. The front end got up, but Blake had to help with the back. Then the front legs collapsed. Finally, the foal stood on shaky stilts and, with Blake's guidance, began to nurse.

Lily found herself smiling with tears spilling down her cheeks. Blake glanced over, and she could easily read the awe in his dark eyes. When he smiled at her, Lily felt something warm and soft wrap around her heart.

Eventually Blake had the presence of mind to ask Lily to snap a few photos of the mare and foal. She took about four pictures before Blake started to swear under his breath. The mare had moved away from the foal, groaning and snapping at her sides, as if in distress. Setting down the camera, Lily stepped into the stall.

"What's wrong?"

"I don't know. She's already delivered the afterbirth. Come over here and hang on to the foal. I want to make sure Bonnie doesn't step on her by accident."

Lily had handled accounts worth millions of dollars without turning a hair, but now she felt herself trembling at the responsibility Blake had just thrust at her.

Speaking softly, the way she'd heard Blake do, Lily approached the foal slowly. It eyed her curiously, but apparently without fear, then sniffed at her outstretched hand and shook its tiny head. Gently, Lily gathered the foal close to her body, bending over it, holding it back from seeking its mother. The foal struggled, but Lily held on and kept stroking its damp, shaggy coat. Its heart galloped under her caressing hand. Did it know something was wrong with its mother? Gradually she felt the baby settling down.

"Well, I'll be damned!" Blake murmured. Lily looked up to see him crouching beside the now prone mare. "She was hiding another one in there! No wonder she got big as a house so early."

A couple of heartfelt groans later, Bonnie's second baby lay darkly wet on the straw.

"Come on, baby!" Blake urged. "Keep breathing. You've got to get up and get your engine started. Mama's waiting. That's my girl. Clear your pipes and get your legs under you."

Lily concentrated on the foal she held, but she surmised from Blake's words that the second foal was in some distress. It seemed like hours before he had the new one up and nursing. When both foals stood by their mother, their muzzles butting her udder, their throats working as they swallowed, Lily leaned against Blake in awed exhaustion.

"Oh, Blake!" she whispered. "They're wonderful! Are twins unusual?"

"Very. Usually they spontaneously abort, or die soon after birth. But I think these two are going to make it. I sure hope so,'' he murmured tiredly. "And I could use a gallon of coffee.''

The element of doubt lingering in his answer made her stomach clench with worry. "Stay with them. I'll get the coffee.''

He hugged her briefly. She could feel the exhaustion in his embrace, and held on even after his arms relaxed their hold on her. When she returned with a steaming mug of coffee, he was snapping photos of the foals with their mother. Lily was amazed at the progress of the foals' coordination and strength in just a few minutes. What she didn't know about nature, she mused, would fill more than the extensive library in Jonathan's house.

"Now what?'' she asked when he set down the camera and accepted the coffee from her.

"Now I wait for the vet and you go back to your warm bed.''

"Nonsense! I'll wait with you.'' His eyebrows rose over the rim of his mug, silently prompting her to justify herself. "I want to be sure they're going to be okay.''

"It could be a long wait.''

"I can handle it.''

"You didn't say that when I brought you the kittens.'' His dimple flashed.

She felt her face grow warm under his teasing. "The kittens were different. You wanted me to take complete responsibility for two infants, and I was afraid I was going to fail.''

"Good thing I knew better.'' He gave her a smug grin. "Grab yourself some coffee, and I'll clear off the cot so we can sit down. It could take Don a while to get here.''

When Lily came back with her mug, she stopped to peek into Bonnie's stall. The foals were lying in the thick straw, close to each other, their sides heaving with their rapid breathing. The exhausted mare stood over them, her head lowered, her eyes half-closed. Lily felt her throat ache as if she were going to cry. There really was something magical about the sight of the newborns that she'd never found in any tax form.

Unsettled by the drift of her thoughts, Lily turned away from the stall. Blake waited for her to sit on the cot before turning off all but a couple of lights in the arena. The heat lamps over the foals glowed red in the darkness. Lily sipped her coffee and stifled a yawn.

Blake sat beside her and wrapped his arm around her shoulder. His embrace felt good and right. She leaned her head on his shoulder, breathing in his scent, mingled with the aromas of coffee and horse. When he eased her cup out of her hand, she smiled to herself and relaxed against him, utterly content, and too tired, too mellow, to question it.

Chapter Ten

Blake waited for the vet to finish examining the second foal's legs before sighing in relief.

"Sneaky little gal, that Bonnie," Don said with a grin. "We'll have to keep an eye on them. They're small, but they should catch up." He snorted. "Jonathan's going to have my head."

"Don't worry. Jonathan has trouble trusting any vet under sixty. He didn't suspect twins, either, or he would have suggested ultrasound when she started to expand like a blimp. Her mother always carried big."

"Well, they're beauties." Don straightened and patted Bonnie's neck. "Speaking of beauties..." He nodded toward Lily, asleep on the cot outside the stall. "Who's that?"

Blake grinned, but it felt more like baring his teeth. "My accountant." The words came out in a feral growl that almost embarrassed him.

Don gave him a long look, then nodded. "'Nuff said."

Blake walked Don to his truck. "Drop by tomorrow and look in on them," he said as Don climbed inside. "I'll give Jonathan a call first thing. He should be back by noon."

Blake waited until the truck's lights had winked and disappeared down the lane before returning to Lily. In the dim light, with the breathing of the mares and the rustling of straw around him, he stood looking down at her. His pulse raced like a teenager's. She looked like an angel, so beautiful and delicate, so silvery in the darkness. He hated to wake her just to send her back to bed. Even more, he hated the thought of being without her. The only solution was to keep her with him tonight.

Carefully, he scooped her up in his arms and headed toward his house. He hoped she would understand. Remembering the sparkle of tears in her eyes when she looked at the foals, he didn't think she'd want to be alone now, either. This was a time to reach out and connect with someone else, not for sex, but to quietly celebrate being alive.

He held her close, savoring the feel of her small, lithe frame against his chest, her delicate scent in his nostrils. Tired as he was, he hardly felt her weight as he climbed the stairs. Dolly lifted her head and yawned noisily from her post outside Carrie's unoccupied room, but didn't bother following him along the hall to his room. When he reached his bed, he set Lily down gently.

Her sweatpants were damp and dirty. With hands that shook, he eased them down over the provocative satin pants she'd been sleeping in. His fingers trailed down her silky, lean legs, sliding the sweats off with her heavy socks. The warmth of her skin stung him like a live wire.

The ladylike splay of her thighs rocked him with possibilities.

He stifled a groan of relief when she sighed and curled onto her side. She looked as if she belonged there. Unable to resist, he bent over her and touched his lips to her temple. Her silky hair smelled more like flowers than horse.

He, on the other hand, stank like a bear. He drew the quilt up to Lily's shoulders and went to his bathroom to shower. When he came out, a towel knotted around his hips, he picked up his pillow and took an extra blanket from the antique rack at the foot of the bed. Much as he wanted to spend the rest of the night holding her in his arms, his destination was the couch downstairs. Somewhere, he had a pair of pajamas, but he couldn't remember the last time he'd worn them.

"Blake?"

Like a kid with a crush, he felt his heart leap when she said his name. "Yeah. Go back to sleep."

"Is it raining?"

"No. I just showered." He knew he should leave the room, but his feet wouldn't move. "I'm going to sleep in the living room."

"Oh." He heard the rustle of the blankets, and the sound made him think of rustling the blankets with her. Heat rushed to his loins, making him glad the room was nearly dark.

"Could...could you come here?" Her voice came out soft and quavery. "Would you...would you just hold me?"

There was nothing overtly sexual about her request, but his pulse raced and his body hardened all the same. He dropped the blanket and threw his pillow back on the bed.

When he drew back the edge of the quilt, his hand trembled.

She only wanted comfort, he warned himself. Human contact. A chance to share the emotions piled up during the foaling. He wanted to bury himself deep inside her and hear her cry out in pleasure, but simple contact was all he would offer her now. When they made love, he wanted to be damn sure she was focused on him. On *them*. Not just reacting to an intense moment that didn't really have anything to do with the awareness that had been simmering between them.

Lily struggled against exhaustion. Her voice sounded far away to her own ears, but Blake must have heard her. She felt the cool air when he slid the cover back. The mattress dipped with his weight. The scent of shampoo and soap and man filled her head. Propelled by impulses and needs she hardly understood, she reached for him in the darkness.

Her fingers touched his bare chest, and his gasp echoed hers. With her eyelids fluttering shut against her will, she flattened her palm over his heart, feeling it beating through her own body. He felt warm and solid and vital, everything she craved with sudden, overwhelming passion. Her exhaustion sizzled away into something hot and urgent, the way water explodes on a hot pan.

He shifted, lying down and gathering her loosely against his side, catching her wandering hand. "Go to sleep, Lily," he murmured. "We can talk in the morning."

"I don't want to talk."

"Okay. Go to sleep."

"I don't want to sleep. I feel..." She struggled to find

the right words. "I feel like I'm really *alive* for the first time. I want to celebrate that feeling. With you."

Blake stroked her hair back from her face. She tried to see him in the darkness, but all she could see was shadow. She could feel him, however, feel how his heartbeat accelerated under her cheek. She could feel his hand tremble on her shoulder. She could feel his body become rigid against her, as if he were holding his breath. What was he thinking?

He stroked her hair again, his rough fingertips grazing her cheek. "I'm glad you were with me tonight." His voice was low, gravelly, intimate.

"Me too. I feel like I've been drinking champagne." Impulsively, she turned her face into his hand and pressed her lips to his warm, hard palm. She inhaled, savoring his scent.

Lily felt his hand tremble, heard his indrawn breath, and slid upward along his side. He didn't move. She held herself over him and lowered her head to seek his mouth. His lips were soft, warm, but unresponsive.

No, no, don't hold back, she wanted to say. *Don't you understand that I need you now? Don't turn away from me, please!* But she couldn't say the words. Instead, Lily opened her lips against his, inviting him to share her passion.

With a low groan, he broke the kiss. "Lily—"

The touch of her fingers silenced him. She stroked his stubble-roughened cheek with trembling fingertips as she sought his mouth again. She felt driven by deep, urgent forces she didn't fully understand and didn't want to question. Not now. Now, all she wanted was the sweet heat of Blake's kisses.

She ignored his passivity and feathered her lips over his. His breath quickened. His heart pounded under her palm. His lips firmed under hers and answered her tentative sips with slow, almost hesitant pressure. His fingers combed her hair back from her face, and sudden sparks raced up her spine at his touch. Her own breath caught.

Blake cupped her head and took over the kiss, his mouth capturing hers, his tongue seeking entrance. Opening her lips for him, Lily let herself sink onto his chest, her breasts crushed against his hard bone and muscle. Needing to be even closer, she slid one leg over his. The towel was rough and damp against her bare skin. She gave herself up to his deepening kisses and shifted closer until the corded muscles of his thigh pressed hard between her legs.

Desire flared, searing the places where their bodies met. *Yes! Yes! This was what she wanted.* Her inhibitions turned to ashes in the heat of her need. She needed to feel her body and Blake's joined in pure primal passion, the most elemental celebration of life.

Finally, with all the polite veneer of carefully controlled relationships stripped away, she understood the power of sex, of raw need. But not with words. Not even with formless thought. With her body and soul, she understood. And she knew that Blake, of all the men on earth, was the one man she could share her passion with.

She tasted his hunger in his kiss and offered her own hunger in return. He was so strong, so vital, and she'd been so empty for so long, without really knowing it. He was life. She needed to connect with him. All her urgency focused on the need to make him understand. Impatient with the barrier of the towel, Lily reached under the quilt and fumbled with it until she found the smooth flesh of Blake's inner thigh. His body jerked under hers. She clung to him and met his tongue with her own, while her hand slid upward to cup the sculpted smoothness of his hip.

"Slow!" he gasped against her mouth.

"No!" she whispered hotly before her lips found his again. She didn't want slow, leisurely lovemaking. She wanted raw, wild coupling. She didn't want finesse. She wanted passion. She wanted to connect with the forces of life itself, and right now, Blake was the embodiment of life.

Throwing off the quilt, Lily pressed closer to him. Still drinking in the sweet heat of his kisses, she brushed her fingertips over his arousal, then closed her hand around him. He groaned as his flesh throbbed under her palm. The sound sent a bolt of desire racing through her like lightning.

Once more, Blake wrested control from her, pushing her away, fumbling with her sweatshirt. Feverish with heat, Lily sat up and helped him pull the heavy top and her camisole off over her head. Then she slid into his arms and shivered as his wet, hot mouth captured one nipple, then the other. The tugging of his lips sent ripples of pleasure and need coursing through her body, to the melting center of her desire. Crying out softly, she dug her fingers into his broad back, holding him, even as she wanted to feel his mouth on the rest of her skin.

Still caressing her aching breasts with his lips and tongue, Blake grasped the waist of her tap pants and slid them down her hips. Lily reached down and pushed them off, eager to feel their bodies touching without any barriers. But Blake's strong hand cupped her hip, holding her back. Her whimper of frustration turned into a gasp as his fingers slid over her belly to stroke between her legs. When she arched into his touch, his groan echoed through her.

She was ready for him. Beyond ready. His caressing fingers were slick with the honey of her own desire. She ached to feel him sinking into her, joining their flesh, creating a fire that was the only way to quench the flames that burned inside her now.

Lily clutched at Blake's shoulders, trying to draw him down over her. When he continued his caresses instead, she hooked one leg over the back of his thigh.

"Blake, *please!*" she whispered, barely able to gasp the words. She was afraid he would take her over the edge before she could feel their bodies becoming one. She didn't want to be alone like that, empty, unconnected.

His mouth found hers again, and he eased her down under his hard body. Instinctively Lily wrapped her legs around him, cradling his arousal against the slick heat of her feminine center. So close, but it wasn't enough.

Blake reached out past Lily, fumbling with the drawer in the bedside table. His movements rocked their bodies intimately together, and Lily felt all her passion being channeled to the place where their flesh met. When he lifted himself from her, cool air swept over her heated skin. She shivered and clutched at his back, trying to draw him into her.

"Wait," he growled. She looked up to see him tear at the small packet with his teeth. The feral, primitive act sent a shiver of a different kind through her.

Then, suddenly, he was *there*, filling her. Pleasure flashed through her as he joined their bodies. He was big, but she wanted no time to get used to him. She rose to meet his thrusts, as if she could become part of him if they only could get close enough.

The pleasure ripped through her, startling her. She grasped at his shoulders and cried out. Blake held her briefly, letting her recover. With tears in her eyes, she covered his face with kisses. Then his mouth captured hers. As his tongue thrust between her lips, his hips began to move. She matched his rhythm until sensations gripped her body and held her motionless. Still he pushed her higher.

With her eyes shut tight, with Blake surrounding her and filling her, Lily gave herself up to the explosion of passion. At the same moment, Blake groaned, and she felt his release as if it were her own.

Stunned and overwhelmed, Lily lay beneath Blake and listened to his harsh, ragged breathing. She ran her hands over his slick, hot skin and pressed kisses onto his shoulder. With his weight on her, with his heat seeping into her, with the waves of her own release still gently ebbing, she felt elementally female, a vital part of the timelessness of life. She felt all-powerful, yet humbled by the power of what they'd shared.

She had no strength and no words to tell him, however. And as reality slowly seeped back into her consciousness, it brought with it embarrassment and anxiety.

Oh, God! What had she done? What had possessed her? She'd given more of herself to Blake than to any other man she'd ever been involved with. She, who had never really enjoyed the awkward, complicated intimacy of making love, had just had wild, passionate sex with a virtual stranger. More than that, she'd deliberately over-ridden his attempts to stop her, as if his feelings mattered less than her own.

She could only pray that Blake would understand that what had happened between them was the result of a moment of madness. That it didn't mean anything. If he was like most men, he wouldn't read too much into an impulsive fling. But she'd be wise to take this uneasy feeling as a warning to finish her business here and get back to her real life as soon as possible.

Blake tucked Lily's limp body close to his and sighed.

He'd suspected she was hiding a passionate, sensuous soul under all that self-control, but good Lord! He felt as if he'd been hit by a train. A glance at his clock radio confirmed his earlier guess. Eight minutes from first kiss to sound asleep.

And oh, Lord! Those kisses! The woman made his blood sing! She was like a spark under his skin, burning every place she touched. And who would have thought she'd touch him the way she did? It was a minor miracle that he'd lasted almost eight minutes.

But that was just the sex, and now he was left with a strange hollow feeling. He had a pretty good idea what had come over her, and he didn't know if he liked it or not. Watching the foaling had opened a floodgate of feelings for Lily, but how much of them had anything to do with him? Judging by the way she'd turned away from him a moment before she fell asleep, he probably wouldn't like her answer to that question.

Then again, it had been inevitable that they would make love. The only variable had been *when*, not *if*, even if Lily hadn't been willing to admit it. The attraction between them had been smoldering from the beginning, but without his realizing it, what he was feeling had gone way beyond the physical. It went so deep that it wasn't going to let go. Any doubts he'd had about Lily being the right woman had exploded the instant their bodies came together. Now all he had to do was convince Lily that what had happened wasn't simple sex.

Not that he was complaining. Physically, the sex had been great, if a little rushed. But it had left him unsatisfied deep inside. He needed to know Lily was making love to *him*, not using him to relieve some private need of her own. That was why he'd tried to put the brakes on when she started kissing him. But it would have taken a stronger man than he'd ever be to stop her when she started touching him like that.

What nagged at him was that sometimes while they were making love, he'd thought she was connecting with him, and sometimes, he couldn't tell where she was. It was a hell of a time to feel lonely, but that was the only word he could find to describe those moments. Still, when he felt her *there,* practically inside him, under his skin, there hadn't been any words to describe it. That was what being lovers was all about, and that was what he wanted from Lily. Nothing less.

He yawned widely and shifted Lily a little closer into the curve of his body. She sighed in her sleep and nestled her trim little bottom against him. He was hard again, wanting her, but he could wait until tomorrow. Then, he'd make love to her right, the way he should have done it tonight.

Call him old fashioned, but he wasn't a one-night-stand kinda guy, and this time, he intended to play for keeps. No doubt Lily had already figured that out. He had a feeling she was going to be in full retreat tomorrow. And he'd be in full pursuit.

As he breathed in the perfume of her hair, he grinned. Her soft murmur was the last thing he noticed before he fell asleep.

Something warm anchored her legs to the bed. Lily awoke stiff all over, and her head ached from too little sleep. At the same instant that she realized she was in Blake's bed, she discovered that Dolly's huge, shaggy head lay across her ankles.

With a scream rising in her throat, Lily clutched at the quilt and heard the telltale crackle of the proof of her irrational behavior last night. Her cheeks burned as she brushed the torn packet off the bed. Burrowing against her feet, Dolly sighed deeply.

The impulse to scream died immediately in the face of reality. The dog wasn't actually doing anything to her, she told herself. And no one was likely to hear her if she screamed. Worse, if anyone heard her, it would be Blake, and he was the last person she wanted to confront.

With a groan, she buried her face in the pillow that still carried his scent. How could she have been so stupid? More to the point, what was she going to do about it? How was she going to face Blake and tell him that what happened between them didn't really mean anything?

Could she look into those warm, *honest,* teasing dark eyes, the imprint of his body still tingling on her flesh, and lie?

She had to, for both their sakes.

Dolly lifted her head and freed Lily's ankles. Quickly, before the beast could pin her down again, Lily drew her legs up and out of the way. She had to get up, but she had no idea where her clothes were, or even if they were wearable. And she really didn't want to encounter any-one—Jonathan, or Carrie, or especially Blake—while streaking across the yard in a sheet.

When she sat up, Lily discovered that Blake had draped a white terry-cloth robe over the bedside table. Gratitude warred with guilt as she shrugged into the robe and raced to the bathroom. Guilt won over gratitude when she found fresh panties and sweats, undoubtably Carrie's, piled neatly on the vanity. A note, in Blake's distinctive writing, said simply, "Good morning."

Dolly trotted at her heels when Lily made her way downstairs. She knew that if she let the dog out, Blake would soon know she was up, but Dolly was insistent about following her through the door. To her relief, Dolly raced off in the opposite direction from the barns, allowing Lily time to escape to Jonathan's house.

Once inside, she started a pot of coffee and fed the kittens. Guilt at leaving them alone all night assailed her, so she spent an extra few minutes cuddling them after they finished their bottles. Then she showered and dressed in a simple white blouse and navy skirt, not bothering with even minimal makeup. She wanted to look as businesslike as possible for the inevitable confrontation with Blake. By half past eight, she was sipping coffee in front of the computer, with Panther curled in her lap and Rascal clumsily chasing a ball of aluminum foil across the hardwood floor.

Instead of seeing the figures for last year's breeding expenses, however, Lily saw Blake's face. She pictured his frown of concentration and concern when Bonnie had been in labor. She saw again his awe and joy when he'd watched the twin foals nursing for the first time. Her memory replayed images of his face when he'd looked at Carrie, reflecting pride and love even when he was exasperated beyond patience at the vagaries of teenage daughters.

Lily smiled as she recalled his teasing moods, dimple creasing his cheek, dark eyes sparkling, warm smile always ready. And she saw again his expression whenever he kissed her, tenderness shining through the sensuality.

Had she once thought he wasn't her type? Too macho? Too ruggedly countrified? Too arrogant? Too different from her familiar world? Lily tapped her pen against the desk and sighed. To be sure, Blake was masculine and rugged and even a touch arrogant, in a charming way. He'd earned his self-confidence by succeeding according to his own high standards, and to hell with image. But he was also intelligent, sensitive, interesting, affectionate, fun. And more. He was honest and honorable.

And because he had all those wonderful qualities, he didn't deserve to be treated as a romantic interlude. Last night had been the result of a flood of emotions she still didn't understand. She certainly hadn't been herself. In her minimal experience with sex, she'd never been comfortable enough to be so aggressive, so demanding. Even now, her face burned with embarrassment at the way she'd *insisted* Blake make love with her.

Somehow, she was going to have to convince him that, even though she'd thrown herself at him and seduced him last night, it had been strictly the heat of the moment. A mistake in judgment, pure and simple. She wasn't looking for either a fling or a relationship.

Restless, she picked up the phone and dialed the number of her mentor at the firm. She needed to touch base with Michael to feel normal, to counteract the effects of making love with Blake last night. She needed the reminder that she had a full and fulfilling life waiting for her at home, in New York City.

"You're still at the top of the shortlist," Michael told her. "It's a hell of an opportunity, Lily. The Hong Kong–based group is in the process of acquiring some major holdings in the U.S., Canada and Australia. We're talking in the neighborhood of several billion dollars. It will take a year or two to restructure their taxes."

It was the kind of assignment she'd dreamed of ever since joining her firm. So why the lack of excitement as Michael spoke?

"You should consider returning A.S.A.P. There are a couple of others who could be tough competition. Jeffrey's one of them," he added pointedly. "I still see you as the strongest candidate, though. You've got the expertise, and you don't have to answer to anyone if they want you. Everyone else has a spouse and family to relocate, which means finding jobs and schools.''

Michael didn't have to spell it out to remind her that she had no one dependent on her to relocate. She swallowed past the sudden lump in her throat. For the first time, she realized that being so completely independent was a two-sided coin. On the one side, she had the freedom to live for herself. On the other, *alone* could turn into *lonely* without much effort. She didn't know if she wanted to thank Blake for that insight, or curse him.

''I'll call you as soon as I can estimate when I'll finish here,'' she promised Michael. ''It shouldn't be more than a week.''

After she hung up the phone, she sat staring unseeing at the computer screen. Why had she exaggerated how long she'd need to finish the work here? She was so close to the end of Jonathan's idiosyncratic but immaculate records. As soon as she finished, she could return home, to protect her career, to pursue her ambitions. Her life would then be free of any emotional entanglements, exactly the way she preferred it.

Chapter Eleven

The work went smoothly for almost an hour. At ten, Lily poured herself another cup of coffee, almost feeling calm. She was beginning to see the light at the end of the tunnel. Then the sound of a door shutting sent her pulse skittering. It could be Jonathan returning from Uncle Bill's, she reasoned, or Carrie, if she had a late opening at school...

But she knew it was Blake, and she couldn't stop her hands from shaking as she hastily saved her work. When she stroked Panther in an effort to calm herself, the kitten chirped in her sleep and started to purr. Instead of finding the contented noise soothing, Lily couldn't help thinking of Blake's stroking caresses. How was she going to keep her cool, when she couldn't stop remembering his hands, his lips on her body, her hands and lips on his?

"Morning," Blake said softly from the doorway to the study.

Lily looked up, her face stinging with heat. He looked

tousled and rugged and sexy in his faded jeans and a chambray work shirt. He gave her a slow smile. She managed a weak one.

"There's a pot of coffee in the kitchen," she told him, hoping he'd settle for that and leave her alone with her guilt.

"Thanks," he said, but continued to gaze at her, one shoulder leaning against the door frame, arms crossed over his chest. Amusement and expectation mingled in his dark eyes.

She needed to distract him. "How are the twins today?"

He grinned, his dimple flashing. "They're fine. Full of energy. Bonnie's already asking about day care."

Lily smiled, momentarily disarmed by the memory of the foals. But as Blake continued to hold her gaze, her smile faded.

The silence stretched between them. Finally, Lily couldn't stand the awkwardness. She forced a quick smile, then turned her attention back to the computer screen, although now she couldn't read a single figure in front of her. Images of Blake filled her mind.

"Turn it off, Lily," he said from right behind her chair, although she hadn't heard or seen him approach.

She kept her eyes focused on the screen. "I have to finish this, Blake. It's—"

His hands fell lightly on her shoulders. Her breath caught in her throat.

"It can wait. This can't."

He turned her chair slowly until she had no choice but to look at him. "Blake, what happened last night was—"

"Was a mistake."

Her jaw dropped. "Thank God, you understand," she breathed.

His lips quirked. "I understand, all right," he drawled, his eyes sparkling. "You want us to forget everything that happened between us last night. You don't know what hit you, because you've never done anything like that before. You don't even really like sex all that much, and besides, we hardly know each other. So you want me to act as if everything's the same as it was before. Right?"

Surprised and grateful, she nodded with eager agreement. He did understand, even more than she had hoped. Even about not liking sex much. But she had to struggle to believe that everything was the same when she remembered the raw passion that had gripped her. She looked up into his gentle face, but what she saw was the arch of his strong neck, the flash of his even white teeth as he'd torn open the condom wrapper in a rush to be inside her.

Desire pulsed hotly through her at the memory of his body crushing her, cradling her, caressing her. How could anything be the same after that? It was impossible, but she would have to pretend it was so. To acknowledge the changes last night had made in her would be to question everything she was, everything she wanted to be. She couldn't do that without giving up too much of herself.

Blake reached into her lap and lifted Panther into his big hands. He gave the disgruntled kitten a quick nuzzle and placed her on the open ledger beside the computer. Then he took Lily's hands in his and drew her out of her chair. Confused, transfixed, she stared up at him.

He smiled. "I said I understand. I didn't say I agree."

She swallowed. "But you said yourself it was a mistake...."

"I understand what happened to you last night, Lily. I felt the same way. Full of awe, and feelings there's no name for. In touch with primitive, primal feelings about being alive. It's raw, powerful stuff. That's why I tried to slow down.''

Lily nodded, her cheeks stinging at the memory of how she'd disregarded his good sense.

''But it was more than that, and it was a mistake not to make sure you knew.''

''Knew? Knew what?''

He stroked her cheek, then cupped her head and lowered his face to hers. His lips brushed hers.

''Who it was you were making love with.'' His words sent a shiver through her. ''I plan on making sure you know it's *me* making love to you, not just some handy male body playing Adam to your Eve.''

His kiss cut off her protest. Frightened by how well he had understood her, how easily he could read her heart and mind, Lily stood perfectly still while his mouth moved on hers. Finally, he lifted his head.

''Relax, Lily,'' he whispered. ''I won't hurt you.''

She believed him, which made everything worse. ''I know, Blake. I know you won't.'' He deserved the truth. ''But I could hurt you.''

Blake cupped her face in his strong hands, and she felt them trembling. She gazed up into his eyes. ''Let me worry about that,'' he murmured.

And then he was kissing her again, and everything around her faded from her mind except the feel of his mouth on hers. She reached up and wound her arms around his strong neck, breathing in his earthy scent. His lips were soft, coaxing. His arms around her held her gently against his hard body. Feeling safe, Lily let herself drift with the sensations his mouth created.

When his tongue slid along her lips, she had to open them for him, eager for the dark, sweet flavor of his mouth. As he probed her mouth, his hands slid down to her hips and he fitted her against himself. He was hard already. He made a low, growling sound as their bodies pressed together, his arousal fueling hers.

Without warning, Blake scooped her up into his arms, his mouth still on hers. Dizzy from his kisses and his sudden move, she clung to him.

She started to protest. "Jonathan—"

"Won't be home for at least an hour and a half."

"Carrie?" she asked weakly.

"Came home, changed, and went to school before half-past eight." He kissed her, and she could feel his smile. "It's just us."

Embarrassed at her surrender, Lily hid her face in the warm hollow of his neck while he carried her up the stairs to her room. He placed her in the middle of the bed and began unbuttoning his shirt. She stayed propped on her elbows, watching. Nervous.

Everything was the opposite of last night's wild explosion of passion. There were no shadows to hide in. The spring sun flooded the room with light. A cool, sweet-scented breeze flowed past the curtains and swirled over her. The frilly, feminine interior of the room, so different from the simple masculine furnishings of Blake's room, made her think of an old-fashioned maiden's boudoir, about to be invaded. And Blake's very deliberate movements, tugging his shirttails out of his jeans, unbuttoning his cuffs, while he watched her with heavy-lidded eyes, reinforced that image.

She could stop him. She knew, despite what he'd said, that he wouldn't make love to her against her will. But what was her will? Did she want to make love with him now, like this, eyes open in the bright light, with no excuses, no reason other than that she wanted him as much as he wanted her? If she could accept that, could he accept that this was all she could give him?

Blake's hands went to his belt buckle. Swallowing hard, Lily sank down against her pillows and closed her eyes. Heaven help her. *Yes!* She wanted to make love with him. Now. Here, in the light. Deliberately, without the excuse of runaway passion.

But she was afraid, too. Last night, everything had happened so fast, she'd simply been too carried away to worry. Now, with nowhere to hide, she felt vulnerable. Her feelings were too visible to Blake's keen eyes. If he could see her fear—or even worse—her need, then her soul would be far more naked than her body.

The whipcrack sound of Blake pulling his belt off startled her into wide-eyed wariness. He stood beside the bed, his gaze sweeping over her, his stance easy, natural, all self-confident male. The open front of his shirt exposed his muscular chest and belly down to the open snap of his jeans. Lily understood that he was meeting her halfway, expecting her to finish removing his clothes. And she understood that the clothes were only symbolic of what he wanted from her.

"Your turn," he told her softly. When her hand fumbled at the buttons at her throat, he smiled. "Here, let me do it." He knelt beside her, his weight on the mattress tipping her toward him. "One button at a time."

Gently Blake lifted her hand away from her neck, but he didn't reach for her blouse as she expected. Instead, he kissed her knuckles, lingering over each one, making her shiver. The slide of his hot, wet tongue into the sensitive cleft between two fingers echoed in the pulsing heat between her thighs.

His gaze was too intense, too demanding. Lily let her

eyes close. Above her, Blake stroked her palm with his thumb, torturing the sensitized nerve endings there.

"Look at me, Lily."

His words—more plea than order—came out in a hoarse whisper she couldn't ignore. His eyes, when she looked up into them, burned with intensity, and something more. Something she'd never seen in the eyes of any other man. But she didn't have the luxury of pondering the differences between Blake and other men. Not now, when he was holding her gaze while he gently cupped her breasts in his hands. The heat of his touch radiated through her clothes. Her nipples hardened, becoming the focus of electrifying need.

"Relax, Lily. Trust me. Let go of that control you think you need. Just let yourself go. I won't do anything to hurt you. You know that." He hypnotized her with his low murmur.

Blake teased her with soft, deliberate strokes simultaneously heightened and muffled by the barrier of her blouse. The heat inside her flared hotter, making her arch her back for more of his caresses. She felt as if she were melting with desire. How could he make her feel so much, when he had yet to unfasten a single button, had yet to touch her bare skin anywhere but on her hand?

As she searched his face for answers, Blake moved so that he straddled her hips, his thighs anchoring her, cradling her. He leaned forward, bracing himself above her. Through all the layers of their clothes, his heat seeped into her flesh. She felt both languorous and restless, dreamy and eager.

Despite the predatory glint in his dark eyes, he started gently, a tentative brush of lips on lips. Lily closed her eyes and drifted into the sweetness of his kiss, letting her lips part when his tongue stroked them. She focused her attention on the silky caress of his tongue and the soft, seeking pressure of his mouth on hers.

Blake unbuttoned her blouse, inch by inch exposing her flesh to his lips and hands. Layer by layer, he peeled away her disguises, her fears, her control. By the time she lay naked under his caresses, her soul, too, had been stripped of the armor of a lifetime of fears. When he stroked her to a shuddering, shattering release, she felt vulnerable and helpless.

But then he gave himself to her, making himself as vulnerable to her hesitant caresses as she'd been to his bolder touches. He was beautifully male, confidently masculine, yet when she stroked and kissed and gazed, he trembled, and she felt him slipping under her control.

Giddy with this newfound power, she gave herself up to giving him pleasure, to wrapping him in sensation. His whispered encouragement, his low groans, renewed her own arousal, until she was sure she could feel every touch, every shock of pleasure, singing along her own nerves.

Blake finally drew her into his arms and captured her mouth with his. She heard the crackling of foil, and closed her eyes to endure the moment that their bodies had to be apart. And then he was cradling her beneath him. She wrapped her legs around his hips and arched upward to welcome him into her body.

"Lily, look at me," Blake murmured.

She blinked up at him, then closed her eyes again. No, she couldn't look at him now. If she did, he would see straight into her soul. Then he would see her coward's heart trying to deny him, even as her body betrayed her feelings.

"Lily."

"I can't."

"Don't shut me out, Lily. Not now. Look at me. I want

you to know that it's me inside you. I don't want you to ever forget.''

"Blake—''

"Look at me, Lily. Look at me, sweetheart.'' He was pressing into her, teasing her with the honey of her own desire. "Now, Lily.''

Unable to refuse him, even though she feared the consequences for her own heart, Lily opened her eyes and looked into the warmth of his. At that moment, he eased into her, joining more than their bodies. The coiling sensations made her arch her neck back and gasp for breath, but she forced her eyes to flutter open as he sank into her. Slowly, his eyes never wavering from hers, he began to move.

"Blake! Oh, Blake!'' The cry burst from her lips as her body gathered itself for a soul-shattering release. Her eyes closed, but she could still see his face as wave after wave of pleasure washed over her.

Lily clutched Blake's shoulders, trembling, whimpering in her effort to catch her breath. He held her tenderly, whispering endearments, kissing her neck and face. She didn't know until his lips met hers that she had tears on her cheeks. The taste of salt melted into the dark, sweet taste of Blake's passion as his tongue echoed the rhythm of his body against hers. Once again, Lily gave herself up to sensations, then rested while Blake rolled onto his back and cradled her in his arms, his pulse resounding through her as if they shared one heart.

When Lily reclaimed her senses, she found she had the freedom to lead Blake in a slow dance of pleasure. With caressing hands and hoarsely whispered words, he praised and encouraged her. She felt all-powerful and giving, unable to hold back from the generous man in her arms. His fulfillment wrenched her name from him in a feral groan.

And as she watched pleasure wash over his face, she felt a sense of rightness that filled her with peace.

But as she slowly returned to the bright spring morning, that sense of rightness filled her with dread. Everything she was, everything more she wanted to be, everything she'd worked so hard for, stood in opposition to that contentment.

Blake caught her face in his hands and kissed her softly, almost reverently. "So good, Lily. So good, and so *right*," he murmured, holding her close.

She buried her face in his warm, musky neck, dreading the moment when she had to tell him that this magic that had happened between them wasn't enough to make her give up the rest of her life.

The muffled echo of a car door slamming jolted her from her thoughts.

"Jonathan!" she gasped, struggling to escape Blake's arms. It would be too embarrassing for her uncle's old friend to find her in bed with Blake, like a teenager sneaking out to neck when she was supposed to be doing homework.

"Relax. I told him about Bonnie's twins. He's going straight to the barn. You've got plenty of time to get dressed."

She pushed away from him, her fears fueling her irritation. "Just once, Blake Sommers, I'd like to see you at a loss for an answer."

His rich chuckle followed her, too infectious to resist for long. Before she shut the bathroom door, she turned and smiled. The sight of him, grinning back, filled her with sadness. She cared for him more than she was ready to put into words, but she was all wrong for him. Blake needed a woman who could give him her undivided attention, one who was willing to let go of her own ambitions just for him. She couldn't be that woman.

Once upon a time, she had dreamed of having everything a woman could have: a loving mate, children, a fulfilling career. Instead, she'd discovered that her career gave her more satisfaction, more sense of self-worth, than any of the relationships she'd been in. And each time she thought she'd found a possible mate, she'd been forced to choose between him and her career. No matter that she'd always tried to compromise. It was never enough. It was always "If you loved me, you'd give it up for me." Never was it "I love you, so I'll meet you halfway."

Blake was everything she could want in a man, but she needed more than even he could give her. Why, to be true to herself, must she give up all but the most superficial relationship with this man?

As she turned on the shower, Lily sighed. The answer to the question lay in the heart of the question itself. To be true to herself. If she couldn't do that, nothing else she ever did would have any meaning. She'd end up spoiling everything with her bitterness, the way her mother had. Better for her to end this now, while she still could see clearly what was happening, before Blake managed to befuddle her completely. As her mentor was fond of saying, there was no progress without cost. She would rather pay now than make Blake pay later.

Chapter Twelve

Blake watched Jonathan examine every fuzzy inch of both foals and grinned, but he couldn't shake the nagging worry in his gut. Lily was up at the house, dressing, and thinking. He didn't want her to have time to think yet. Moments after making love to him with a sweet, sexy rightness that he'd only dreamed about, she'd pulled back into herself. He'd felt it as surely as he'd felt the instant she gave herself over to their lovemaking.

It was as if he'd asked for too much. At least she seemed to think he had. Was it too much for her to acknowledge that he was the man making love to her? He knew it was her, Lily, and no other woman he'd ever known or was likely to know. She wasn't the type for faceless one-night stands, so why was she so spooked by him wanting more?

He needed to understand, so he could do something about it. He wasn't about to let her get away. Not when he wanted her, and she wanted him, whether she could admit it or not. But time was running out. He figured it was a minor miracle that she was still spending nights at the farm now that spring was finally here, and driving was safe again.

He knew damn well that Jonathan's audit was small potatoes for Lily. At the rate she'd been working, she'd be finished with it within days. He had a plan for extending her stay, a legitimate need to get the farm's business computerized, despite Jonathan's old-fashioned love of pen and ink and huge ledgers. He knew Jonathan was also fascinated by the computer, and would be amused to learn how to keep his books electronically. Getting her to set up a system and teach Jonathan how to use it would buy him precious days to work on her. If he could convince her to accept such a simple challenge.

But he didn't want to hide behind excuses. He preferred to be straightforward. It wasn't a computer or accounting expert he wanted—needed—to make his life complete. It was Lily.

But how did Lily feel about him? Attracted, sure. Interested in his mind. Definitely responsive to his body. But what about her heart? What about her life? What did she want and need?

He'd coasted along for so many years without feeling this deep-down need for any woman that he'd begun to think he never would. Now that he'd fallen like a load of hay off a runaway wagon, he had to face the probability that she didn't need him the way he needed her. He had to face it, but he didn't have to accept it, damn it!

Lily waited until Jonathan waved goodbye to the local reporter before signaling Carrie to take dinner from the warming oven. Blake's firm step sounded on the back stairs at the same time the older man entered the kitchen, a silly grin on his lined but handsome face. He winked at Lily and did a little soft-shoe shuffle. Carrie giggled.

"Too bad Jonathan isn't excited about those foals," Blake drawled, coming up behind Lily.

He snitched a slice of carrot from the salad bowl she was arranging, then lingered to smile down at her. Her heart lurched when their eyes met. She could feel the pulse in the base of her throat. No matter what her brain said, her heart and her body persisted in this conspiracy to react to Blake as her lover.

"Tease away, my boy!" Jonathan crowed. "I'd kick up my heels if I thought I could land on my feet instead of my seat. I can't wait for Dora to see those foals. Did I tell you she phoned to say she'll be driving up with the trailer when she ships the new mares up to us?" He paused to pat Lily's shoulder. "Dinner smells wonderful, my dear."

"I made it," Carrie announced. "Lily's teaching me to cook."

Blake muttered something that sounded like "Thank God!" and Jonathan offered hearty encouragement to Carrie. Standing a bit off to one side of the sudden activity in the big, homey kitchen, Lily realized that they looked and sounded like a family. A peculiar family, perhaps, but a happy one. And, in a small but gratifying way, she was part of that family.

The thought shook her. Long ago, she'd given up wanting to be part of a family. She'd finally come to terms with the fact that her parents were dysfunctional before anyone had read that word in the popular press. Over the years, all her friends and acquaintances had had their share of unhappy families, and some had gone on to perpetuate that unhappiness in marriages that were supposed to be better. Now, for the first time in years, she felt the tug of wanting to belong, to be part of a family.

The very thought made her dizzy, as if she were standing too close to the edge of a cliff. A very steep cliff. And she had no confidence that, if she ever dared to step over the edge, she'd land softly and safely. On the contrary, if she strayed too close to the edge, all her own dreams would shatter on the rocks below. If she let herself give up everything for Blake, it would be the same as if she'd thrown those dreams off that cliff herself. The blame, the responsibility, the choice, would be hers alone.

"Come to the table, my dear," Jonathan called. She had to smile at his jovial mood. "Let's all have a glass of champagne in honor of the birth of Bonnie's healthy, beautiful twins."

"Me too?" Carrie asked, her gaze on Blake.

Blake glanced at Lily and raised his eyebrows. Was he consulting *her*? As if she had any say in decisions he made about his own daughter?

"Lily, tell him yes," Carrie wheedled.

Lily shrugged. "It's Blake's decision." She took her seat at the foot of the table, opposite Jonathan. "I'm just the accountant."

"But he *listens* to you."

"If you ladies are finished discussing me, I'll give you my answer." Blake's twinkling eyes didn't match his stern tone. "Yes, one glass."

Carrie beamed at her father, who winked at her, then turned to grin at Lily. Still unnerved by her roller-coaster emotions, Lily forced an answering smile. Blake poured glasses of very expensive French champagne for all of them, and they raised their glasses.

"To new life," Jonathan said. "Or, in this case, to new lives."

The champagne tingled on her lips and tongue. Blake sipped from his tulip glass and licked his lips, his eyes meeting hers, catching her watching him in fascination. Flustered by her conflicting emotions and his knowing look, she looked away.

Determined to keep her distance from Blake, Lily smiled at Jonathan and held out the platter of chicken to Carrie to serve. As the meal went on, the men heaped lavish praise on Carrie's efforts at cooking. In spite of her reluctance to become too involved, Lily felt her own proud smile widening as she watched the girl soaking up their compliments. But when she saw the way Blake was regarding her, she knew she'd have to stop being selfish and break away before she hurt everyone more than necessary.

After Blake and Jonathan cleared the table, Carrie served a barely scorched peach crumble while Lily poured coffee. No one mentioned the discreet piles of blackened crust while praising Carrie's efforts. Lily had heard enough about Carrie's previous failures, both from Blake and the girl herself, to understand their gratitude. She wondered if they understood that, with two excellent cooks in the family, Carrie had been too intimidated to feel comfortable in the kitchen.

"Lily's a terrific teacher," Carrie announced, deflecting another round of compliments from Jonathan.

"A teacher can't teach if a student can't learn," Jonathan declared. "So you must have more ability than you think."

Carrie grinned. "Maybe, but I still plan to be a vet. I'll just be a vet who doesn't have to eat TV dinners." She picked up her dishes and pushed back her chair. "Lily? Is there a chance you can go shopping with me? Maybe in Rochester? I need a dress for the spring dance."

"I think there's more than a chance," Lily replied with a smile. She was going to miss the energetic teenager when she returned to her life in New York City.

"Great! Thanks." She rose and put her dishes into the sink before moving toward the back door. "Well, I've got an English essay to work on. Good night."

"Wait a minute, young lady," Blake ordered. "Who are you going to the spring dance with?"

Jonathan eased toward the hallway and nodded silently to Lily. She smiled back, knowing he was going to the barn to check on the twins. And, she suspected, to escape the scene that was about to occur. She probably should excuse herself, as well. Blake really needed time alone with Carrie, to regain the balance of their relationship. And she needed to ease herself out of it.

"With whom, Dad." Carrie put her hand on the door-knob. Lily could see that Carrie really didn't want to answer the question, and could guess what she would say. Blake wasn't going to like it. "I'm going with Rick." Carrie said lightly as she opened the door.

"No, you're not. I told you I don't want you seeing that boy."

"I'm not 'seeing' him, Dad. I'm going out with him. If you'd just give him a chance, you'd see he's a really nice guy." She shrugged. "Anyway, it's all arranged."

"Then *un*arrange it!" Blake practically bellowed. Lily flinched. "Do you hear me?"

"Yes, Dad. I hear you. I imagine they can hear you in China, too," she said, with the superiority of adolescence. "But I'm still going with Rick. I gave my word, and you always say it's important to keep your word."

Carrie slipped out and closed the door behind her, ignoring Blake's repeated demands that she stay and listen to him. He swore and pounded his fist on the table, rattling the dishes and cutlery. Lily jumped in her chair. He glanced at her, looking surprised, as if he'd forgotten she was there. She gave him a hesitant smile, uneasy with his anger. It was a side of him that she'd never suspected.

"Sorry. Damn! What can I do, Lily? I don't want her near him. I don't care how nice she thinks he is. His father is in jail for passing bad checks. His older brother has been in and out of jail for breaking and entering and disturbing the peace. His mother is on probation for driving under the influence. I feel sorry for the kid, and I sincerely hope he can break away, but I don't want my daughter mixed up with him."

Lily took a deep breath, unsure of her footing. Carrie already had confided much of Rick's background to her, explaining that she was one of his few friends. The date to the spring dance was a gesture on Carrie's part to show Rick that she believed in him. She was trying to convince him to stay in school, to go on to learn a trade. Lily admired Carrie's faith and loyalty and good sense, but she also understood Blake's protectiveness. Somehow, without betraying Carrie's confidence, she was going to have to find the words to bridge the gap between Carrie's good intentions and Blake's.

"Blake, remember what you tell your students when a horse gets too strong for them? Don't pull steadily. Check and release." He looked startled. She smiled gently. "Check and release. Otherwise, you get into a tug-of-war and—"

"You can't win," he finished for her, then sighed heavily. "You're right. I have to tone it down. But damn, Lily, I can't help worrying. I know firsthand what can happen when two kids get carried away. Kids today start fooling around with sex even earlier than they did when we were young. She's got her whole future ahead of her. I don't—''

"Blake?"

"What?" He shook his head and grinned sheepishly. "Okay. You're right. I'll talk to her. Calmly."

"No, Blake. *Listen* to her. She's got some very wise things to say to you. Give her a chance. You've done such a good job of raising her. She won't let you down."

Abruptly, Blake pushed his chair back and stood. He held his hand out to Lily. When she gave him her hand, he tugged her to her feet and pulled her into his arms. "Forget the dishes for now."

Lily wound her arms around him and leaned her cheek against his chest. His warmth and scent surrounded her. She wanted to offer him the support of her friendship, as Carrie was doing for Rick. But the fact that, last night and this morning, they'd been lovers couldn't be denied. Nor could the way her pulse was racing, the way her skin tingled with his lightest touch.

Blake tipped her head back and covered her lips with his. The yearning in his kiss stole her breath. She wanted so much to give him what he needed, what he was asking for, but she was a fraud. She didn't have what he needed, and it was just a matter of time before he discovered that she was letting him down. This was the time to start pulling away. If she waited too much longer, she would hurt him even more. She didn't want that on her conscience. She didn't want any regrets to follow her home to New York.

He drew back. "Mmm... My place or yours?"

Her heart leaped at his words, but her head repeated the refrain: *No regrets.*

"Neither, Blake. I'm sorry, but with Jonathan and Carrie both home..."

He kissed her neck, seriously damaging her resolve. "I can't imagine either one of them objecting, as long as we're discreet. They've been playing matchmaker since you first showed up."

She smiled into his shirt. "I know. But..."

"It's not like I plan to ravish you in the kitchen. I might fantasize about it, but I have some self-control."

His hand slid over her bottom, lifting her against him. His arousal stirred answering desires deep within her. Fighting her heart and body, Lily pushed at Blake's chest. "Blake, the books are almost ready for the audit, and I have work waiting for me at the office. I'm going back to the city Saturday, after I take Carrie shopping."

"Going back?" He released her, then grasped her shoulders. "No. You can't go back. Not now, Lily."

"Yes, now. Before we get involved."

"Sweetheart, we *are* involved."

She couldn't look into his eyes. If she did, it would be impossible to hang on to her resolve. The silence between them stretched until Lily could feel it vibrating.

"Lily, talk to me." He led her into Jonathan's comfortable living room and pulled her down beside him on the sofa. With one arm around her, he held her close. "Jonathan said you had at least another week free. I was hoping we could spend some time together after you finished the books. Maybe you could come to a horse show with me, to see what they're like. Why are you running away now?"

The sadness in his voice broke her heart. How did you hurt someone gently?

She searched for a way to help him understand. "I'm not running away, Blake. I have a full, rewarding life in New York. All my friends are in the city. I love my work. I'll be made a partner next month. I make good money and I have a beautiful condo. There's a strong probability of an assignment in Hong Kong for a year or more. I can take it because I don't have to answer to anyone else. I can follow my own dreams, not someone else's. That's my *life*, Blake. Not an escape. I want to go home, to live the life I've made for myself. That's not running away.''

His fingers sifted through her hair. She fought the urge to lean her head into his hand, the way the kittens did, seeking comfort and affection.

''That's all about material things. Money. Condos. What about us, Lily? That's part of your life now, too.''

''I never intended for there to be an 'us.' I tried, Blake. I really tried.'' She had to pause to subdue the catch in her voice. ''I never meant to hurt you, but you're too damn nice and fun and sexy to resist.''

His brief laugh sounded hollow. ''Terrific. You're leaving me because I'm irresistible.''

''See what I mean?'' She turned in his embrace and looked up into his face. This was so hard, but she knew it would only be worse for both of them if she let him convince her to stay. A quick, clean break was the only way to be fair to him. She owed him that much.

''Damn it! This doesn't make sense. Explain to me why a warm, giving woman refuses to let love into her life. Make me understand how you can turn your back on what we have here. Because you know as well as I do that we have something very special going on between us, and I don't just mean sex. Talk to me, Lily. Don't just shut me out.''

His plea made her heart contract. ''Blake, when I was barely Carrie's age, I made a promise to myself. I broke it once, and almost lost everything. I won't break it again.''

"How can a promise you made to yourself when you were a teenager have anything to do with us?"

She took a deep breath. "I already told you my mother was very self-centered. Because I loved her, I tried to please her, to make her love me. I nearly died starving myself for gymnastics, because she wanted me to go to the Olympics. It devastated her to find out I wasn't good enough."

He massaged the stiffness between her shoulders. The gentleness of his touch made her want to cry. Why couldn't he make this easy for her by being difficult? Why did he have to be so damn nice?

Drawing a deep breath, she went on. "Eventually, I figured out that it wasn't my fault that I couldn't please her." She gave Blake a weak smile. "But the bottom line is, I tried because I loved her, and she used my love to manipulate me. The day I figured that out, I vowed I'd never let it happen again. But I couldn't turn my love off like a tap, so I let her continue to twist me around her fingers until her dying day."

Blake made a noise that sounded like a hiss. Before he could remind her that he wasn't her mother, she added, "A few years ago, I started dating one of the rising stars at the firm, and broke that promise spectacularly. I thought I was in love, but the truth was, I was just terribly hungry for affection, for what I thought was love." She felt him stiffen and decided to get the rest of her story out quickly.

"And then, one day, I woke up to the realization that Jeffrey was using my expertise to his own benefit. He didn't take it well when I refused to let him take over my most prestigious accounts. He told me that if I loved him, I'd do anything to make him happy, and I suddenly realized I'd fallen into the same trap I'd been in with my mother. I told him I wasn't responsible for his happiness, and broke our engagement. He, of course, told everyone that I'd succumbed to the pressures of too much work, which prompted some of my accounts to transfer to him, in case I had the nervous breakdown he was predicting. It's taken me a long time to recover from the damage he did to my reputation. I'm not willing to jeopardize it again. Can't you understand?''

When Blake smoothed her hair, she closed her eyes and leaned her cheek against his hand for a moment.

"I remember way back," he said, his voice low and caressing, "Bill saying he had his only niece working for him. I never suspected she'd be such a knockout, or I would have found a way to meet you. None of that would have happened."

Lily tipped her head up and smiled. "I don't think I would have been very interested in a single father on a horse farm. Even then, I knew I had to keep my nose to the grindstone."

He touched the tip of her nose with his finger. "Doesn't seem to have done any damage," he murmured. "I would have done my best to distract you."

"With Mother booking herself into expensive spas and clinics, I couldn't afford to be distracted. Every penny I made went to charlatans, right up until the day she died of undiagnosed pneumonia. And then I had a stack of bills to pay."

"No insurance?"

She shook her head. "When I paid the last bill, I swore from then on, I would be able to live for myself, and I wouldn't compromise on anything I really wanted. Jeffrey made me forget for a little while, until he reminded me rather painfully that I'd lost track of my goals. I know that sounds cold and heartless, but it was the only way I could think of to protect myself from being used."

"It'll be a frosty day in hell before you can convince me that you're cold and heartless. We all saw through your act."

She tried to pull away then, his perceptiveness making her feel vulnerable. But Blake held on to her hand, raising it to his lips. The gesture brought tears to her eyes. She blinked them away, determined not to let his gentle understanding lure her away from pursuing her dreams.

"You had it rough, Lily, but all that's behind you. It's time to think about the present, and the future. I want you to stay and make me part of your life. I want to be part of yours. We're good together."

"Oh, Blake! It's not as simple as that. There's nothing here for me. What would I do?"

He looked away, and she knew she'd hurt him badly. Then he cleared his throat. "You could computerize the farm. You could take on clients around here. You could keep learning to ride, and start showing some of the horses. You could be Carrie's friend. She needs that. You could be my friend. I need it, too. We could start a new family, you and me. Lovers and partners. No one using anyone."

The sweet vulnerability behind his words left her speechless. She'd never meant to let things go so far, and yet, the part of her heart that craved love and acceptance swelled with yearning, impossible yearning.

Blake tipped her face up to his and brushed his lips over hers. His voice grew husky. "There's love here, Lily. You didn't say anything about love in the city."

She forced herself to harden her heart. "I don't want love. All it's ever meant to me is sacrificing too much and getting too little back. I can get that back in the city, Blake. But if I stay here, I have to give up everything

I've earned. I'd have to give up who I am. Love can't replace my work or my independence.''

"No. You're right about that.'' He released her. Although their sides still touched, she felt the distance between them growing by the second. "I guess it's a matter of deciding what's most important,'' he said. "And it looks like you've made your choice.''

A coldness settled inside her. "I'm sorry, Blake. I tried not to let it go this far, but—''

"Yeah, I know.'' He stood up, making the coldness spread deeper. His quick grin was ironic, not showing his dimple. "I'm irresistible.''

Lily blinked at the sudden sting of tears. Why did it have to come down to this impossible choice? What was right for Blake was so wrong for her. What was right for her made no sense to him. There was no middle ground. She forced herself to meet Blake's eyes, even though doing so made her want to throw herself into his arms and forget everything else.

"I'll move back to Uncle Bill's tomorrow and commute until I'm finished with the work. The weather's been nice, and it won't take me more than two days. I should spend more time with him, anyway.''

He nodded, his expression guarded. "I'll tell Carrie you won't be able to go to Rochester with her.''

"Why? I promised her, and I intend to keep my promise. We can go shopping on Saturday morning. Unless you don't want me to see her anymore.'' The thought of not seeing Carrie again hurt almost as much as not seeing Blake again.

"No. She considers you a friend. It will mean a lot to her.''

The front door closed softly. Jonathan passed by the doorway, waving as he went. He called a good-night behind him, leaving them alone again. A moment later, a door shut upstairs and Rascal and Panther raced down the stairs. Lily smiled weakly at their antics, then choked back a sudden sob when she thought about leaving them at the farm. Oh, Lord, she was even going to miss Dolly. And the horses.

And Blake. Leaving Blake was going to be like leaving part of herself behind, but so would leaving her life in New York.

"Good-night, Lily. Let me know if you need help moving your stuff out. Otherwise, I'd just as soon end it here and now."

She nodded, unable to speak. His decency, his dignity, made her feel sick with guilt.

Lily bowed her head, listening as Blake's footsteps faded and the back door closed. Then, alone in the big house, she let the tears slide down her face as she sobbed silently. Oh, God, why did it hurt so much to do the right thing?

Chapter Thirteen

On their way out of the shoe store where Carrie had finally found a pair of dressy shoes that complemented her new prom dress and wouldn't cripple her while dancing, Carrie turned to Lily, her dark eyes, so like Blake's, sparkling.

"This was great! My friends' moms have taken me shopping before, but I always felt like an outsider. I still have to get stuff for college, so I don't look like a hick. Do you think we can do that after graduation?"

Carrie paused to breathe, giving Lily a perfect opening to tell her she wouldn't be around that long. But Carrie launched another rush of words before Lily could stop her.

"Oh, God, Lily! I want to get into M.I.T. so badly, and I'm afraid I won't get in because I want it so much. Dad just tells me not to worry, like that will help. I'm so glad you'll be here for me to talk to."

Lily felt her heart sink. Obviously, Blake hadn't told

his daughter that their brief romance had ended abruptly several days ago. Part of her was upset with him for leaving her with the unpleasant task of bursting Carrie's bubble. But part of her understood that since it was her decision, it was her responsibility to explain it to the teenager, who had begun to believe in the fantasy of someone to replace her lost mother.

She put a hand on the girl's arm to prevent her from taking off on another verbal tangent. "Carrie, honey, I hope you'll always feel you can talk to me and ask me for advice, but I'm afraid it will have to be long-distance from now on."

Carrie stopped short on the sidewalk, causing people behind them to grumble about moving around them. She looked at Lily, silent questions and reproach in her eyes.

"I'm going back to New York City today," Lily told her, as gently as she could.

"Do you have to?" Carrie's voice came out very small. Heart aching, Lily nodded. "Oh," the girl said softly, then turned her head away. A muffled sniff alerted Lily that her news had hit Carrie hard. Without thinking, Lily put her arms around Carrie and held her while the girl sobbed silently into her shoulder. Finally, she lifted her head and sniffled, then stepped away when Lily relaxed her embrace.

"I'm sorry Lily. I'm being a big baby. I knew you would be going eventually. I just hoped..." Her voice trailed off, and then she shook her head. "The way things were between you and Dad. I hoped you liked it here so much that... You know."

"I know, honey. I know."

They walked the rest of the way to the parking lot in silence. Then Carrie turned and looked earnestly into

Lily's eyes. "I wish you could stay. Dad and I are going to miss you."

"I'll miss you, too, but..." Lily swallowed hard. "I'm still planning to fly up for your school career day. And after the term is over, pick a time, and I'll bring you down to the city for a few days. We'll go to museums and plays and shop till we drop."

Carrie laughed. "I'm going to hold you to that!" Then she looked at Lily, her face expressing sudden seriousness as only an adolescent's can. "I'm scared, Lily. I really want to be a vet. I know that means years of school and working long hours and not much time for a social life. But I don't want to give up falling in love and being a mother. What if I end up waiting too long, and then have nothing? Look what happened to my mother! She wanted everything, and she lost it all."

Lily suppressed a shudder at the thought of all that Carrie's mother had lost—had thrown away. "You have lots of time, Carrie. You have to live your own life, make your own choices, not try to make up for the mistakes of others."

Carrie nodded solemnly. After a moment, she said, "Lily? You should listen to your own advice, too." She smiled sadly. "I wish Dad could have been the right man for you."

Ah, but Blake *was* the right man. The right man at the wrong time and in the wrong place. Lily might find another man, in the right place at the right time, a man who suited her life-style, but she'd never meet another man even remotely as right for her heart as Blake.

"Thanks, honey" was all she could manage to say around the sudden constriction in her throat. "Now, I have to say goodbye to my uncle and get to the airport, and you have to drive home before Blake and Jonathan start worrying.''

After Carrie unlocked the doors of Blake's Jeep and stowed her purchases inside, Lily gave in to the compulsion to fuss with Carrie's hair and wipe away the smudges of her mascara. But when just being next to the familiar car brought tears to her eyes again, she knew it was time to go. She gave Carrie a last hug, then waited, fighting the lump in her throat, while the girl drove away.

Blake had been right. She *was* involved. Involved with him, with Jonathan and the farm, with Carrie. How had things gotten so complicated and contorted, Lily asked herself, when she'd only intended them to be simple and straightforward? No amount of caution and self-control would undo her feelings. With Blake, it could never be out of sight, out of mind. She couldn't make a place for him in her life, but he would always have a place in her heart.

Had she really thought she could leave without regrets?

Two weeks later, Lily braced herself to face Blake again. She had managed to arrange the meeting with the IRS auditor the day after Carrie's school career day, so she would have to take only the minimum amount of time away from the backlog of work that had been waiting for her when she returned to New York City. Now, driving away from the school with Carrie, she only half listened to the girl's enthusiastic chatter about the success of the career-day workshops and seminars. All she could think of was that she was staying the night at the farm, and in the morning she'd have to face Blake when she met the auditor.

As if reading her mind, however, Carrie announced, ''Dad and Uncle Jonathan flew to New Jersey yesterday to help Dora Simpson and her sister Joan get ready to move out of their farm. Uncle Bill told them you could handle the audit without them. He was supposed to tell you."

Carrie spoke very casually, but Lily could feel the girl's eyes on her. "They're really nice ladies. Dora and her husband have been very important to the breed, so Dad rallied a lot of Morgan people to help. He'll be back next week with the horses he bought to start his own breeding program. It's really exciting. He's got his own prefix now, to register foals under."

So Blake had found a legitimate excuse to avoid her. Uncle Bill hadn't warned her the day before, when she stayed at his place. Lily knew she should be grateful that Blake wasn't going to force a confrontation, that in fact he'd gone out of his way to prevent one. But in her heart of hearts, she suspected she'd hoped he would offer her a compromise that would work for them both. Now he'd taken away the temptation to change her mind. Yes, she should be grateful.

"Understandable," Lily managed to comment. "How are the twins?" She couldn't ask about Blake, couldn't speak his name. It would hurt too much.

"They're amazing! Wait till you see them tomorrow! And the other foals. They're all on the ground now, and Dad and Jonathan say they're the best crop we've ever bred."

Lily steered the car through an intersection, weighing her next words. "Carrie, this audit is pretty serious business, and the auditor will want to get it done as quickly as possible. I doubt I'll have a minute to breathe, let alone to see the foals. And I have to get back home as soon as we're finished. I'm up to my chin in work."

"Oh." There was a world of disappointment in that one subdued sound.

Lily's heart ached. "I'd love it if you'd get me some photos of the foals and the mares and stallions, so I can put together an album. Rascal and Panther, and even Dolly, too. Okay?"

Carrie promised she would, then chattered nonstop for the rest of the drive, describing the antics of the foals, kittens and dog, which suited Lily fine. She would have been hard-pressed to keep up her end of any conversation, especially when they drove up the familiar curving lane to the yard.

Carrie walked Lily to the door of Jonathan's house and unlocked it for her. "Lily, thank you. I know you're giving up more vacation days for Uncle Jonathan and me, and I really appreciate it. He does, too. He'd rather chew tinfoil than admit the audit has him petrified. And I was really proud to introduce you today and see how the kids respected you. Even the guys."

"I was glad to do it, Carrie. You're a very special friend."

"You are, too. Don't forget us, okay? I mean, just because things didn't work out with Dad, you know?"

Lily nodded and blinked away the sting of sudden tears. "I could never forget you, Carrie. I'm only a phone call or a postcard away. Promise you won't forget that, okay? I really want you to visit me. Promise?"

"Promise," Carrie echoed in a small voice. She started to walk away, then stopped. "Lily, I'd like you to come to my graduation? I know you're busy, and you might not be able to get back here again so soon, but if you can?"

Deeply touched by Carrie's request, Lily put her hand on the girl's arm. "Thank you for asking me, Carrie. I don't know if I can, but I'll try." She blinked away a sudden threat of tears and smiled. "I promise I'll try very hard." In fact, she vowed silently, nothing short of a national disaster would keep her away from Carrie's graduation. Not even seeing Blake again.

Carrie nodded. "Okay. I'll send you an invitation." With a muffled sniffle, she ran to her father's house and dashed inside.

The next morning, as Lily had predicted, the IRS auditor turned out to be a dry stick of a man. But the audit went smoothly, and not a penny was found to have been misappropriated. Lily flew home a day earlier than she'd anticipated, torn between relief and disappointment that Blake hadn't returned early.

Alone in the Simpsons' stallion barn, Blake paused before bringing out the young stud he'd bought from Dora. He wanted to be perfectly calm when he approached the snorty little black stallion, and at the moment he was feeling anything but calm. He'd just passed the phone over to Jonathan, after listening to Carrie babbling about how successful the school career day had been.

Damn, he felt as if he were betraying his daughter, but he really hadn't wanted to hear how wonderful Lily had been. He was deeply proud of Carrie's achievement in organizing the event. But it galled him no end that his daughter had a case of heroine worship for a woman who expounded on the glories of a career that excluded everything he'd tried to teach his daughter was important in life: love, family, nature.

But, double damn, he missed Lily! Call him stupid and bullheaded, but he still wanted her. She was generous and stubborn and loving and beautiful, and she made him crazy like no other woman ever had. His body ached for her. His ears waited for the sound of her voice, her laughter. His mind missed the sharpness of hers. His eyes missed her beauty. His soul missed the sweet warmth of hers, trapped under all that ambition.

Well, he could miss her till the cows came home, but he wasn't going to change her mind about her damn career. Not that it would make a difference if he could. She wouldn't give up her partnership, her perks and her condo in New York, for him.

Maybe he was being petty, but it bothered the hell out of him that his daughter took Lily's side. Carrie talked about the courage to make choices, to make sacrifices, but she was too young to understand what she was talking about. She hadn't lived long enough to see that an expensive condo or travel to exotic places couldn't keep a person from being lonely deep inside.

On the other hand, there was no way life on a horse farm could compete with the money, the life-style, the jolts per minute of a career like Lily's. If Carrie visited Lily in New York city, would she be seduced away from her goals, her dreams? From him? Technically, she was old enough to decide for herself, and there was nothing he could do to stop her. He'd probably drive her farther away if he tried. His daughter had accused him of taking the easy choice, claiming Lily had shown the courage to make the difficult choice. But she was too naive to see the difference between easy choices and hard ones.

Well, Lily had made her decision, and so had he, damn it. Decisions that left zero room for compromise. So he might as well just get on with his life, the way he always had. And right now, he had a new horse to introduce himself to.

The young stallion nickered softly inside his stall. Blake let out a breath, as if that could blow away all the turmoil in his soul, and opened the thick wooden door.

General G's Lad, with his intelligent dark eyes in a classic Morgan face, gazed at him quietly. The horse extended his neck and sniffed at his shirt, then rubbed his muzzle on it, streaking dirt across the front. With a grin, Blake scratched the wide forehead under the thick forelock, then moved to the stallion's side and stroked the warm, solidly muscled neck.

"Hey, fella. You're going to sire some beautiful babies someday soon. You won't have to worry if they love you, or if they're taking bad advice, like I do," he muttered. The youngster blew out a breath and lowered his head to grab gently at the knee of Blake's jeans. Blake moved out of reach, absently admiring the deeply angled shoulder and the arch of the stallion's neck.

"And then there's Lily. Damn, but I screwed that up. I didn't expect to fall for her, but I did. Like a ton of bricks. And I didn't think I was falling alone. You know what I mean?"

As if he understood the question, Lad snorted and slowly shook his head. Blake grinned. "'Course not. You're too young to know how the ladies can tie you in knots without trying." He gave the glossy neck another pat. "And I'm old enough to know better."

Lad nodded. "Thanks a bunch," Blake muttered, giving the stallion a final pat before leaving the stall. "I guess you can't always get what you want." As he slid the door latch closed, Lad thumped the bottom board with one foot, and gave Blake a level look. "Yeah, you're right. The next line of that song is something about trying hard and getting what you need."

Not bad advice, and straight from the horse's mouth.

Two weeks after Jonathan's audit, Lily punched the keys for Uncle Bill's number on her cordless phone, then paced the width of her living room and waited for him to answer. One ring. She paused to straighten the frame of a small, delicate watercolor iris on the cream-colored wall. Two rings. She changed the angle of a stem on one of the silk plant arrangements.

Three rings. Funny, she'd never noticed that although she surrounded herself with things from nature, they were all artificial. It felt *wrong* now to touch a leaf and not feel a cool, living plant. And there was no scent from any of her perfect imitations of nature. The lilacs had been starting to bud in Rochester when she'd left, as if the spring blizzard had never happened. Now, more than halfway through May, the Lilac Festival was already over. In the city, spring was exploding everywhere, but sometimes Lily couldn't help feeling that the flowers and trees were out of their element. A deep breath of springtime in the city certainly owed more to General Motors than it did to Mother Nature.

Four rings. She paced back toward the kitchen alcove. Where was Uncle Bill? Was he all right? His doctors had said he was fine again, that she needn't worry about leaving him on his own. But doctors could be wrong. Maybe she should have stayed another few days at least, to make sure he was okay. She'd ended up spending so much time at March Acres that she really hadn't spent as much time with him as she should have. And he'd probably tired himself out gallivanting off to New Jersey again with Jonathan last weekend.

Five rings. She glanced at the sleekly modern black-and-white clock over the sink. Nine o'clock on a Wednesday evening. He should be home. Like her. Although not necessarily as alone as she was. Once again, she noticed that her apartment felt strangely empty. She'd taken to leaving her stereo on all day, so that there was some sign of life when she came home after work. Maybe she should get herself a kitten or two from the pound. Where on earth could Uncle Bill be?

Six rings. Now she was really worried.

"Hello?" The familiar voice sounded slightly breathless.

She halted her pacing. "Uncle Bill, where on earth were you?" To her horror, she sounded exactly like her mother!

His chuckle crackled in her ear. "Jonathan and I were out stargazing with the telescope I gave you when you were fourteen. I found it in the basement."

She smiled. She certainly did remember that telescope. Her mother had ranted for days about Bill's foolishness, complaining repeatedly that paying for gymnastic lessons would have been a much better use of his money. But she and Uncle Bill had spent wonderful hours stargazing, hours she had always treasured.

"How have you been? Are you resting the way you should?"

"In a manner of speaking. I moved to March Acres last week." He chuckled dryly. "Jonathan insisted I need company and something to take my mind off my preoccupation with my health. I'm having my calls forwarded until I get a new number here."

Lily opened her mouth, but no words formed. Finally, she managed to say, "Oh! That's great! That's...really great!"

"Those kittens of yours have taken a shine to me. I don't think I'll ever find half the things those little characters mistake for mice. They race around here like the devil was after them, and always look surprised when things come crashing down in their wake. But I have to admit, they grow on you."

"They do, don't they?" she agreed, but the image in her mind wasn't of rambunctious kittens. She couldn't think of Rascal and Panther without thinking about the night Blake had brought them to her bed. And thinking about Blake sent a shaft of pain and longing through her heart. Time wasn't doing anything to dull the regrets, the second thoughts. Nor had time provided any creative solutions. Blake was still the right man, at the wrong time and place, and now things were even more complicated.

"Of course, Jonathan and I have both been widowers so long that we may get on each other's nerves."

"Probably." She smiled. "But the farm is a lovely place."

After a short pause, he said, "So it is, child. So it is."

Lily blinked away unexpected tears. "How was your trip to New Jersey? Jonathan didn't talk you into buying a horse, did he?" she teased, hoping her voice didn't betray her longing.

"New Jersey was fine. Dora and Joan are delightful ladies, gracious hostesses," her uncle answered. "And don't think that old character didn't try to convince me to buy a horse." A dry chuckle came down the line, making Lily smile. "I have to say, I'm having more fun than I have in years. Now, my dear, what prompts this call?"

She took a breath, then released it. "Two things. One is, Carrie invited me to her graduation, and I want to surprise her, so I'll need you to keep my secret." Thereby making it unnecessary for her to phone Carrie and risk having Blake answer. "And two is, I was officially offered a long-term assignment in London today."

"London? What happened to Hong Kong?"

"Jeffrey happened." She hoped her uncle wouldn't press for the details of how her former fiancé had outmaneuvered her.

After a pause, Bill said, "Well, London is nothing to sneeze at, is it? I never liked the idea of you going half-way around the world. Never liked Jeffrey, either," he muttered. At her startled laugh, he chuckled. "Tell me about this assignment."

She gave him the names of the multinational firm involved in the assignment and smiled at his long whistle. "I know. They don't get much bigger. The bottom line is, they need someone to work out new tax structures. It's at least an eighteen-month project. Possibly longer. They'd want me to relocate to London, but I'd be traveling to their Paris, Brussels and New York offices once a month or so."

"Wonderful, Lily! I'm very proud of you. Very proud indeed. London! And Paris and Brussels. Sweetheart, you deserve this. I can remember how you used to talk about your dream job, and this sounds like someone finally heard you. When do you start?"

"Early September, although I'll have to move sooner."

"I hope you'll have time to visit before you leave. I still owe you a champagne toast for being made a partner."

Her little laugh came out surprisingly like a sob. "Of course! I haven't left yet. I just wanted to make sure you thought it was a good idea for me to accept the assignment."

"Well, I can't see any reasons why you shouldn't accept it. You don't have any ties—" he cleared his throat "—except me, and I'd love a chance to visit London. Or Paris. Or Brussels." His chuckle made her smile briefly. "If you're hesitating because of my health, don't. The doctors say I'm fit as a fiddle."

She bit her lower lip. "I can't say I'm not concerned,"

she answered truthfully. "It's pretty far away, if you need me."

"Nonsense. This is the assignment of a lifetime. You've always worked hard, and you gave up a lot to take care of your mother, not to mention that weasel Jeffrey nearly scuttling your progress. Show those partners of yours that you're better than Jeffrey can dream of being."

She smiled, feeling a little teary at his loving pep talk. He and Aunt Martha had always been so good to her, so supportive, so encouraging. But this time, she wondered if that was what she needed. She knew she should be ready to burst out of her skin with excitement at this offer, she should be packing already, but she felt curiously as if she'd lost something, rather than gained something. What was *wrong* with her?

There was one explanation for her indecision, but she didn't want to think about him.

"Thanks, Uncle Bill. I guess I need time to get used to the idea of my dream coming true. Like the Chinese proverb about being careful what you ask for, in case you get it."

He chuckled. "We only get one ride on this carousel, at least only one we know about. Make the best of your ride, Lily. Grab what you want, whatever it is, with both hands."

"I will, Uncle Bill," she said. "Thanks."

"For nothing, sweetheart. I'm glad you'll be coming to Carrie's graduation. She'll be thrilled. There's plenty of room at the farm for you to stay over. I promise not to spill the beans, and I'll start chilling the champagne now. We'll have a lot to celebrate."

Her throat tightened, and her eyes stung. "Great. Give

my love to Jonathan and Carrie, and…and the kittens.'' Her voice nearly broke. "And…and Dolly. And Patsy.''

"And to Blake, too?''

She swallowed hard, fighting the sting of tears. "I'll see you next week, Uncle Bill.''

Lily disconnected and set the phone down on the glass and acrylic end table. That uncomfortable nagging feeling surfaced again. When she closed her eyes, she could see again Blake's dark eyes, warm with affection, sparkling with challenge. And she could hear his low voice asking the question that she had once thought she could sidestep so easily: What about love?

anywhere in Jeannie and Carrie's apartment, but there
was more to hear. "And," said Dell, "it goes on."

"Arthur Hines' son."

She swallowed hard, drained the glass of tea.
"Are you nervous? Here you—"

"I—" Blake focused on the handle down on the glass
and on the table. Then too much. He tugging nodding
and agreeing. When she closed her eyes she could see
again Blake's rather gray, warm with affection, spun into
with their lies. And she could not know what, asking
the question that she had once more she could almost
so easily. What about later?

Chapter Fourteen

Blake looked around him, absorbing the atmosphere of
anticipation. The high school auditorium was filling rapidly with the families of the graduating class. He grinned
and nodded at a number of parents he'd met over the
years. Somewhere backstage, Carrie was probably pacing,
or giggling with her friends, waiting for their cue to line
up.

God! He couldn't believe his baby was about to get her
high school diploma! Wasn't it just yesterday he'd walked
her into her kindergarten class for the first time, and tried
to sneak away so she wouldn't cry to see him go? He
smiled wryly to himself at that memory. Carrie had been
so excited about going to school that she didn't notice
he'd left her. In fact, she'd cried when he came to pick
her up, blubbering that she wanted to stay.

Well, they'd come a long way, his little girl and him.
They'd done a lot of their growing up together, learning

by the seat of their pants. So far, Blake thought with a swell of pride, so good. Very good. She'd never let him down. Never let herself down. He only hoped their relationship would weather her quest for independence. Hell, he hoped *he* weathered Carrie's quest for independence! He'd shared almost half his life with his daughter. The next few years, with her away at university, were going to feel pretty damn weird. Not exactly empty, because he still had the horses and his students, but less full.

Against his will, his thoughts immediately strayed to Lily. They did that whenever he thought about what was missing in his life. Damn the woman! She was gone, but her presence lingered in his mind like a haunting melody, teasing him to remember what he couldn't have. It didn't help that the woman who sank into the seat beside him just as the auditorium lights dimmed wore the same damn perfume as Lily. As if a switch had been flipped on, his body immediately hummed with memories of the sight, the feel, the sound, the scent of her.

Just then, Carrie's classmates began filing into the auditorium to sit in the front rows. The kids were arranged alphabetically, but that didn't stop him from straining to see his girl as soon as the first students marched in. When he finally found Carrie in the line, he gave in to the grin that was bursting inside him. That was his baby there, in a cap and gown, looking a little nervous, a little excited, and very grown-up.

The principal spoke first, but Blake was too lost in his own thoughts to pay much attention. He replayed memories of Carrie as a baby, a toddler, a child. Now she was a young woman. He'd watched her grow, guided her, protected her, and probably sometimes overprotected her, mostly by himself. Sure, Jonathan and his wife had been like a second set of grandparents for her, but he'd had to make all the major decisions, had to take all the responsibility for the results, himself. He was proud that she'd turned out so well, proud—and maybe even a little smug—at having succeeded with no experience and little help.

But now, surrounded by two-parent families, he felt that he'd missed something important along the way. A partner. A wife. A mother for his child. Not Sandy. Once the initial attraction faded, there had never been anything between them except the baby they'd made by accident. But he felt the lack of someone special to share his enormous pride, his hopes and fears for his daughter. He'd wanted that person to be Lily. Still did, if he was being honest, but he knew it was hopeless to think she'd ever give up her fast-track career to move to the farm. According to Bill, she was on her way to Europe for a year or more. Opportunity of a lifetime, Bill had gloated. No kidding. And no way he could compete.

As the names of the graduating students were called, there were occasional cheers, smatterings of applause, and almost constant flashes from cameras. In front of him, Jonathan sat poised with his own camera, waiting for the right moment. And then Carrie's name was called. Blake watched her cross the stage to take her diploma and shake hands with the principal, and a riot of emotions bubbled inside him.

"Congratulations," the woman beside him said, her scent wafting to him when she leaned toward him.

His thanks died unspoken as he looked into Lily's eyes.

She couldn't tell if Blake was angry or simply surprised that she'd come to Carrie's graduation. He gave her a curt nod, then turned back to watch the last few students receive their diplomas. Lily felt as if she were sitting next to a tiger who might at any moment discover that the door to his cage was open. The rest of the ceremony couldn't go fast enough for her.

This was a mistake, she told herself. *He resents my coming. He'll be upset with Carrie for inviting me, which will spoil her pleasure.* She decided to leave as soon as the formal program was over, and phone her uncle to tell him she'd be staying at a motel before returning to New York City on an early-morning flight.

But before she could sneak away, the instant the graduates sent up a collective cheer for themselves, Jonathan saw her and greeted her with a wide grin and a hug that briefly trapped her against Blake's solid body. After that, there was no escape. Jonathan kept her hand tucked in the crook of his arm, and promised to repay Bill for not sharing the surprise of her coming. He introduced Blake's parents after an awkward pause that made it obvious that Blake wasn't going to. Shaking their hands, Lily felt more than ever that she shouldn't have come.

Then Carrie swooped down on them, laughing, crying, and hugging Blake, Jonathan and, finally, Lily.

"I'm so glad you could come!" Carrie exclaimed, hugging her a second time before turning to Blake. "Dad, is it still okay if I go to Debbie's party? After I spend some time with you guys?" She flashed a mischievous grin, then went on without giving her father a chance to answer. "I heard a rumor that there was cake back at Jonathan's," she confided to Lily. "You're staying at the farm, aren't you? How long can you stay? Will we be able to spend some time together before you have to go home?"

Painfully aware of Blake's disapproving glare, Lily forced a smile. "I have an early flight back," she fibbed, "so I probably should stay at a motel near the airport."

"Nonsense!" Jonathan declared. "I won't hear of it!

Your usual room is ready, and Bill is waiting for us. The sooner we get to our little celebration, the sooner the graduate can join her friends.'' He winked at Carrie, then offered her his other arm.

As they walked out to the parking lot, Lily felt the heat of Blake's glare in the center of her back. This was not going to be a very comfortable evening, she decided. When Carrie announced that she wanted to ride to the farm in Lily's rental car, Blake grunted before turning on his heel and stalking to his Jeep. With a shrug, Jonathan followed him. The elder Sommerses strolled arm in arm to their own Jeep, talking quietly.

It took several extra minutes for Carrie to exchange hugs with other students, handshakes with their parents. When she finally sank into the passenger seat and shut the door, she heaved a dramatic sigh, then gave Lily a smile that was positively glowing. Following the line of cars out of the parking lot, Lily was perfectly content to let Carrie do all the talking. That way, she could concentrate on calling herself a fool for hoping Blake would be glad to see her again.

When Carrie finally seemed to wind down, Lily asked, "How is it working out with my uncle and Jonathan sharing a house?"

A laugh burst out of Carrie. "Didn't Uncle Bill tell you what those two characters have done?" Lily shook her head. Carrie groaned. "Remember Dora Simpson and her sister Joan? Dora had the Morgan farm in New Jersey, and her husband died last year." Lily nodded. "Well, Dora and Joan moved in with Jonathan and your uncle."

Lily almost hit the brakes. *"What?"*

"Jonathan and Dora and Uncle Bill and Joan." Carrie giggled. "Isn't that a riot?"

After a moment of considering the situation, Lily

smiled. "I think it's sweet," she told Carrie. "I'm glad none of them will be lonely."

"Except Dad," Carrie muttered.

Lily wasn't sure she was meant to hear that comment, so she didn't respond, but the idea troubled her. It wasn't just Blake who was lonely, she mused.

Fortunately, she didn't have much time to dwell on loneliness. As soon as she and Carrie walked into Jonathan's house, she was swept into the laughter and conversation that flowed and swirled around the small gathering. After introductions, Jonathan opened a bottle of champagne and Carrie was handed a knife to cut a cake decorated to look like a partly rolled diploma.

Joan and Dora served the cake. When everyone had a glass of champagne, except Carrie, who had poured ginger ale into her wineglass in anticipation of getting the keys to the Jeep later, they all looked to Blake for a toast. He cleared his throat, raised his glass and said gruffly, "To Carrie. Congratulations."

They waited, but he said nothing more. Finally, Jonathan echoed Blake's words, far more sincerely, Lily thought, and they all sipped at their drinks.

"And to my lovely niece, Lily, for being made a partner in her firm, and for getting that London assignment," Uncle Bill declared, raising his glass again.

While the others drank to her, Lily glanced at Blake. He stared into his champagne, not toasting her success. No matter how she tried to convince herself that his good wishes meant nothing to her, his silence hurt.

"And one more toast to Carrie, upon her acceptance at M.I.T.," Dora added, beaming at the girl.

"Oh!" Lily turned to Carrie. "You didn't tell me! That's wonderful!" She lifted her glass in a salute, then took a sip along with the others. She couldn't help noticing that Blake sipped his champagne, but looked far from pleased.

Gamely Carrie tried to keep an animated conversation going while they ate the cake and finished their champagne. All the while, Blake stood apart, watching, hardly speaking, and then only if someone asked him a direct question. He set down his cake after one bite, then silently accepted a cup of coffee from Joan. Barely twenty minutes into what was supposed to be a family celebration for Carrie, he pushed himself away from the wall he seemed committed to supporting and tossed the keys to his Jeep to Carrie.

"I've got some things to take care of. Have fun," he told Carrie, then caught her in a tight hug that brought tears to Lily's eyes. When he stepped back, he added, "But for God's sake, be sensible." He glanced around the room, not meeting anyone's eyes, and said curtly, "G'night."

A long, strained silence followed the sound of the front door shutting behind Blake. Carrie's face showed her hurt and confusion. Finally, Lily stood up. "Excuse me," she said. She gave Carrie's arm a gentle squeeze and, ignoring Jonathan's wink, walked out into the balmy evening to beard the lion in his den. Her only dilemma was, she didn't have a clue what she was going to say to him.

Blake stomped into his office and slammed the door behind him, even though he was alone in the house. He flung himself into his chair, then jumped up to pace. His head was pounding, and the single bite of cake he'd eaten lay like a brick in his gut. Anger choked him. Anger at Carrie for springing Lily on him. Anger at Lily for invading his life yet again, giving his daughter false hope, reminding him of all that was out of his reach. Anger at himself for hurting Carrie. That was the worst.

A sharp knock on his door interrupted his pacing. "What?" he snapped.

The door opened slowly, framing Lily in the shadowed light of the hall. His heart did a slow roll and began pounding against his ribs. To cover his foolish reaction, he let his anger surface.

"What do you want?" he growled, hoping his lack of manners would drive her away.

It didn't. She stepped into the office, her eyes fixed on his. "Go ahead and be mad at me all you want, but don't you dare take your anger out on Carrie!"

He opened his mouth to protest, but Lily kept talking. And with every word, she walked farther into the office, closing the gap between them until she was barely two feet away. "She's a sweet, lovely girl, and you should be very proud of her."

Again he tried to interrupt, but Lily ignored him. By now, she was staring up at him, sparks of anger in her eyes. "She doesn't deserve to be hurt because you're acting like a jerk."

"I know, damn it!" he practically shouted when she paused for breath. "I know," he repeated, in a gentler tone.

Her eyes widened. "Oh," she said softly. "Well..." She took a step back. "Then I'll just say good-night."

Acting on impulse, with his brain frantically logging reasons why he was crazy, Blake reached out and grabbed Lily's shoulders. The silk of her bare arms felt as soft as the silk of her sleeveless blue dress. She stared up at him, her lips parted, the pulse in her throat surging against the delicate skin.

He told himself that if she gave him the slightest hint

of resistance, he would stop. But when he bent and pressed his lips to the hollow of her throat, he heard her gasp softly, and then she seemed to drift toward him. His arms went around her, and she leaned into him, pliant, boneless. Even when he scooped her up into his arms, she didn't protest, didn't stiffen. Instead, she looped her arms around his neck and rested her head on his shoulder.

"Lily, are you sure?" he asked, his voice catching.

She tipped her head back to look into his eyes. "I'm not sure of anything except that I want to make love with you one last time," she said softly. "Please don't hate me for being greedy."

Her words stunned him. Hurt him a little, too. "Hate you?" He shook his head. "I don't hate you. I tried, but it kept coming out just the opposite."

Her midnight eyes filled with tears. "Oh, Blake, I'm sorry!"

"Don't be. Just tell me again that you're sure. If you have any doubts, tell me now, while I can stop. Otherwise...." He let his voice trail off, honor-bound to give her the choice, but reluctant to convince her too well.

A tear escaped from the corner of one eye, but she smiled. "I'll take the otherwise, please. I have no intentions of asking you to stop."

That was all the answer he needed. Without another word, he carried her upstairs to his bedroom and kicked the door shut behind him. Anticipation hummed in his veins as he lowered her to the middle of his bed and looked into her eyes. Oh, God, he wanted her! Wanted her beyond his bed, far beyond tonight, beyond forever, if that was possible. And if he couldn't have her, he would brand her with his loving so that she would never be able to make love to another man without feeling *his* touch on her, body and soul.

He fumbled with his shirt buttons, cursing under his breath when they refused to be undone. Finally, he just tore the shirt open, sending buttons pinging onto the floor and all over. Lily's eyes widened, but she didn't move from where she knelt in the middle of his bed. He yanked his shirt off, tearing out the cuff buttons when they trapped his hands, and threw it across the room.

Then he reached for Lily's hands and lifted them until he could press them flat against his bare chest. That first contact seared him, shocked him, and then he felt the electricity of need pulsing between them. He closed his eyes briefly, allowing himself to simply feel. When he opened his eyes again, Lily had shut hers. Still pressing her hands against his chest, he leaned down and brushed his lips over hers. Her lips parted on a sigh, luring him back for more.

Somehow, he managed to get rid of his shoes and kneel on the bed with Lily while still teasing her mouth with his. When he closed his hands around her shoulders, she slid her arms up around his neck, leaning into him so that he could feel her warmth and the silk of her dress and the soft swells of her breasts. With trembling hands, he lowered the zipper of her dress and traced the delicate line of her bare back through the open fabric, discovering that she wasn't wearing a bra.

Reverently he drew back and slipped the dress down her arms. In the dim light, her skin glowed like polished alabaster. Her breasts were small, the nipples pale. He knew she was watching him look at her. When her nipples beaded in response to his gaze, his reverence gave way to his need. His low growl sounded feral, but Lily looked back steadily while he eased her down onto her back. She didn't close her eyes again until he kissed her face.

With her delicate scent in his nostrils, he trailed kisses

over her face and down her neck, then teased the surging pulse at the base of her throat with the tip of his tongue. He was so hard that he trembled and ached, but he willed himself to be patient, even when Lily stroked his back with delicate touches of her fingertips.

Carefully, he took one nipple into his mouth, reveling in the way it hardened even more under his tongue, in the way Lily arched and gasped softly. His hand found the other breast and teased it until she writhed and whimpered, and then he switched mouth and hand. Her muffled cries made him smile, despite the way they fed his hunger.

When he sat up and drew her dress down over her hips and legs, his hands trembled. When he had dropped her dress on the floor and slid off her filmy black panties, he felt the trembling taking over inside him. He sat back and looked at her, trying to memorize every line of her pale body. If this was all he could have of her, he wanted to savor every moment, to remember.

Lily lifted one hand toward him. He caught it in his and brought it to his lips. "Not yet," he whispered. "This is for you."

Keeping his own hunger in check, he bent over her and made love to her with his hands and his lips. Her skin tasted like honey. He couldn't get enough of her. Couldn't give enough to her. By the time he had kissed and tasted his way to her belly, she was whimpering and sighing his name, but he wasn't ready to stop. Not until he'd branded all of her with his loving.

Her legs parted at the first touch of his hand. He teased his way up her inner thighs until he found the soft golden curls that hid her secrets. Inside, she was hot and tight and slick. He trailed kisses down to the silky, honeyed flesh, and caressed her there, holding her hips so that she couldn't twist away from him, loving her until her body arched up to him and she cried out. He held her gently while she trembled, stroking her back and shoulders until she lay quietly against him, her fingers tracing idle patterns on his arm and chest.

When her caressing touches changed from idle to purposeful, moving down to the waistband of his slacks, Blake smiled.

"Let me," he murmured, starting to get up.

Pulling away, she pushed him down and smiled. "No. Let me."

He smiled and lay back, watching her face as she unfastened the button. His smile faded when she slid down his zipper with deliberate slowness, turning the act into a tantalizing caress. Her fingers teased and tormented him, but just when he was reaching out to stop her, she tugged his trousers down his hips and off. He heard his change spilling and rolling across the hardwood floor and, for some crazy reason, thought of champagne bubbles. Yeah, that made sense. Lily was as intoxicating, as delicate, yet potent, as champagne.

He hooked his thumbs into the waist of his briefs, impatient to be inside her. Lily's hand molded to the ridge of his hardness, then moved down to cup him through the fabric. He stopped thinking, stopped breathing, as her touches set off tiny explosions along his nerve endings. Blake shut his eyes to savor the sensations she created with the slightest contact. Her silken hair slid along his belly and his thighs, and then he felt the heat of her mouth. She played over him with shy kisses and soft bites, wringing a deep moan from him when she slid his briefs down so that nothing came between them.

The temptation to let her finish what she'd started was strong, but his need to bind her to him was stronger. With his own breathing echoing harshly in his ears, he caught her in his arms and eased her over onto her back. Cursing his own awkwardness, he fumbled in the nightstand drawer until he found a condom, then tore open the wrapper with his teeth. To his surprise, Lily's hands covered his, then took over, turning the interruption into another caress.

He braced himself above her and schooled himself to take his time, to kiss her soft mouth, to nuzzle her breasts, before he joined their bodies with slow, deliberate care. He sank into her as if he were sinking into flames, and her soft cries fueled the fire within him. He felt her pleasure ripple through her and let himself follow. And then he held her close, while their hearts raced and their breath caught and slowed. When he kissed her face, he tasted salt tears, but when he brushed them away with his fingers, she smiled straight into his heart.

As he drifted to sleep, his body almost numb from release, he gathered Lily close and smiled smugly to himself. The evening had turned out a hell of a lot better than he'd dared to hope. No woman made love like that without giving her heart. In the morning, they'd talk, really talk, and he'd convince her that she wasn't making a mistake to love him.

When Blake woke up at six the next morning, Lily was gone.

A week after she snuck out of Blake's bed in a fit of cowardice, Lily tapped on Michael Mason's half-closed door. At his answer, she stepped into the beautiful corner office of one of the firm's most senior partners. As her mentor, Michael had shown her the ropes and had always encouraged her, as Uncle Bill had, to try for the gold. She was now a partner herself, but she felt unsettled by the way Jeffrey had wangled the Hong Kong assignment and maneuvered her into the one in London. She wanted to make sure this was the best move for her at this time.

Her conscience still stung over the way she'd run out on Blake, too, and she knew the two concerns were tightly intertwined. It had been a mistake to give in to her greed for one more time in Blake's arms. He'd read too much into it, and she'd suspected he was going to use her feelings for him to convince her to give up her career.

Why couldn't Blake see that it simply wouldn't work between them? He wasn't a selfish man, yet he wanted her to give up everything she had gained, everything she could gain, for him. She'd had enough of that kind of love for a lifetime. No matter that she loved him, she would never ask him to give up his way of life for her. But that issue was private and nothing to do with her career. Summoning a smile, she firmly relegated her thoughts of Blake to the back of her mind.

Michael sat behind a gleaming antique partners desk, tapping a slim gold pen on the edge of his blotter as he studied a document. In his mid-fifties, he was a handsome man whose appearance testified to his success. His light blue eyes and neatly styled salt-and-pepper hair emphasized the slight tan acquired golfing with clients.

Lily had always thought Michael was the epitome of image-packaging. Youthfully trim, he wore his conservatively tailored suits with just the right dash to turn women's heads and tell men he was in control. The silver-framed portrait of Michael with his elegant wife, Amanda, beautiful daughter, Jessica, and handsome son, Michael, Jr., like the silver Jaguar sedan and the mansion in the suburbs, said he had it all.

"Come in, Lily, come in. Congratulations!" He leaned back in his massive leather chair and gestured for her to take one of the smaller leather chairs in front of his desk.

She sat down. "Thank you."

"Don't thank me. You've earned every chance you've gotten. Don't let Jeffrey's Hong Kong coup get to you. The truth is, I always intended you to get the London assignment. It requires a finesse Conklin hasn't got."

Her surprise must have shown, because Michael gave her a moment to let his words sink in. "You've moved ahead faster than the other women in the firm because you play your cards well. You're bright, no doubt of that. A team player with creativity. It's mutually beneficial that you're also independent. No strings. No commitments except to the firm."

Michael shook his head as if bemused. "We've lost six good women in two years, because their husbands were transferred, or because they decided to stay home with their kids."

He said the last as if the women had opted for drinking hemlock. Only a short time ago, she, too, had felt amazed that her female colleagues were willing to give up so much for their families. Now, Michael's disparaging tone made her vaguely uneasy. She didn't want to consider the reasons for that.

Michael gazed into her eyes, his expression piercingly direct. "One of the things that swayed the client, Lily, is your ability to look and act like a lady, and play like a man. You always give a hundred and ten percent to your work, and that gets noticed. It certainly proves that a woman can get ahead, as long as she's willing to make sacrifices. You've always made the right ones, Lily, and I'm confident that you'll continue to go far."

Sacrifices? What sacrifices had she made in order to progress? She believed she was living her life without giving anything up, without trading anything for success. All these years, she'd worked toward her most precious goal: her independence. Now she had it. What did Michael think she'd sacrificed along the way?

Long after she left Michael's office, Lily continued to mull over the question: *What had she given up?*

Nothing. She had everything she'd ever wanted. She made her own decisions, from what to eat and what movie to see to where to go for a vacation and whether to take a posting in London. She didn't have to answer to anyone. She didn't have to compromise or give up anything, because there was no one to make demands on her. No one with a different agenda, different needs, to make her feel selfish when she put her own needs and goals first.

Her thoughts strayed to the family portrait on Michael's desk. And Blake's question reverberated in her mind: *What about love?* Why, she wondered, could Michael have the perfect career, plus a beautiful family, while she, like so many professional women, had to choose, or compromise? Or sacrifice?

She'd told Blake she didn't want to love anyone, but her heart hadn't listened. She did love Blake. But the only way she could fulfill that love was to give up everything she'd made of herself. She'd succeeded where her mother had only fantasized. If she gave it all up now to make a life with Blake, would she eventually become as bitter and selfish as her mother? She would end up hating him for seducing her away from her dreams, and hating herself for hurting him.

Or, if she refused to sacrifice her career for love, would she end up full of regrets, like Carrie's mother?

She had to give her decision about the London assignment to the client by the end of the week. The only logical thing was to say yes. She couldn't worry about having regrets in twenty years. The present required her immediate attention. Who could predict what the future would hold? As Uncle Bill had said, this was the chance of a lifetime.

And what about love? Love was a nice concept, but in practice, love had been a source of pain and disappointment. Love had made her vulnerable, which frightened her. It was too easy to manipulate someone who wanted to be loved. Experience had taught her it was safer not to love, not to need love. Somehow, she'd find a way to put her feelings for Blake—and for Carrie—into a neat little corner of her heart where they wouldn't prompt her to do anything foolish.

Chapter Fifteen

Blake leaned his hip against the kitchen counter and sipped at his breakfast coffee. His mind was only half on what Carrie was saying. The rest of his thoughts strayed, as usual, to Lily. It was a week since she ran away in the middle of the night, but his anger still simmered.

He hadn't figured her for a coward, but she hadn't stayed to give him a chance to speak his mind. Or his heart. Sure, she'd had it rough in the past, and she'd been unfairly manipulated in the name of love. But couldn't she see that this was different? He loved her for who she was, damn it, not what she could do for him.

"Dad, are you listening?" Carrie demanded. "I was asking you a question."

He pulled his mind out of the fog, but he didn't have a clue about what Carrie had been saying. He figured it had something to do with borrowing the Jeep, or doing some last-minute shopping before she flew to Vermont to visit his parents for a couple of weeks. That was mostly what she talked about these days, when she wasn't talking about getting ready for her freshman year at M.I.T.

"Sure, honey. Whatever you want." He took another sip of his coffee.

"So I'll start by piercing my navel and getting a Morgan tattooed on my shoulder. Just a small one. A bay, maybe. What do you think?"

The coffee slid down wrong, and Blake coughed wildly. "What?" he finally gasped.

She gathered up her breakfast dishes and gave him a mildly exasperated look. "Snap out of it, Dad. Either pick up the phone and call Lily, or get on with your life." He winced at her words, but he gave her credit for being wiser than her old man.

Carrie sighed. "Right now, you're useless. I was asking you if I could ship my horse to Massachusetts while I'm at school. I've got names of several dressage trainers and Morgan farms within a reasonable commute."

"Providing you have a car," he reminded her, "which you may not, at least for your first term."

"Well, Grandpa offered—"

"Forget it," he snapped. "Your grandparents can't afford to give you a car."

"Fine," Carrie said airily. She gave him a quick kiss on his cheek. "I've got chores, and then I'm going for a trail ride," she told him on her way out of the room. "Don't forget to sign those checks on the kitchen table. They need to be mailed before the end of the day."

Blake grunted and took a last drink of his now tepid coffee. His daughter was getting very bossy, he noted, and very sure of herself. She was going to turn into a strong, interesting woman sometime very soon.

Like Lily, he couldn't help thinking as he shuffled

through the checks Carrie had filled in. Mechanically he signed his scrawl on each one, then glanced at the open magazine Carrie had been flipping through during breakfast. It was one of those woman's magazine she was always quoting. A cartoon caught his eye. Well, he could use a good laugh.

A man at a bar was describing his ideal woman: strong, independent, exciting, a vixen in bed, a lady in the living room, a tiger in the boardroom. A woman who had her own career, made her own money, knew her own mind.

Very much like Lily, Blake thought as he read the next frame. The punch line was that the man wanted her to give up all that for him. As punch lines went, it wasn't very funny. The guy was obviously a jerk.

Shaking his head, Blake rinsed his mug and went outside. He had to get stalls ready for the new horses he—and the bank—had bought last week from Dora Simpson in New Jersey.

He was halfway down the path to the mares' barn when he stopped short. Damn, that cartoon wasn't funny at all! That guy—that jerk—was *him!*

He didn't know if Carrie had left that cartoon out for him to see, or if it had simply been there, but he felt like he'd just received a message from the cosmos! Then he started to laugh, and couldn't stop. Dolly barked at him, her expression faintly condemning. Well, he couldn't blame her. No dog liked to have a jerk for a master.

Still chuckling, he caught up with Carrie in the barn and drew her aside to thank her. And to explain the sudden inspiration that made him think he wasn't as dumb as he looked.

At noon, after speaking with Michael, Lily was still mulling over the question of sacrifices as she walked in

Central Park. On a day like this, Lily usually didn't want to be anywhere else in the world. But today she noticed she could hardly smell the flowers over the exhaust fumes. Or hear the birds over the car horns and truck engines. She tossed the napkin from her lunchtime hot dog into a garbage can, frowning at all the debris scattered around it.

It wasn't just the sounds and scents of nature that she missed. It was Blake, teasing, challenging, teaching, loving, that made her ache with longing.

Her final decision about the London posting was due Friday, although everyone assumed it was already a "done deal." That gave her two days to weigh her options. But did she have any options? On the one hand, she worried that she would lose touch with home. On the other hand, did she have anything here to lose touch with? Only Uncle Bill, who was already planning to visit her in London.

She sat on a bench that had just been vacated by three elderly women, and watched the pigeons bobbing hopefully around her. After so many years of dreaming and planning, she no longer knew what would make her happy. What was happiness, anyway? Was it independence, freedom of choice? Or was it family and close ties? Was it satisfying work, or was it loving and being loved? Or was it some elusive balance of all those things?

And what was love? How could something so vague and changeable be worth risking everything? What if she gave up her job, her life in New York, her friends, her independence, and then he stopped loving her? It could happen. She'd learned early on not to take love for granted. Counting on love to last was a leap of faith she couldn't afford. What if no one was there to catch her?

Suddenly, Lily heard the sound of hooves crunching on

gravel. Her heart skipped, although she knew there was no way on earth Blake could appear on horseback in the middle of Central Park. Even so, when a pair of enormous dark bay horses rounded the bend, ridden by New York City police officers, she felt a wave of disappointment. The policemen paused to let a small group of chattering children gather around and pat the horses. Lily wanted to join them, just to feel the warm, smooth coat of a horse under her hand again.

Feeling only a little foolish, Lily strolled closer to the horses, trying to appear casual. Finally, she gave in to the impulse to run her hand over one horse's muscular, velvety neck, and felt a flood of memories wash over her. Horses and Blake. Horses, Blake and love. Oh, God, she missed him! She needed his love, and she needed to love him. But she was still too afraid that love wouldn't be enough to bridge the distances and differences between them. Oh, God, what should she do?

She blinked back the tears that clouded her vision and rubbed the horse's broad forehead.

"Lady, are you all right?" the officer asked her, leaning down from the saddle.

Lily rubbed her open hand over the big horse's soft muzzle and breathed in its comforting, earthy scent. Its warm tongue slid wetly over her wrist and across the silk of her blouse cuff. Blake had been right when he expounded on the ability of horses to heal troubled spirits and awaken inner joy and peace.

Lily looked up at the officer, who was frowning with concern, and smiled. "I am now, thanks," she told him.

Blake leaned on the top rail of the back stallion paddock. That new little chestnut mare they'd bought from Dora had poor Pride going in circles. She should be ready to breed, but she was making the stallion sweat with her indecision. July was hardly too late in the year, but females could be damned unpredictable. Pride was strutting his best stuff, flagging his tail and arching his neck, but little Miss Dainty wasn't impressed by the stallion's floating trot and macho displays.

Pride halted suddenly and snorted. Boy, he knew how that felt, Blake thought. Confused. Frustrated. And no little bit stung in the old ego. What's a guy to do when his best isn't good enough for the lady he wants? How's he supposed to know when to keep trying and when to back off?

In apparent exasperation, Pride stuck his muzzle in the air and trumpeted a long neigh that drew responses from all over the farm. Dainty turned her glossy rump in his direction and peered back over her shoulder. What a flirt! And it worked, Blake noted, feeling both amused and chagrined at how easily the males of any species seemed to fall. With a shamelessly eager snort, Pride trotted toward the mare. The instant he nuzzled her, she stamped, wheeled and bolted away with a squeal.

Blake smothered a snort of laughter. Poor Pride. He had a bad case of spring fever, but Dainty was apparently immune. Was she holding out for a better mate? Or a better offer from this one? Would the males of any species ever understand the females?

Dainty settled down to graze in the far corner of the pasture. Pride snorted a time or two, circled the enclosure in his floating trot, then paused to rip up a chunk of long, juicy grasses. Instead of devouring them, however, he cautiously carried them to the wide-eyed mare.

"Well, I'll be damned," Blake muttered. Dainty extended her delicate muzzle to sniff Pride's bouquet of grass and dandelions. Ears flicking, the little mare munched the ends of the grasses until she stood nose to nose with the quivering stallion. "That crafty old Casanova!"

Then, as Blake watched and grinned, Dainty stood quietly for the stallion. Whatever sweet nothings Pride had murmured in the language of horses had obviously convinced Dainty to accept him. Blake swallowed against the sudden thickness in his throat. When it was right between partners, nothing was more beautiful, nothing was more sacred. The way it had been between Lily and him.

He saw her face whenever he closed his eyes. He relived making love with her every time he dreamed. He imagined he could hear her voice, her laugh. He'd finally given in to the knowledge that he'd never get her out of his heart. A dozen times a day, he wanted to show her something special, or ask her advice, or just touch her.

It was too late now. He'd have to wait until she came back from that damn European assignment. Not that he had the patience to wait eighteen to twenty-four months. Hell, he was tempted to show up at her London office to show her what he'd been doing since June, when she ran out on him in the night. This time, he wasn't asking her to do all the giving while he did all the taking.

In the meantime, he was so intent on thoughts of Lily that he could practically *feel* her with him. Talk about spring fever... Pride didn't have a monopoly on that ailment.

"Looks like all it took was the right incentive to convince the lady to meet him halfway," a soft, familiar voice said behind him.

His heart gave a buck that knocked him breathless. He turned slowly, afraid she'd disappear. But no, this was no hallucination gazing up at him with wide, lapis blue eyes.

The need to hold her and taste her sweet mouth ripped through him, leaving him shaking.

"What the hell are you doing here, damn it? You're supposed to be in London," he muttered, chagrined that she'd rendered his plan to surprise her totally useless.

But he didn't care why she was there. It was a miracle that he didn't want to spoil with an explanation. As long as she wasn't a figment of his overheated brain. He reached for her, not willing to wait for some intangible female signal that she would accept him the way Dainty had accepted Pride. If he didn't take her in his arms *now*, he was going to spontaneously combust.

Lily lost herself in the liquid darkness of his eyes. Blake gripped her bare upper arms in his gloved hands. The roughness of the leather on her skin seemed to strip away her remaining defenses. She could barely breathe. She couldn't stop trembling. She couldn't even smile. He looked so intense, sounded so angry. Had she made a mistake in coming back? As he stepped closer, she let her head tip back and shut her eyes.

He whispered her name and hauled her closer, standing her between his braced legs to bring them belly-to-belly. His hands slid up to cup her face, the deerskin gloves erotically rough as he caressed her skin. Sensing his gaze, she opened her eyes to meet his. He gave her a slow, feral smile that shook her to her core. As he lowered his face to hers, she let her lids drift shut again.

Clutching at his shirt for stability, Lily absorbed the warmth, the dust, the sweat, and inhaled the mingled scents of skin, sunshine and horse clinging to him. All her senses recognized him as her mate, the man she loved. Oh, God! How had she thought she could live without him forever? How had she lived without him for even four weeks?

He was hard where their bodies met, stirring the flames of her answering desire. She could feel tremors rippling through her, and didn't know if they were his or hers. Breathlessly, she parted her lips in anticipation of tasting his.

A distant groan of masculine satisfaction shattered her languor. Blake drew back slightly, his body rigid. Startled, Lily opened her eyes. The expression on his face was a comical mixture of laughter and frustration. The tension left his body, and his dimple showed as he nodded his head toward the pasture where Pride had been courting the chestnut mare.

Lily followed his glance. Pride and the mare stood quietly together. The stallion's eyes had closed, and his neck had drooped so that his head rested heavily against the little mare's shoulder. It was a surprisingly romantic and touching scene, Lily decided. And rather erotic. As if he'd had the same thought, Blake pressed into her, tightening his hold, branding her with his heat and hardness. Desire flared within her in answer.

Once again, Pride heaved a sigh of utter contentment. Lily looked up at Blake and caught him suppressing a grin. She felt herself blush, and a tiny snort of laughter escaped her. Blake's lips struggled to stay straight, but then a laugh burst from them.

It was too much. All the tension and anticipation of finally seeing Blake again dissolved into laughter. She clung to him and laughed until tears streamed down her cheeks, all the while feeling his laughter vibrating through her. When she caught her breath at last, he sighed deeply and cradled her head against his pounding heart. Content for the moment, Lily simply nestled closer.

Blake savored the feel of Lily leaning against him. He let his hands roam over her back, the gloves dulling the sensations in his hands but not those in his imagination. She wore tight jeans and a dark tank top, and her pale hair hung loose over her shoulders and his arms. He wanted to get back to where they had been when Pride interrupted. With any luck, he could sneak her up to his room before anyone noticed they were missing. He would have laughed at his adolescent eagerness if he weren't in pain. Everything he'd ever said about patience being a virtue was a crock. Anticipation stunk. Instant gratification held definite appeal. He wanted Lily now. Now, and forever.

He prayed he hadn't read her wrong again. Maybe she wasn't there for him after all. Maybe she'd only come to the farm to say goodbye to her uncle, and allowed another moment of lust to overcome her. After all, he hadn't exactly said, "May I?" when he grabbed her. If he didn't want to make a fool of himself all over again, he'd do well to take things a little slower.

It took more willpower than he'd thought he had, but he released her. The next move was hers. She still hadn't told him why she was there.

Sudden uncertainty made Lily resist the impulse to reach up and touch Blake's face. He looked so grim, as if he were unhappy that she'd surprised him. She had no doubt that he was still physically attracted to her, but maybe he no longer wanted to be. Maybe he was still angry about the way she'd deserted him back in June. Oh, God, they needed to talk! But all she really wanted to do was feel his arms around her and taste his kisses. Instead, she clasped her hands together and held herself stiffly, resisting temptation. If she'd been wrong, throwing herself at him would embarrass them both.

"The farm is beautiful now," she ventured, deliberately choosing a safe topic. She knew how much he loved the farm. She wanted him to know she felt its magic, too. "It's hard to imagine that only a few weeks ago, everything was coated in ice and mud."

He shrugged. "Yeah. Time changes a lot of things." He turned away. Leaning his elbows on the fence, he gazed over the field.

Her heart plummeted. Was he trying to tell her that time had changed his feelings for her? Certainly, their lovemaking had been spectacular, but sex wasn't love. She'd never really let him talk to her about his feelings. She'd been trying too hard to deny hers. But she'd thought he was trying to tell her without words that his feelings ran deeper than simple lust. Had she been wrong about that? Or had she destroyed his feelings when she snuck away, a thief in the night?

Afraid everything was falling apart before they had a chance, she put her hand on his arm. The heat of his skin seared her fingers. Daringly, she let her simple touch become a caress, tracing the hard, smooth bulge of his biceps. He kept his profile toward her, but she saw his Adam's apple rise and fall.

"Blake, I—"

Something bumped her from behind, startling her, propelling her toward Blake. She was too stunned to do more than gasp. A heartbeat later, she fell clumsily into his arms. He clutched her against his chest and steadied her. She wrapped her arms around his neck and held on tight, struggling to breathe properly.

From behind her, she heard heavy breathing. Or rather, panting. Still holding on to Blake, she turned her head to see Dolly grinning maniacally up at her. With a sigh, she relaxed against him.

"Are you all right?" Blake murmured.

With his strong hands sliding over her back and arms,

she was absolutely fine. He'd removed his gloves, and she felt herself leaning into the touch of his work-roughened palms on her skin.

"Mmm-hmmm..." She let her hand drop to Dolly's large, ugly head, and stroked the coarse hair between her ears.

Blake held her away from himself and gazed into her eyes. "I'm hallucinating. You just patted my dog."

Self-consciously, Lily laughed. "You're not hallucinating. I finally got disgusted with being such a wimp. So I found someone who could help me get over my fear of big dogs."

"You went to a shrink?"

"No. I went to a dog trainer." His eyebrows rose. She laughed. "We have dogs in the city, you know. I passed puppy kindergarten with flying colors, but I'm still working on the advanced classes."

As she'd hoped, Blake chuckled. Still grinning, he shook his head. "You are one amazing woman, Lily Davis. You've got guts. I like that. And," he said, his voice dropping into an intimate growl, "I like you."

The way he looked at her made her heart gallop in anticipation. And fear. Abject, clawing fear of failing, of falling alone. But she had to know now.

"Only *like?*"

His eyes went darker, and all traces of teasing left his face. "More than *like,* damn it! I love you."

Relief flowed through her so forcefully that her knees weakened. She would have crumpled to his feet if he hadn't been holding her. Light-headed, she gazed up at him through a mist of tears.

"I love you, too, Blake." The words came out in a rush. "I tried to run away from it, but it followed me everywhere, until I had to come here—come home—to tell you.''

He framed her face with his strong hands, and tremors rippled through her. Holding her gently, he lowered his head. The first touch of his lips on hers lasted barely a second, but it was enough to imprint her with his taste.

With a sigh, she brought her hands up to rest on his shoulders. He brushed his lips across hers, teasing, caressing, awakening her senses. Lily stood quietly, letting herself savor this leisurely, sweet reunion. Blake caught her lower lip between his teeth, and suddenly she was no longer content to passively receive his kisses.

She curled her fingers into his shoulders and pressed her mouth to his. She felt the soft fullness of his lips, the sharpness of his teeth, under her own lips. He made a low sound deep in his throat and wrapped his arms around her. He was hard when she pressed against him, and the slide of his hot tongue within her willing mouth echoed the slow rocking of his hips. Desire flowed rich and thick inside her.

When he drew his mouth away, a whimper of protest escaped her. Blake scooped her up and carried her to his house, with Dolly bounding happily around them. Once inside, he shut Dolly out. Lily clung to him as he mounted the steps, releasing her hold on his neck only when he lowered her to his bed. Impatient to be joined with him, she began working on the buttons of his shirt. He stroked her hair and set the nerve endings in her neck on edge.

''What about London?'' he asked in a strangled voice.

She looked up. ''I declined the assignment.''

His eyes widened. ''For me?'' The touch on her cheek quivered.

''For me. For you. For us. For all the promises I refused

to let you make before.'' She smiled. ''I want them now, Blake.''

''But what about your career? I thought that was so important to you.''

''It still is.'' She drew his open shirttails out of his jeans and started on his belt buckle. ''I'll be working part-time as a consultant.'' Her fingers fought with the snap on his waistband, but she finally won. ''I may have to fly into the city occasionally for meetings with clients or the partners, but most of what I'll be doing can be done by computer, modem, phone or fax.'' Slowly, she drew his zipper down over his rigid sex, smiling at his low moan. ''It was the only way they could have me,'' she told him.

''What about me?'' His eyes were nearly closed, and his voice was harsh, yet tender. ''How can I have you?''

She knew this was the leap she had to take, and she prayed he'd be there to catch her. ''Any way you want me.''

His eyes opened, and he gazed into her upturned face. ''Only one way I want you, Lily. Always and forever.'' As he spoke, her eyes filled. ''My friend, lover, partner, wife.''

A tear slipped down her cheek. ''And the mother of your children?''

With one warm fingertip, he wiped away the tear. As she watched, he swallowed and nodded. ''Oh, Lily!'' he whispered. ''Nothing could make me happier.'' She closed her eyes to savor the sweet promises in his eyes, and placed her hand over his to press his strong palm against her cheek. ''But I hope you aren't counting on living here with me.''

Her eyes flew open. *''What?''*

His grin looked a little sheepish. ''I guess I didn't say that right. I bought Dora Simpson's farm in north Jersey.

In partnership with your uncle Bill and the bank. Jonathan will leave March Acres to Carrie, and I'll start my own breeding and training farm close enough to New York City for you to keep your job if you want.''

Feeling somewhat dazed, she asked, ''You did that for me?''

''For you, for me, but especially for us.'' He slid his hands down to lift her top and ease it over her head. ''When I finally stopped sulking, I realized I was being a selfish jerk. I was asking you to give up everything you'd worked for, while I was going to eat my cake and have it, too.'' He knelt before her and trailed teasing kisses across her breasts until she forgot what they'd been discussing. ''I can meet you halfway.'' He left a trail of wet kisses between her breasts, down to her waist.

With a soft sigh, she twined her finger in his silky hair and tipped his face up. ''I'd rather meet you all the way,'' she whispered.

Blake closed his eyes as if savoring her words. Then he bent his head, and hot kisses followed his hands as he slid the rest of her clothes off her. Lily promptly lost interest in everything but the fact that they were making love. She felt pliant, dreamy, floating on love and sensations.

He held her hips in his strong hands, and she felt the intimate heat of his mouth. The fire inside her built until she couldn't draw a breath without crying out softly from the intensity of sensations. And still he caressed her with his mouth and his hands, fueling a white-hot fire to forge their union.

Finally, Blake reached for the top drawer of his nightstand. Trembling with the beauty of her love for him, Lily stopped him.

''This might be a good time to start that family we both

want,'' she murmured, answering the question in his eyes. ''Maybe I'm greedy, but I want it all with you.''

The sweetness of his kiss sent tears of happiness slipping down her cheeks. And then, gently holding her in hands that trembled, he claimed her as a stallion claims his mate. His teeth closed softly on the back of her neck and sent shivers rippling down her spine. She felt his love filling her, a gift, a promise, a timeless bond.

Epilogue

Lily leaned her head on Blake's shoulder as he brought the antique courting buggy to a halt in the parking lot of March Acres. Pride stood quietly in his harness, occasionally swishing his ground-sweeping black tail at a late-summer fly. The pink, green and white ribbons Carrie had braided into his mane fluttered on the breeze, but the stallion seemed as unbothered by them as he was by the honking horns following them into the yard.

It was a perfect day for a wedding, Lily thought contentedly. A perfect day for their wedding, and for a horse-drawn procession back to the farm. Although, she reflected, she was too happy to have cared if the day had dawned cold and black with rain. She smiled at Blake. He looked incredibly sexy and dashing in his gray morning coat and formal trousers, a white carnation in his lapel and the ring she'd given him shining on his left hand.

Jonathan and Joan followed in a reproduction doctor's

buggy, and halted Patsy beside Pride. Patsy arched her neck, showing off her ribbons, then stamped one hind leg to discourage another fly. Behind them, Carrie guided matched bay Morgans, pulling another antique buggy. Uncle Bill and Dora sat behind Carrie.

The first of the cars, Blake's Jeep festooned with ribbons and bows, eased past the horses. Blake's parents waved from inside. "Don't move, anyone!" Blake's mother called. "I have to get this on film."

For the next few minutes, Lily watched her new mother-in-law with amused affection as the older woman efficiently directed her husband and two other sons wielding video and still cameras. Blake's two sisters, their husbands and his sisters-in-law gathered their assorted children to crowd around the buggies for photos.

"Enough, Mother!" Blake's father finally announced. "Let these horses rest, and let the rest of us get at some of that food you've been preparing all week."

Rick Preston, hired for their new farm at Lily's suggestion, hurried to hold Pride's bridle. After Blake climbed down from the buggy, Lily took his offered hand. Gathering the white lace skirt of her ankle-length dress in her free hand, she let herself drift into the arms of her incredibly handsome new husband.

Blake held her against his chest and kissed her softly, sweetly, but she felt the banked fires that promised to flare into passion once they were alone.

"I love you, Lily Davis-hyphen-Sommers," Blake murmured, nuzzling her neck under the netting of her veil. "How are you feeling?"

She smiled, thinking of the new life growing within her. "I feel wonderful."

"Let me know if you get tired. This could turn into a three-ring circus."

"Nonsense. Carrie has everything under control."

She turned to watch her stepdaughter lifting her little cousins in their party dresses. Shrieks of happy laughter filled the air. Lily nestled against Blake, savoring the last of their moment alone, before their guests surrounded them. He lifted her left hand to touch his lips to the wide gold band on her third finger.

"I hope you'll never be sorry you gave up anything for me," he murmured.

She looked up into his face and smiled. "I have more than I ever dreamed of, Blake." She drew his hand up to her lips and kissed his palm. "I've still got my partnership." She dropped another kiss into his warm hand. "I've got a wonderful husband." Again, she kissed his palm, lingering just a little longer than the first time. "I've got a terrific stepdaughter, and a child of our own on the way."

For each item in her list of happiness, she dropped another kiss into his palm. When she looked up at him, he was grinning. "And I've got a huge, ugly dog, several fluffy cats, and now my own beautiful Morgan mare waiting for me back in New Jersey."

By now, he was laughing. "What more could a woman ask for?" he teased.

"Nothing," she assured him. "I've got everything I ever needed and didn't know I wanted." She pressed her hand to his chest, where his heart beat steadily. "Like love." Through a mist of happy tears, she smiled up at Blake. "Especially love."

* * * * *

Morgan Horses

The Morgan Horse is truly the American Horse. Two hundred years after the birth of the stallion, Justin Morgan, his many descendants still bear the stamp of his small, powerful physique, his generous nature, his intelligence, and his versatility. "Figure," as Justin Morgan was first known, sired offspring in New England and Canada that resembled him no matter what kind of mare he was bred to. What started as a fluke of nature became the first native breed of horse to the United States of America and the only breed ever to be named after the founding sire.

From plowing the rocky farms of New England to racing in harness, from bridle paths to cattle ranges, from cavalry charges to show rings, the Morgan has shared in the history of the U.S.A. General Sherman rode a Morgan in the Civil War. And a Morgan gelding was the only army survivor of Custer's last stand. Morgans contributed to the development of such uniquely American breeds as the Tennessee Walking Horse, the Standardbred racing trotter, and the American Saddlebred. Today, Morgans can be found as hunters and dressage horses, as endurance and trail mounts, as driving and ranch horses, in rehabilitation programs and show rings...and as family pets.

To learn more about "The Pride and Product of America," contact The American Morgan Horse Association, P.O. Box 960, 3 Bostwick Road, Shelburne, VT 05482.

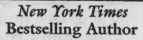

Bestselling author

JOAN JOHNSTON

continues her wildly popular miniseries with an
all-new, longer-length novel

The Virgin Groom
HAWK'S WAY

One minute, Mac Macready was a living legend in
Texas—every kid's idol, every man's envy, every
woman's fantasy. The next, his fiancée dumped him,
his career was hanging in the balance and his future
was looking mighty uncertain. Then there was the
matter of his scandalous secret, which didn't stand a
chance of staying a secret. So would he succumb to
Jewel Whitelaw's shocking proposal—or take cold
showers for the rest of the long, hot summer...?

Available August 1997
wherever Silhouette books are sold.

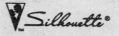